THE JACKAL'S HARE

Patty Smith

The Jackal's Hare.

Note: Event descriptions and entities included in the story are based on the lives of real people. Most events described in this novel took place. Cian is a fictional character and some of the details and events surrounding this character are the work of the author's imagination, any resemblance to actual persons, living or dead, is entirely coincidental.

Smith Publishing in Golden, Colorado. Printed and Bound in the United States of America.

Publisher: Smith
ISBN-13: **978-0692475300**
ISBN-10: **0692475303**
Cover and Interior Design by: © Patty Smith

For DARCEY, my Parents, my Husband, and Children ~ Meine Eltern: Ihr seit meine Inspiration. Paps, Danke Vielmals, this book could not be possible without you!

Thank you to my husband **Kevyn** for your encouragement and my children **Natasya** and **Ely** for your patience. My first readers **Susy** and **Hans**, thank you for your comments. **Adrienne Zeller** thank you for your advice on the book cover. **Katja Stafford** you are an amazing friend, thank you for your editing work – You all rock!

Chapter 1

I nearly died once on a dreary afternoon in Yemen.

Soon after, I made a great sacrifice an icy-cold morning in England. Prior to my bi-polar experiences in Sana'a, I lived a steady mundane life in Munich. No day was ever ecstatically great or ever too shockingly awful. I was twenty years old and any future waited to unwind at my desire. It was then; when my family moved to Sana'a without me and my sisters had already created lasting relationships. Warm wind had stolen the conditioned air by drawing it out through the narrow opening of the car window and replaced it with the foul smell from the garbage heap on the corner. Tanner had parked the truck facing the storefront. A small place looked like all the other shops in Sana'a. A blue metal door marked a business inside. My sisters talked fast with anticipation stopping only to sing along with the chorus of '*No woman, No cry*'

"I'll just be a minute," Tanner had said and waved slamming the truck door shut.

Mo's short and thin figure was back to pre-pregnant phase or maybe even thinner than before she was pregnant. Her bleached platinum blond hair wound tight around pink curlers cradled inside a large flowery silk headscarf.

Later, she would take the scarf off and unfurl her hair revealing a Marilyn Monroe hairdo. Most of the time, she did not care about her looks and would go to the supermarket in PJs and a headscarf. Her hair was thin and brittle from weekly platinum bleaching. She thought wrapping it under a scarf would keep it from breaking. Her head bobbled heavy on her skinny neck when she turned to talk to Ronny.

"So, tell me about you and Tanner," she had said with a smirk on her face ready to take Ronny's confession.

Although Ronny was three years younger, she was almost an inch taller than Mo. As a teenager, she was still growing. Her milky skin, lighter, pallid, contrasted with her long midnight black glossy hair. She vigorously fluttered her hands, touched, occasionally slapped, and sometimes punched Mo when she spoke. Privileged with dark ponds framed in black generously lined curly lashes, emphasized by flawlessly shaped full eyebrows that would never need plucking, rendered her to appear Arab. Her bossy and know-it-all nature rubbed some people the wrong way, mostly because she was often right in what she said.

"Now is not the time," Ronny waved her hand dismissively, "I am sick of this place. I am not going to waste my time."

She loved to read, a habit she inherited from Paps and she had a photographic memory. It was easy for her to engage in conversations with complete strangers. Her perfectly developed figure landed her a job as a model in Munich.
She worked for an entire year and saved up quite a bit of money. She would be spending most of it on chocolate bars and gummy bears that she hid from us in her bedroom closet. Sharing was not her thing. These next few years would be the best she had ever looked.

"Okay, never mind, you don't have to get so snippy about it. Have some fun!" Mo said.

They would take the pizza to the American embassy and spend a nice afternoon playing pool together at the Marine bar. Ronny had twisted herself in the front seat to face Mo sitting in the back. The front truck window exposed a squatted Yemeni man. His weight balanced heavy on his heels and his upper back rested against the wall of the pizza business. A white shirt-dress bundled above the knees. A dark suit jacket folded over the dirty sidewalk and covered the sides of his thighs. His arms stretched long between his legs. A thin, loose, cotton, short-underwear, large around his skinny thighs offered a view. He reached into one leg opening and moved his hand onwards with increased frantic flogging while smirking into the truck.

"Oh my god, Ronny, don't turn around," Mo breathed in disgust, "You won't believe what that guy is doing! Just don't turn around."

Her gaze unintentionally trapped in the moment. Unnerved, she slumped her body into the leather until the headrest of the front seat blocked her line of sight. Of course, Ronny turned around to witness the man reaching his peak,

"Ugh, you could have said what he was doing. Now I have this image burned into my memory."

Tanner exited the restaurant not looking left or right. He balanced the pizza boxes in one hand while searching in his pocket for the truck keys, forgetting that he left them in the ignition.
"Quit fumbling around, hurry lets go," Ronny yelled out of the cracked window.

Patty Smith

"What's the hurry?" Tanner stepped into the jeep.

Ronny grabbed the boxes placing them onto her lap, "You don't want to know," she said giggling into her fist attempting to hide her amusement. Her plum lips pulled into a line. "There is a story to tell Chloe when she calls, she may change her mind about coming to Sana'a," she murmured. That evening Ronny shared the story with such detail it edged into my mind as though I had experienced it myself. However shocking, it was not enough to deter me from moving to Sana'a. Gulping for air, I strained to slow the thrashing in my ribcage. The intense light of the airport aroused my senses, I felt drunk with excitement. My arms pushed firm on the cart in front. I welcomed the bitter chilled air; it dried the sweat of my neck and forehead. My body desired a place to rest and my mind required a break from worry. I swung my arms clutching a dense lump, my only belongings, first one, and then the other onto the scale. I had packed the heavier items into my carry-on bag, a foolish attempt to avoid paying over weight on my suitcases. That caused my black Samsonite bag and small purse to pull heavy on my shoulder.

"500 Marks for overweight luggage," said a stiff demanding voice.

Her hair pulled back tightly into a ponytail caused her eyes to squint and her eyebrows to lift into her hairline. An impeccable Lufthansa agent with her uniform pristine and her shirt pressed into a cocky state. Just like the one that humiliated me during my job interview. When I took off my shoes to step on the scale she proclaimed before all other candidates that I should have worn a panty hose, that my suit was too lively, my earrings too big, and I was just slightly too heavy. It was a dream destroying moment. Paps wrote the application letter that requested for an exception to Lufthansa's minimum twenty-one age-rule.

I was just eighteen and Paps was either very convincing or the Airline was desperate for someone who spoke three languages. I got the interview, not the job. It was nearly the amount of another flight ticket. Grudgingly I dug into my purse for the bills.

"Wow, that's a lot of money."

There goes the gold necklace and good-bye to the shoes and clothes I planned to buy.

"Well, it is what it is. You packed too much luggage and now you pay for it."

You could always count on a German to say something without using a filter. Shaking her head, the check-in agent signaled for the suitcases to be loaded. I watched a man hoist my luggage onto the belt behind the counter. A defining moment, there was no turning back. No returning to my nice apartment in Munich that was perfectly situated close to city center and had a breathtaking view of the English garden's lush green lawns and tall trees capped by Munich's baroque churches and modern apartment buildings. I would miss Gianna and our long evenings sitting at her place or mine. Our rituals: Taking a nap after work, selecting the clothes we might wear, the clothes we might trade for the night, riding the U-Bahn to her apartment early Friday and Saturday evening where we listened to music, and her cooking for the two of us as we talked. She was definitely more comfortable in her skin than I in mine.

Gianna sat in her bra and sweat-pants, cross-legged on her metal-wire chair. She lit one cigarette with another inside her very tastefully decorated studio apartment. A hairdresser, she was unhappy with her profession. Her dream was to become a professional singer. She briefly dated Rob of the Milli Vanilli duo and counted on that connection to help her along. Her voice was enjoyable and fragile. She held the microphone so close that her bottom lip stuck to the metal.

Patty Smith

Sticky strings vibrated at the corner of her mouth as she strained to sing with Whitney. Her dusky straight hair parted and hung like a curtain across her face exposing just one eye and the corner of her mouth. Her Italian olive skin covered by heavy makeup in preparation for our disco night. We pooled our money for a cab to the first venue then rode the U-Bahn in-between our disco hops. We often visited three to four discos in one night.

The end of our outings often depended on us finding one special individual. A handsome dark dancer that Gianna had a crush on and who sadly ignored our presence. I could have probably left more things behind. Most of my belongings I managed to sell and some I gave away. My houseplants found a new home with Gianna. The money I made from the sale of a few furniture pieces my parents left was now with the Lufthansa agent. My parents sent all of their belongings on a ship to Hodeida, the northern port of Yemen and the military paid for the cargo. Had I left with them, I would have been able to take all of my clothing, including the bit of furniture I owned. Living in my parent's old apartment was certainly fun and convenient. It was close to the U-Bahn (German Subway) and minutes from Munich City Center. Paps had the idea to rent out the other two bedrooms; it took care of the entire apartment rent.

While the concept was great, I found it challenging to share a space with complete strangers. My first tenant was a young Egyptian man, Mehmed, who Paps vetted and pushed on me. With his new obsession over the Middle East, he was convinced that Mehmed was the right tenant. He went as far as giving him the task to watch over me. I guess Mehmed took the request literal. One night, I was in my bedroom getting ready to change my clothes when Mehmed walked into my room without knocking. I was in my underwear.

It was my predictable behavior to change out of my work clothes as soon as I arrived at home. He knew that, had watched me do it numerous times. I would come home in nice clothes and go straight to my room, a minute later, I came out wearing sweats. I jumped onto the center of my bed from the floor and screamed loudly in surprise.

"Get out!"

He proceeded to approach me with his hands raised. Moving toward me in that manner felt threatening.

He was not waving at me;

It looked as though he reached out to grab hold of me. I did not think I could scream any louder but I did, realizing a gut wrenching shrill. It was as if I woke him from a daze. He stopped dead and apologetically turned around, left the room slamming the door behind him. Now thinking back it was probably a cultural misunderstanding, the fact that he approached me with his arms raised that is. The walking into a woman's bedroom without knocking part, that was unacceptable. I did not feel safe around him anymore. I called Paps that evening in Sana'a and explained the situation. He got on the phone with him and they spoke in Arabic. The next day when I returned from work he was gone. I spent that night at Gianna's house just to be certain he did not return on the pretense that he had forgotten something. The following day, I found a completely cleaned out room and the key left on the kitchen table.

Patty Smith

Chapter 2

Andreas had come to learn much about the country and its fabulous tales of the Queen of Sheba and her love affair with King Solomon. The German military deployed Andreas to the Yemen. He was to manage a program by the German government that included the outfitting of Yemeni military hospitals, medical assistance, and training. The Germans donated medical appliances for the various Yemeni military hospitals and he was to manage the donations. His wife Sofia, Ronny, Mo, and Mo's one-year old toddler accompanied with him. Chloe his oldest daughter initially stayed in Munich then changed her mind and joined the family a few months later. Besides geopolitics, Andreas knew that the personal interest politicians in the pre-Islamic Sabaic, civilizations played a role in his assignment. He had eagerly volunteered for the job and trusted that if there were more to his appointment he would discover the details soon.

Andreas and Ernst were the only two German military people to have worked in the Yemen since the first German military mission after the famous 1915 shore party at Hodeidah led by Lieutenant Helmuth von Muecke. Ernst, the engineer, was to maintain the medical hardware. Andreas was in charge of medical organization. The MoD (German Ministry of Defense) made final decisions on technical investments. That meant his new position demanded he submit budget proposals. Andreas usually had his way. Skilled at arguing and churning words he convinced the MoD that his own ideas were theirs.

He was frugal with the millions of budget dollars and strived to repair existing equipment rather than replacing it with new. The Yemenis liked his attitude and what followed was a myriad of repair jobs. A fire inside the fuse box of the Siemens DR 1 CAT shut the machine down, the only one of its kind in the country. He quickly ordered its repair to spare people the travel to Egypt for a CAT scan. His job included solving complex problems, such as when he was tasked to find unutilized equipment and ready it for use. That is when he encountered two complete sets of endoscopic surgical equipment for the removal of kidney stones, a donation to the hospital years ago, still in original packing. He contracted a Bulgarian urology professor to set up the equipment. The professor successfully used it for all of his operations.

"The Yemeni people have tremendous problems with large kidney stones due to the high calcium content in the drinking water," the professor explained, "It reacts with the chemicals of the Khat plant Yemenis chew daily."

Soon after the family's arrival in Yemen, Andreas and Ernst determined to reconstruct three badly damaged OR hospital wings. One included an eight-bed intensive care unit inside the military hospital in Aden. They managed to fully rebuild and equip the hospital wing according to European standards. These projects consumed much of their efforts and stipulated that the Yemeni military agree to provide the workforce necessary to complete the job. Upon addressing their first job, they found themselves faced with a shortage of essential tools. What tools they had were often broken.

Military support personnel supplied by the Yemeni Army also posed a challenge because of their notorious absenteeism. Andreas arranged to mediate that issue by contracting day laborers who had their own tools, only to realize it came with its own set of skirmishes. He ordered a flooring job in one of the operation rooms and was horrified to find a random un-matching tile job installation. It appeared as though the person who did the work was drunk.

"This floor looks crooked," he said when he inspected the first room.

Patty Smith

The worker disagreed with Andreas. "I am not drunk. So do the job yourself," the worker said and walked of the job. Emotion sometimes took over Andreas' tongue and challenged his ability to express himself cordially. He was patient, remained calm, and would stick with a problem; it was one of his strengths. Without a tile layer and left with a ruined tile job, Andreas measured every unused tile himself. After neatly sorting them into matching piles, he discovered that the shipment had contained tiles sizes ranging from 49 to 51 centimeters long. He hired a new worker. Each OR was finished with matching tiles, one had small subway tile, the other traditional one-square foot tile, and the third was a mix of accent tiles. Andreas was surprised when he received the assignment. It was unusual that a higher-ranking soldier was not sent. A position such as this would have normally required someone with a Lieutenant colonel's rank.

He figured that it was due to a shortage in colonels volunteering to go to the Yemen for a several year assignment. To make himself stand out from the few other applicants, he sneaked into an Arabic course at the federal language school in Huerth (close to Cologne). Most Yemeni people spoke little or broken English. Yemen's military soldiers trained in Moscow, they spoke Russian and drank Vodka. The country was pretty much untouched by Western culture. Only most recently with the overthrowing of its monarchy the Yemen opened its borders. In 1962, the powerful Imam was overthrown and in his place, a republic was born. Knowing to speak Arabic put Andreas in a favorable position. As a rule, Yemenis reacted quite friendly to the new German military presence. His quirks, like his passion for chess, helped him to create relationships and solve chancy situations. He quickly connected with the nephew of the foreign minister.

They routinely played chess together. When the foreign minister discovered that Andreas played the violin, he asked him to give his daughter private violin lessons. It was important to have good relations with Yemenis so that he could move freely about the country to do his business.

Word about the German spread and tribal leaders invited him to Khat chewing sessions. He built contacts by providing tribal leaders with little hard to get presents. Gifted a hand held electronic blood sugar instrument to a Sheikh who suffered from diabetes. Therefore, it was that increasingly more tribal leaders asked for his help. Another Sheikh had a heart condition, he arranged with friends at the Ethnological Museum in Munich and they agreed to finance the Sheikh's heart operation.

The military hospital provided free treatment for military, their civilian relatives, and virtually everyone. It caused for a very busy hospital at all times. Early mornings crowds gathered at the main gate for treatment. One day, with little advance notice, Andreas received notice that a German parliamentary delegation would be touring the hospital. He expected the delegation might ask embarrassing questions. Possibly ones that would negatively affect the relations he had built with Yemenis. So it was, during the tour of the hospital the German visitors began to ask patients if they were content with the largesse of the German taxpayer. In anticipation, Andreas had resourcefully prepared. Prior to their arrival, he cleared the regular patients out of the wards and replaced the patients with English speaking soldiers. Who answered questions as instructed. That evening, after the delegation left, Andreas celebrated with a small drink of whiskey. For a brief moment, he propped his feet up on the large wooden desk he procured for his office.

He leaned back into the hard metal chair content with his little charade. Then suddenly, he jumped to his feet realizing that it was late. Sofia would be worried. He rushed out of his office forgetting to put the whiskey bottle back into the metal cabinet.

The next morning, he entered his office to an appointment with a Yemeni captain. He found him sitting in his metal chair behind his desk completely drunk. A lengthy phone call from Germany had held him up at home. He was late for the appointment. When the Captain Ali arrived to his office on time, a nurse let him inside to wait.

Patty Smith

The captain must have killed time by emptying the bottle of whiskey. Andreas stumbled upon him with his head propped onto the palm of his hand, his other arm curled on top of the desk cuddling the bottle of whiskey like a long lost pet.

The Yemeni's condition was a problem both for him and for the captain. Among the hospital personnel worked Islamist fundamentalists - though some Yemenis liked to drink especially to induce sleep after a Khat session - drinking alcohol came with the punishment of severe flogging if someone took offense. Andreas convinced him of the need to go home, offered to take him, but the captain could not remember the way to his house in the old city (also called the Suq-al-Milh or Salt Market). Andreas knew to approach problems a step at a time, he just needed to get him to his car first, and then out of the hospital. He would drive him to a friend, the house of Saleh a young lieutenant he knew from his Arabic studies in Germany.

Saleh worked in the Yemeni military. Surely, his friend would know where the captain lived. When he arrived at his friend's home, they encountered some heavily armed civilians standing in front of the building. It was a bad idea to be driving around with a drunk Yemeni captain, he thought, and probably just as stupid to let him out right there. He looked at the captain, he laid hunched down in the seat next to him, his face green, and he was close to vomiting.
"Stay in the car," Andreas said, leaned across the passenger seat to take hold of the door handle.

Andreas' words fell on drunk ears. The captain had already perked up and opened the door of the jeep, stumbled wobbly onto his feet, propped himself against the open door, and staggered toward one of the officers. With glassy eyes he mumbled, "Ya khabibi, my sweetheart," making amorous advances toward him.

The man pushed him off in disgust, loomed next to the Jeep's window, and leaned in, "We will take him out of the city and shoot him and leave him in a ditch for the dogs," he said firmly.

Andreas pleaded for the captain's life on grounds of illness.

"This officer suffers from temporary insanity due to illness and is under my protection," Andreas said with the most honest expression he could muster. Then he added, "The director of the military hospital, Colonel Yahiya, will be extremely upset if he lost his medical records officer." After a lengthy discussion that felt initially unproductive, the men gave Andreas permission to drag the captain back into his car. The two set off again driving the streets of the old city, slowing down when seeing a person, rolling down the window just slightly to ask the question if the captain looked familiar, until he astoundingly found somebody who knew where Captain Ali lived. Naturally, the captain did not remember anything about the incident the next day. The word got around among the hospital staff and they thanked Andreas for saving the Captain's life.

Patty Smith

Chapter 3

A loud hustle of hurried frantic yet organized movement between gates and up and down escalators filled the airport. Just like traffic on the German autobahn: you move slowly on the right, you pass to the left. I ran feverishly through the large cold halls afraid I might be late for my flight. I would have been happy staying in Munich if Farris had moved into my apartment. Living together would have been a small step toward marriage. It would have solved the problem of finding the right renters for my apartment. The next tenants were difficult to find. Due to the previous incident, I looked for girls my age only, young ones, so that I might have some sort of connection.

Two girls, sisters from East Germany, rented both of the bedrooms I advertised for rent. I kept the third bedroom for myself. I struggled to understand why the sisters took both rooms when they spent all day stuck inside just one. My curiosity won over my respect for other people's privacy as I looked for ways to peek into the girls' rooms. I should have had no complaints; they paid their rent on time. They were generally no bother, except around my pet. I kept a small cat named 'Qis mat', which means destiny or fate in the Persian language. Farris and I found him on a dusty road somewhere in Turkey. We placed the cat inside the car and brought him back to Germany.

Upon my arrival from work one afternoon, I called out Qismat but he was nowhere to be found.

Like so many other afternoons, he would suddenly reappeared like Houdini out of nowhere. I always thought he was hiding from me. That day, I saw Qismat slowly tiptoe through a tiny crack in the door to one of the girl's bedrooms. My interest peaked.

It was a rare occasion that both girls were away on a family visit in Berlin.

"Woops, the draft must have blown the door open," I said loudly pushing the door wide open.

Qismat furled himself around my legs and followed me inside. The room was a dump. Piles of dirty laundry covered the floor, full trash bags in a corner, and a stained sheet covered a blow-up mattress. What shocked me the most was discovering that the only piece of furniture was a large cat play structure and a bowl full of cat food right next to it. Qismat had been lured away, seduced. The selfishness of the animal hurt my feelings. I saved his life and he abandoned me for a bowl of cat food and a climbing tree! When I announced my plans to move, I was not surprised they asked to adopt the cat.

Farris, my boyfriend, owned and managed three posh restaurants in Munich where the rich mingled with artists and a crowd of long legged Claudia Schiffer wannabes that sipped on long drinks waiting to be picked up appearing uninterested. Two years ago, I met Farris at one of his restaurants. Gianna introduced us. We instantly liked each other. He, the Iranian born, was looking for a restart in Germany, me the Mexican born aimed to grow roots in a Bavarian city. Both of us torn between cultures and trying to fit in. I hoped he would propose irrespective that we belonged to completely different worlds. We had discussed the future before while we were together in Turkey. I dropped hints whenever I saw an opportunity.

"Wouldn't you love to live here in Turkey?" I had said to him while we enjoyed a sunset out of his balcony.

Patty Smith

"I could open up a restaurant and make a living here," he said.

"Is that your plan? To live in Turkey one day?" I asked. His family had recently invested in a large beachfront home in the ancient City of Smyrna nowadays called Izmir.

"Well of course. It is an excellent business location with all the tourism and why else would we have bought a place here?"

"It sure is beautiful here," I said looking out at the warm waters of the Mediterranean.

Izmir was a modern city and women rarely covered themselves. The entire two weeks I walked around in shorts and tank tops. Life would have been amazing. I could have easily lived in Turkey and have done something special like researching the 4000-year-old Greek temples of philosopher academies, the cradle of Western civilization. Maybe I would have learned to whirl dance with the Sufi Dervishes. I could have also just been happy as his wife, have children, and help him run his restaurant. I wanted for nothing more.

"How soon do you think you'll be moving to Turkey?"

"Not anytime soon," he said preoccupied with a new crossbow he had purchased. "So tell me about your new job," he asked and once again finagled himself out of discussing the subject just as he had done every time before when a conversation had the slightest inclination toward a specific answer about plans for the future.

I was finished with dropping hints and knew I would have to give him an ultimatum. One evening I took a leap. We had just returned from our trip to Turkey. It felt like the perfect setting. Summer was ending and the weather had slightly changed to a comfortable cool. Sitting closely together holding hands at one of his restaurant tables, I spoke about my decision to leave Munich, a hasty unprepared thought that left my words without inspection.

"I've decided to follow my parents to the Yemen," I said with a small voice studying his face for a reaction. He released my hand, pushed his chair from the table, walked a step, and looked back over his shoulder.

"Great, if you are really unsatisfied with your life here in Munich, perhaps moving to the Yemen is a good idea," he muttered sounding annoyed.

Perhaps he had a point; I should have been satisfied with my life. I had landed a job as a secretary for one of the leading fund managing companies in Germany just that summer, earned a handsome salary and was able to enjoy the fruits of my labor in Munich. Life with Farris was easy. He treated me like a princess. Sometimes he surprised me at work by picking me up in his black BMW Z1, and then invited me to eat wherever I desired. Any attempt to pay while I was in his company offended him. That summer he left me speechless when he paid for our entire vacation to Turkey. We boarded a ferry cruiser in Italy that took us to Turkey via Greece. We drove his car onto the ship in Rimini and stopped off for a day of sightseeing in Athens. We explored ancient civilizations, the perfect backdrop for a proposal.

The Acropolis was once a rocky hill then transformed into a unique citadel, it sat high above the city of Athens. We walked holding hands through gigantic columns up enormous rocky steps. I had fallen in love with his tall stature, strong masculine build, his remarkable blue eyes against his thick dark lashes, and his tremendous kindness and intelligence. I adored him and looked at him for direction.
Reflecting back, most likely my devotion turned him away from me.

We wandered around Athens gawking at statues and architecture when I asked him, "Have you thought of starting your own family?"

"Of course I have," he said sitting down on one of the gigantic steps leading up to the Acropolis.

"What are your thoughts?" I asked sitting down next to him.

"What do you mean?"

Patty Smith

"I mean, will you have kids?"

"Of course I will."

"When?" I continued to dig for a specific answer.

"When it's the right time to do so."

"When will you know it's the right time to do so?" I
asked with a firm tone.

"I don't know, I guess when I *do* know, *that* will be the
right time."

I stopped probing for fear about what he might say.
Staring into nowhere, he added, "When I find the right person,"
indicating that I was not the right one.

We returned to the ship for another day out toward Turkey.
During the three days we spent on the ship, Farris waited on
me hand and foot, brought me coffee and a croissant to bed
every morning, right after placing towels on poolside chairs.
He paid no attention to other girls. Everywhere we went
together, I caught the looks and smiles of other woman. I
knew he certainly captivated their attention. Perhaps they
wondered what I had to offer.

He certainly made an impression, especially driving his
brand new and very expensive Z1. I do not deny that I enjoyed
the luxurious feel of driving in it. At the push of a button, the
doors slid down, disappearing into the chassis of the car.
Another push and the entire roof collapsed tucking into a small
compartment. I felt like a celebrity as we drove down the ramp
of the ship with the doors submerged into the bottom of the
car.

Farris liked to splurge and he had the money to do it.
Our disco-jumps in Munich typically ended at an early morning
restaurant for breakfast. Gianna and I often had a group in tow
and Farris would pull out a roll of bills from inside his pocket
and pay everyone's meal at the table.

He did the same thing when we were out with my family. He surreptitiously found a way to settle the bill by paying the waiter on his way to the bathroom. Paps usually did not stand a chance.

"That's how you do it," Mom said embarrassed. She threatened not to accept Farris' invitations any more.

"You don't wait for the waiter to bring you the bill," she would say.

It happened only a few times then Paps learned to speak to the waiters ahead of time. Farris and Paps would then get into a macho tug-of–war over the bill. Farris was only twenty-two, two years older than I was. Iranians married early; however, I figured he had acculturated to the German way of marrying late. I could hear my Moms words on the phone when I told her I was ready to leave Munich.

"Why should he buy the cow if he can get the milk for free?" she would say. Perhaps his young age was the reason marriage was not on his radar. It was on my radar along with a loud alarm ringing in my mother's voice.

Mom was overjoyed with the idea to have all of her daughters living with her again. I secretly hoped for a way out, thought they might try to convince me otherwise, to my surprise, they were both thrilled. We discussed selling all of my things and Paps purchased the ticket to the Yemen. Everything went so fast that I forgot to apply for an entry visa to the country until it was too late. Perhaps my subconscious kept me from thinking of such an important step. I moved briskly through airport halls ready to depart from Munich and leave everything behind. Wearily I climbed the escalator up to my departure gate. I took a deep breath and boarded the flight to Sana'a.

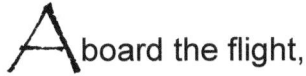Aboard the flight,

I thought about Farris again. My effort to coax him into making a real commitment backfired.

I made the threat to move to the Yemen and then actually found myself toying with the idea. Every passing day I grew increasingly excited about a new life. In time, Farris would realize his loss and ask me back. My ego would not allow me to rescind my intentions to move unless he asked me to come back. Even Gianna thought it was insane.

She called me every night and we squeezed as much fun as we could into my last days in Munich. The thought of needing to mold myself into someone else flooded my body with panic. I knew moving to Yemen would require that I adapt to an unfamiliar culture. Sadly, I felt that it was the only way. I had to leave to have a chance at a meaningful commitment. Either our relationship would stand the test of separation or separation was to be the end of our relationship. Hours later, the pilot landed the plane skillfully in Cairo Egypt. A slew of people de-boarded the plane and I followed the crowd to the transit hall. It was modest with one gift shop and a small bistro that sold snacks. I looked around the one shop to pass the time and picked up a plastic pyramid trinket to purchase.

"You must pay with American Dollars."

A short man with tight black curly hair and a three-day stubble addressed me. I handed him a ten-dollar bill, the only American money I had on me. He advised me that there would be no coins in change given back.

"Are you telling me that you will round up from 5.52?"

"Yes, I give you four dollars in return."

Feeling taken advantage of, I placed the trinket back down onto the shelf, and walked away without buying anything. A slim tall young man in his early twenties dressed in an old pair of jeans and brown steel-toed boots smiled. With a noticeable British accent, he whispered in my direction, "You will find that everything here has a tourist price and a local price."

I returned the smile, slid down into a hard plastic chair, and found a small travel brochure someone left on one of the seat next to mine. A photograph of square buildings surrounded by picturesque mountains was on the front cover:

Shem originally founded the home of the legendary Queen of Sheba known as Sana'a. Shem was Noah's oldest son.

According to a legend, the spot where Sana'a now rests is not far from the mountain where the ark washed ashore after a flood and chosen with the help of a bird. It is the oldest living city in the world and dates back to the Sabaean dynasty 2500 years (about 10,000 years old). Tucked away in the mountains, it has earned the nickname "Hidden Jewel of Arabia" because of its beautiful buildings. Nine-meter high clay walls surround Sana'a. It is home to over 100 mosques, among them the seventh-century al-Jami al-Kabir (the Great Mosque), one of the oldest in the Muslim world. Elaborate friezes and stained-glass windows decorate over 6000 multi-story clay homes. These homes are the first skyscrapers in the world.

An uncomfortably smelly crowded flight to Sana'a was my next fortune. Every seat was booked and some had women with infants on their laps. Next to me sat a large Arabic woman. Her face covered in a black veil that held on with bobby pins to the sides of her hair. She wore a long black robe-like dress adorned with buttons that closed it all the way up to her neck. No skin exposed, except on her hands, and parts of her wrists. She pushed the tray table into the seat and her sleeve lifted revealing plentiful gold bangles. I leaned forward to catch a glimpse out of the small window, in hope to catch a glimpse of the mountains. I had read that Sana'a sits 7500 feet high. The pilot announced our approaching landing and I searched to see the skyscrapers naively expecting tall city structures. I spotted a few buildings obscured by the rock around, perfectly blending into the landscape.

Patty Smith

I was impressed that homes withstood the test of time, numerous rainy seasons and hot dry blasts of desert winds blowing from the Rub' al Khali, and yet wondered what happened to an ancient civilization that was once ahead of its time. My bladder felt the rebound of a bouncy jerky landing. The entire flight from Cairo to Sana'a I had not gone to the restroom. Vigilantly watching the occupied sign above the bathroom door, I had jumped at the opportunity to use it once and happened upon a urine splatter covered space.

The strong smell burned inside my nose, made me nauseous, I could not bring it upon myself to go, so I returned to my seat. Looks pierced my back. I stuck out like a sore thumb with my uncovered straight long ash-blond hair. What I felt was a perfect outfit for travel - a black pair of 501 Levi's jeans, black studded leather belt, biker boots, and my black tailored ¾-length trench coat – gained attention. Females de-boarding the plane appeared to be in the company of other women and at least one male. Most travelled with a hurdle of children, whereby boys walked alongside male adults and girls next to women. Infants hung tied to the hip or back of their mothers. I found it irritating that there was no order in the de-boarding process.

As soon as plane tires touched ground, people stood up in the alley, and pulled out their belongings from overhead compartments. The woman next to me jumped up as if on a spring, pushed past my knees into the alley. I scooted into her seat near the window after a man hit me in the head with his elbow when pulling a heavy bag from above me. I looked up to tell him it was no problem. He ignored my attempt. My row was in in the center of the plane. I vigilantly watched for the front rows to clear out, the cue for me to get up, then people from rows behind mine began pushing past my row. Loud chatter in Arabic and warm air from the front open door overflowed the cabin.

I struggled to wedge myself into the current of people, someone knocked my foot with a large suitcase, and I sat back down until all rows behind me cleared. Bar for a family in the very back row wrestling with several pieces of luggage and boxes, I was the last person to exit the plane. The crowd moved down the small air-stairs leading onto the tarmac, I followed. We walked across the blacktop to enter the airport building. Once inside, I felt my bladder calling for urgent relief, I shifted my weight from one foot to the other hoping to get through immigration quickly.

"Yalla," a man motioned for me to get out of the crowd that formed and slowly inched toward a narrow door. I looked at him eyebrows raised, surprised, hesitating to leave the flow to freedom. He asked to see my passport, quickly scanned the pages, and signaled with his hand.

"You go there," he pointed to a glass-door leading to what appeared to be a waiting room on the other side of the arrival hall.

"Why do I need to go there?" I asked knowing well that it was due to not having a visa.

He pointed again without responding. His dark formal suit-jacket oddly paired over a white shirt-dress that ended just below the knee. The dress narrowed at his lower waist with a green-gold decorative wide belt, a large curved dagger holster attached to the side of it. The holster, of some sort of stamped and decorated silver metal, matched the dagger handle resting upon it. I later learned more expensive dagger handles are from rhino horn, a major factor in illegal poaching of the African rhinoceros. Black socks pulled up to his knees. His feet inside worn old dress shoes covered in sand dust, the old leather bore the sign of a lazy man who slipped into his shoes by stepping onto the heels.

"Yalla," he said again while he waved his arms around as if hurdling cattle.

I refrained from asking him more questions and entered the waiting room. My passport was still in his hand, he directed me into a large room, and a dread that he might lose my passport crept into my mind.

Patty Smith

I walked into the space, noticed several other people sitting around as though they had been there for a while, and told myself it must be where they directed all foreigners. A family held a picnic. On top of a thin blanket, they stretched out on the tile floor. Kids tugged at some sort of flatbread wrapped in newspaper out of a plastic bag. They must be Indian or maybe from Africa, I was not sure of their origin.

I reckoned they were not Yemeni since their skin was much darker than the skin of the few Yemeni people I had seen. Their dress was also different. Two women with colorful head coverings and lively clothing sat with their children. I rested on a chair in an empty row feeling fortunate no one chose to sit in either of the empty spaces next to mine as more people entered the waiting room. For a good hour, I waited without a sign of Paps. Staring out across the seats, I scanned the arrival hall through the glass for someone who looked like an airline official so I could ask a question. At last, a person in a Lufthansa jacket appeared at the glass door. He approached me with a smile, looked like he was willing to help me.

"You will be flying back to your home on next flight," he said.

"What? Why? I am not sure I completely understand. Are you saying that I will be returned without a chance of speaking to my father?" I said in an irritated tone, angry that I had no opportunity to speak with my family.

"You do not have a visa to enter the country," he said in a barely audible voice as though he was sharing a secret with me. He kneeled down to my eye level and repeated, "You will most likely be sent back home on the next flight out of Sana'a."

"Okay, I heard you the first time. My father told me it was all right to fly without a visa. He said that he would be arranging my visa once I got here," I jumped to my feet.

"Have you spoken to my father?" I asked feeling extremely frustrated deciding that if he wanted me on the next flight, he would have to drag me back on.

"His name is Andreas Scherer." I strained to calm myself, in a friendlier tone and attempting to hide my irritation, I said, "I am German. My Dad is working here in Sana'a. He is doing important work for the Yemeni hospitals."

I studied his face to read his demeanor but could not determine if he believed me.

"He is managing an aid project from the German government, providing for the people of the Yemen," I said in an even softer tone.

The creases in his face softened.

"You need to be patient, yes? I will find out where your father is. I will try to find out what your options are," he said while he began to walk away.

"I have no home to go to. My entire family is in Sana'a," I shouted after him.

The flight was long. Although I repressed the feeling to use the restroom for over an hour, the urgency had grown stronger than ever. I looked around the space for a sign of a restroom and discovered an unmarked door that might lead to one. I carried my carry-ons to the door ecstatic to find it was a restroom. Yet again, a strong smell of urine greeted me, this time it was insufficiently stout enough to deter me. In shock, I discovered only a hole in the ground surrounded by tile flooring, and no toilet paper or paper towels. A small half-filled metal water bucket sat underneath a faucet next to the hole in the floor. Paps had told me about the bathroom situation although I had not imagined it would be the case in an airport. His words resonated in my mind.

"The squatting toilets are actually pretty common worldwide as they are used in India, China, Japan, but also in France, and southern Europe. They do have enormous health benefits as they prevent constipation and stress on the colon through easier defecation and they prevent hemorrhoids!"

I found it difficult to squat down with my jeans around my ankles without peeing on pants.

Patty Smith

Without the time to fidget with my jeans I completely stripped out of them to use the restroom. I squatted half-naked, my pants and underpants wedged into the handle of the door. I took so long that I feared someone might soon knock on the door.

There was no sink to wash my hands, so I used the cold water from the low faucet to wash my hands and freshen up my face. I had used tissues from my carry-on to dry myself and dropped them into the hole. Dried my hands with another tissue, there was no trash can around; I wadded up the paper and throw it down the hole. Fearing that all the paper may plug and flood the room, I chose not to pull the flush. Pleased I had packed my toiletries into my bag, I sprayed a cloud of body mist into my hair, my armpits, and legs, showered in body mist, and then sprayed some around the hole.

I rolled my ponytail around the elastic band and tucked the ends into the bun. With another tissue, I blotted off lipstick excess and accidently pulled the toilet flush. Realizing my mistake, I quickly left the restroom. I returned to my seat feeling much better and stretched out into the row of chairs, a blessing they were without armrests. A deep growling woke me from a disturbing dream. My stomach was glued to my backbone I was so hungry. I only ate the breakfast on the first leg from Germany to Egypt and a small bag of nuts I saved for the second leg to Sana'a.

Chapter 4

Like a fish in an aquarium, I sat surrounded by glass walls on three sides. I scanned the holding area and spotted access to the restroom in the far corner the only other door led back to the main arrival lounge; not a single vending machine in sight. Through the large glass window, I realized that all the other passengers had cleared out of the hall. Unable to tell if it was still daylight outside, I checked my watch and calculated that I had spent seven hours inside the holding room. That meant I would not be flying back given there was only one flight per day. I rolled over the seats feeling the plastic edges dig hard into my ribs. I would probably spend all night inside the airport. The upside to my situation was that it gave my father more time to negotiate my entry. I felt confident he would find a way to get me out of there. After a few moments, I heard my name called and turned to see the Lufthansa agent was calling me to the glass door.

"You will need to place your bags on that table over there," he said.
"I can leave?"

He nodded. Two men opened my purse and black carry-on. They proceeded to empty the contents and separated out magazines, a book, and a video tape. I kept silent for fear I would be sent back home. The man that handed me my passport then pushed my bags toward the table edge and motioned with a head bob, "it's ok to go," he kept his voice impassive.

Patty Smith

Slinging my purse over one shoulder and simultaneously zipping up the carry-on, I rushed to the exit door before he could change his mind. As I entered the main lobby, my parents and Ronny greeted me with a loud "Hello." Paps hugged me first, "I have to deal with the release of your luggage," he said with a big grin on his face, "I bet you thought you were flying back. Your bags have been set aside somewhere all these hours," he said and left. Mom, Ronny, and I exchanged hugs. As usual, Mom looked great; she always dressed up no matter where she went.

"I can't believe you waited this long for me," I said.

"Oh no, we left and went home while dad sorted things out. He just picked us up half an hour ago. Mo and Rubén are at home," Mom said, turned to an Arab man and asked him to bring the car around the front door.

"The German embassy driver is helping us out here and there and is our chauffeur for the night."

"Well, really?" I said raising my eyebrows.

"It is just temporary," she explained, "I got my license and you can get yours if you like, but it's safer to have a driver that knows the city for now."

Ronny nodded in agreement. To the right of the main lobby, a large group of men bowing with their arms stretched forward caught my eye, "What the heck," I said watching them come up onto their knees, and throwing themselves to the ground once again, "Oh, they're praying."

I had seen this before on my trip to Turkey with Farris. I chuckled loudly. They prayed to a wall with a large hand drawn advertisement for Canada Dry.

"This would make a great photo. I could send it to Canada Dry," I said, "a large group of Arabs praying to their favorite drink."

"It's bizarre, when it's time for prayer, people will pray where they stand," Ronny said.

A few minutes later, Paps joined us pushing a small cart with my bags, "Did you have to pay for overweight?" he asked.

"Robbery," I said, "You don't want to know how much."

Dry cool darkness welcomed us outside the airport.

A plush Toyota Land Cruiser that Yemenis had nicknamed Leila heluwe - sweet Leila after a voluptuous Egyptian singer, swung around the traffic circle and stopped at the curb in front of us. My parents had left our more spartan Ford Blazer at home.
"I could get used to this kind of service," I said and stepped into the car.
Paps loaded my bags that weighed a ton into the truck. We drove to the Taj Sheba hotel. My family had been living there for the past couple of months while they searched for a rental home. Along the way, we exchanged stories about my trip and about their two-month stay at the hotel.
"You are going to like the Taj Sheba, although we are probably not staying much longer," Mom said.

Mom, Ronny, and I sat closely in the back seat. Paps had taken over driving the truck and the driver gave him directions.
"We have two adjoining rooms," Ronny interjected.

"You can sleep in our room, but you'll have to put up with Rubén waking up early."
Rubén was Mo's baby boy. Ronny my youngest sister and Mo my middle sister both lived with my parents.
"How in the world did you manage to get me off the return flight?" I asked, "How did you do it? They were pretty steadfast on sending me to Egypt on the next flight out."
"Making a stopover in Cairo, Egypt on a Friday which is the Muslim Sunday and all embassies closed made it extremely challenging." Paps said.

"The local Egyptair office had a deal with Sana'a airport immigration. They were not to notify anybody and instead put any traveler without a visa right back on the next return flight," he said into the rearview mirror with a smirk on his face.

"Yes, I know that, that's why they stuffed me into the transit hall for so long, but it was a Lufthansa agent that spoke to me not someone from Egyptair. Is that because my ticket was purchased through Lufthansa?"

"I assume that is so. Lufthansa does not fly out of Sana'a," Paps said.

"I knew they would try to send you back. That is why I told you to act like you felt sick when you arrived," he said and raised his brows as he does when I choose not to listen.

"Sorry, I completely forgot about that. I did spend an awful long time in the restroom; perhaps they thought I was feeling sick after all?"

"I demanded that the German embassy doctor should see you. Anyhow, the ruse worked and they put you into the transit room where already a Brazilian was waiting a couple of days for his family or his embassy to cough up the funds for his return flight."

He turned to focus on the road in front of him occasionally looking at me through the rearview mirror as he continued to talk, "On another occasion, I was asked to look after the case of a Syrian teacher who had travelled on a fake German passport from Sana'a to Switzerland. He claimed political asylum in Switzerland after he threw away his passport. Unfortunately for him, the Yemenis had made a copy of his original passport and so he was returned to Sana'a and remained there until his fake passport business was sorted out."

"Wait, I'm confused," I interrupted.

"I do not understand how this story connects to my situation."

It was typical for Paps to go off in a completely different direction when he talked, speaking round, and round until you forget your original question. He ignored me and continued, "For three days I provided the guy with food, but grew a bit tired of the situation with no solution in sight. This was when I decided to convince the Yemeni immigration officer in charge to let me put the person under house arrest in a hotel with a military guard. The rest was easy, I explained my plan to the teacher gave him a little travel money and bribed the military guard to leave the hotel room unattended for a little while. The last I heard he was safely back in Syria!"

He kept rattling unaware I was growing impatient and began to tune him out. Feeling the effects of my long flight, dazed and tired, I looked out the window. Dark shapes passed on the other side of the glass.

"Now back to you," he said in a serious voice regaining my attention, "Since the immigration officer told me that you would not be seen by a doctor but be put on the next flight to Cairo, I invited him to chew Khat with me, which he gladly accepted as I have the good quality adh-dharij Khat."

He turned his attention away from the road, "There are differences in quality and price as with red wine! Our conversation drifted to the Queen of Saba and her liaison with King Solomon. Then I threw in some Arab poetry I knew," He turned forward occasionally glanced into the rearview mirror, he shifted his voice, and recited:

"She looked at me with a wink from her eye,
She only looked but did not say a word
Frightened from her family
Then I understood that the wink from her eye said
be greeted and be welcome my dear beloved!"

"Gee dad, I can't believe you had to romance the guy to get me off," I said amused.

"Islam is rather prudish. In public, people love to hear pre-Islamic poetry. The immigration officer was no exception and soon we negotiated a solution for your entry visa," he said with a smirk on his face, and then added,

Patty Smith

"I simply made a handwritten notice into my civilian passport. I used the regular passport not the red diplomatic one. The note said that you were my daughter and thus included in the diplomatic visa."

A simple poem and a penciled note into his own visa was how Paps got me into the country. After about a 20 km car ride, we arrived at Taj Sheba hotel, centrally located and within walking distance to the old town city center. It was far past midnight and I was beyond exhausted. Without paying much attention to my surroundings, I quickly followed my sister into the elevator at the end of the grand entrance of the hotel. On the fourth floor, we walked down the hall to our room and tiptoed into a pitch-dark room negotiating our way around the edges of a large bed.

"You want the taco or share the bed with Mo?" she whispered tapping me on the shoulder.
"I'll take the taco," I said softly and plopped down onto a lumpy mattress fully clothed.
The muffled sound of honking cars, people shouting and crying out to prayer through an intercom roused me in the morning.

"Allah u akbar, allahu akbar."
Blades of sun pushed their way through narrow cracks in the dark-out curtain of the hotel room. I pulled back the drapes, cracked the window open, and pushed my face through the small gap. Below, people hung halfway out of their cars, shouted at each other, waved their arms, signaled for others to yield, or signaled to turn. A loud metal mess mutated along a paved road in front of the hotel. I later learned that this main street was one of very few paved roads in the city. The city's infrastructure was vastly antiquated. Sana'a birthed just a few paved roads with and an even fewer amount of traffic lights. Streets filled with minibuses, cars, vendors, goats, and people; the right of way given to the biggest, fastest, or loudest.

A constant sound of horns and yelling wafted in the air. In the distance, a traffic officer perched at an intersection and conducted traffic like an orchestra. He transformed chaos into a first class performance where traffic moved very quickly around. It seemed he enjoyed himself, guided vehicles while he danced away like Michael Jackson, swayed his white gloves, and swung his raised leg at the knee. Roundabouts were ubiquitous in Aden, the second largest city of Yemen; it was a former British Crown Colony.

Unlike Aden, Sana'a virtually had no real roundabouts, only intersections, some with stoplights, and all with big mayhem. Left lane cars made right turns and traffic-conductors jumped in front of cars to stop them. Occasional shootings left unfortunate overeager drivers dead; road rage. Turquoise blue metal doors framed the street below, a few of them, left open to reveal businesses. Like I had seen at the airport, men walked the streets in the traditional white long robe-like dresses with formal suit jackets, wide belts, knives, and headscarves wrapped around their heads like bandages. Some men wore colorful skirts as an alternative to the white robe. The attire was typical of Arabic countries, inherited from Bedouins, Paps had told me on the ride home.

Mostly men walked the street holding hands with each other, some squatted against walls, and others pushed loaded wooden carts amidst chaotic traffic. I closed the drapes, Ronny, Mo and Rubén still slept like rocks. Quickly, I dressed and walked down to the main lobby of the hotel for a better view outside, leaving a note on the dresser.

A beautiful round tufted settee was at the center of the lobby, like something out of a Tiffany's Jewelry store. Comfortably, I sat down feeling exquisite. I never shopped at Tiffany's; I had however, seen models lay across large turfed velvety furniture in magazines. Near the hotel entrance, beggars camped and approached visitors to the hotel. A family with a few children lay on the slim sidewalk and appeared to be near starving. A grey haze in their eyes, bodies' skinny with pronounced bellies, and bones protruded through paper-thin skin. One on top of the other they tugged at a small dirty blanket. Ronny and Mo appeared in the lobby.

"Let's step out of the hotel and walk the sidewalk for a few minutes," I said excited to scope out my new home.

"Not sure if that is the best idea," Ronny said uninterested.

"I guess you're right. Maybe just for a moment and we ought to let Mom know we're stepping out," I said.

"Why? Let us just go. We won't go far," Mo said and began to walk toward the front door.

Ronny and I followed her outside. We stepped onto the sidewalk and strolled just a few feet away from the entrance. A man to the left was missing all of his limbs. Another dawdled between cars. A blind child tapped a stick holding out a hand. A woman, I saw her often from that day forward, near the main intersection, grasped at stopped cars. She rolled her body to the side from a seated position to a folded-over one and walked on all fours, not able to straighten out her back. She stretched and tilted her neck and craned her head toward open car windows. Further down, on Ali Abdul Mogni Street, we came upon a man missing his legs up to his torso. He pushed himself around with his bare hands, his torso sat on top of a piece of plywood with large casters. The morning heat swayed above the black asphalt.

"We better turn around," Mo said, "They are probably waiting at the restaurant for us."

Seeing so many people struggle was difficult to process, I walked in silence all the way back. Upon returning, we tussled to pass children that crowded around the hotel entrance. They ran, thrashed their bodies at us, and clutched at our legs.

They heaved at our clothes and stepped in front of us pressing their palms against our chests. Feeling horribly that we did not have any money to give we smiled breaking past them. Inside the restaurant, we shared our experience with our parents.

"Most of the children are refugees from Somalia," Mom said, "You should always carry change to give the poor.

Ronny and I were driving alone and when we stopped at a light and a girl began lifting herself up to my window. I didn't have any money to give her and so she spat into my face."

"Yes, I was so angry with her, I jumped out of the car, chased her, and gave her a spanking," Ronny said proudly. "Ronny, you should not have done that," I said with a nice voice trying not to upset her. She typically did not take criticism very well, especially if it came from me. She rolled her eyes in disagreement.

"Yemen is one of the poorest countries in the Middle East, and with so much unemployment, the average annual income per person is only about 300 USD," Paps educated us. "The life expectancy is only around the sixties here and the infant mortality rate is very high, I think it's about 53 for every 1000 babies," he said.

I was surprised to hear Paps did not have exact numbers, he usually knew all sort of random facts. I assumed it was because data in a county like this where much remained unreported had to be hard to collect. A delicious breakfast buffet with spreads of exotic fruits, teas, coffee, European breakfast items such as cereals, waffles, baked goods, and Arabic dishes invited us to begin our day. I had looked forward to the opulence of the Taj Sheba, although it was difficult to enjoy knowing that people starved right outside the hotel's doors. My family members were ready to move into an actual home. The staff had gotten to know everyone well and greeted my family by name. They liked Rubén particularly well as waiters stopped to poke his belly and play with his hands. Rubén comfortably waddled around the restaurant toward staff when called, explored the potted plants, and pulled leafs of the small palm tree by our table.

"Rubén, stop that," Mom corrected him, "look what I've got here," she redirected his attention to a rubber toy ball by waving it in his direction.

"Mom, I don't know if that's such a good idea, he'll be throwing that thing all over the place," I interject.
"Hey, need I remind everyone that he's my kid and I say he can have the ball," Mo frowned at me and got up to pull Rubén away from the plant.

Patty Smith

"Sorry," I said surprised with Mo's reaction then excused myself from the table to fill my plate from the breakfast buffet.

Most of the hotel staff was from India and quite respectful always bowed, nodded, and said, "you're welcome," in response to everything. I walked back to the table with a full plate of tropical fruits. With a slight bow, the waiter offered the open menu and said, "You're welcome.

"Would you please bring me a glass of orange juice? The juice on the buffet table has not been replenished," I said. The waiter shook his head.

"Okay?" I said under my breath, thinking they must be out of orange juice, "What kind of juices do you have?" I asked searching the pages inside the large menu.

"Kiwi, Lemon, Apple, and Orange juice," he listed. "Orange Juice?" I asked.

He shook his head and said, "Yes, you're welcome."

I was thoroughly confused. My family laughed.

"The head-shaking means 'yes' in India," Mo clarified. I ordered the orange juice and the waiter walked away.

"I'll be surprised if he brings me juice," I whispered. My sisters and I spent the morning at the hotel lobby, we watched people check-in and out, perused Yemen approved magazines (the men confiscated mine at the airport) and played a gigantic game of backgammon. Hotel band members were the only other young people around, although they choose not interact with us.

"Just boring adults," Mo said with a scowl and told me about the school both of them attended.

"It's like a private school, has an American education system. All our classes are in English. They let you take tests over and over until you get a hundred," she complained.

Both Ronny and Mo attended the Sana'a International School, which they felt had much lower standards compared to schools in Germany. They joked about feeling as if they were taking special education classes.

"That sounds like a pretty good deal to me," I said somewhat distracted by the flow of people in the lobby.

"Chloeee! That means it really doesn't matter if you study hard the first time," Ronny said with an insulting undertone.

"I get your point," I said kindly.

"Then we get home at three pm and we still have more work to do because the school didn't teach us like they're supposed to," she continued, "Paps had to buy us a science kit and put us in distance learning lessons so we can learn proper science and social studies to keep up with German standards."

"I'm going to stop going to school," Mo said, "Paps said I could continue through the long-distance learning program. That way I can be at home and spend more time with Rubén."

That afternoon, we all piled into the truck and drove down a dirt gravel road toward the mountain range. After a short bumpy ride a suburban neighborhood appeared. Large castle like homes stood tall and square, each house in its own large lot enclosed by hefty concrete walls, topped with barbed wire or glass shards. Walls concealed most of the structures, but one could still discern that homes had similar building style: boxy and square with enormous colorful arched windows reminding me of churches' stained glass. Large metal gates marked main entrances. Some had small guardhouses staffed with armed guards.

"This is the neighborhood we'll be moving to?" I asked in awe of the wealth.

"With three young and unmarried ladies at home, I have to make sure we live in a highly-guarded neighborhood," Paps grinned. We came to a dead-end. Only two large homes flanked the road majestically and tall. To the left the house we were going to view, to the right another. The large metal gate opened to a friendly paved patio lined with patches of flowerbeds, to the side of the home a larger square of green grass. Grey pavers made up the walkway. Two steps led to a big landing surrounded by small walls topped with a smooth grey stone.

Patty Smith

The wooden front door stood majestic and heavy. The two story home offered a large hollow entry that spilled into a long wide hallway. I could see all the way to the very back of the home and counted seven doors left and right.

"Holy smokes, how many bedrooms does this house have?" My voice echoed inside the entryway.

"It has seven bedrooms, some upstairs, some downstairs. Two large family rooms, one up and one down, totaling eleven rooms all together if you count the office and the mafraj downstairs," Mom said.

We had never lived in such a gigantic home and it truly felt surreal. It was at least four times the size of our previous home in Canada. That had been a gigantic upgrade for us at the time. We felt as though we had won the lottery when we arrived in Canada and had our own home for the first time. This home felt like a castle. In astonishment, we walked inside the empty house. Thick brick walls and tall ceilings kept the temperature cool inside. Large thick white glossy stone stretched through the entire home, much larger tile than what I was used to seeing in Germany.

"It's marble," Mom said.

Walls glistened in bright white.

Every window, crowned with decorative Plaster of Paris, had colorful stained glass. Crown molding made of the same white intricately designed plaster surrounded every room. The two main living areas upstairs and downstairs had additional Plaster of Paris medallions at the ceiling center. Large colorful designs casted onto the tile floors once the sunlight broke through the windows. Like a kaleidoscope, the patterns on the floors changed as the sun shifted.

"This room will be used as a mafraj," Mom planned as she walked the space. "We will need to have a mafraj. Paps will have to take measurements and I will have to order it custom for the room."

I shrugged my shoulders, "What's a mafraj?"

"It is large sitting area. Mattress-like cushions are pushed against the perimeter of the room," Mo said pointing to the corners of the room, "It would probably look well right there between the windows," she looked at Mom for confirmation.

"Maybe," Mom said.

"We have seen one. Every home in Yemen has one. They are kind of fun. They have these boxy cushions," Ronny said.

"Every so many feet a cushion sits on top of the sitting mattress."

"They serve as armrests," Mo interrupted and added, "The Mafraj comes in this intricate decorated material."

"Yea, they're all made of some bright color velvet," Ronny said twisting her mouth, "*We* will get it in gold," she giggled.

"We looked around in the fabric shops and the materials are so *kitchig*," Mom typically threw in a word of German or Spanish mid-sentence it did not matter what language she was speaking at the time.

If she could not think of the word, she used whatever language came to her first, *Kitchig* meant distasteful.

"The center of a mafraj typically has at least one large water-smoking pipe," Mo said raising and lowering her eyebrows a few times in my direction. I knew she was hinting to smoking something else perhaps.

"I will get one or more smaller tables to hold the tea," Mom said ignoring Mo.

Paps walked into our conversation, poked his head inside the room, and said, "This is where I'll be holding business meetings and important men to men conversations, as is custom here." He stepped all the way inside,

Patty Smith

"Yemenis receive all male visitors in the mafraj. Women and children are separated and spend their time in the kitchen when they visit," he said.

"You're kidding right?" I could not help but laugh, "I hope you're not expecting your daughters to come and serve on you while you chew Khat with Yemenis in the mafraj!"

"Don't worry, there won't be any Khat chewing in our house," Mom assured tapping Paps shoulder. I had already heard that Yemeni people had a specific Khat-chewing time in the afternoons. Kind of like a Mexican siesta.

"Have you tried it?" I asked Paps.

"I've tried it once, but had to drink so much sweet tea to wash down the bitterness. Khat leaves are ripped off branches and chewed into a pulp," he said creasing his nose, "The bitter green leaf juice is sucked out of the leaves and washed down with dark sweet tea. The leafy mush stored inside the cheek and more and more mushy chewed leaves added."

I leaned against the wall to get comfortable. I knew this explanation was going to take a while.

He continued, "Yemenis are the only Arabs to chew Khat. It is an essential part of their society. Khat leaves contain a stimulant and deemed to have amphetamine properties. Most adult Yemenis chew the leaves every day, the morning is spent going to the Khat souk to buy Khat and then meeting up with groups of Men to hold a Khat chewing session."

Mo had pointed out a group of Khat chewing men earlier on our way to the house. I thought they looked like lopsided hamsters with only one cheek puffed out. Then, walking into the house, I spotted an older man, a guard to the house next door, who had obviously been chewing for many years. The skin on his cheek stretched paper-thin. A huge bulge of Khat forced his face to look pregnant. Three tennis balls would have found sufficient room inside.

We carefully scrutinized everything in the house. Scanning the various rooms on the first floor, Mom and I then proceeded to ascend the large stairs to the second floor.

My sisters had sprinted up to the second floor and chased each other in and out of rooms up and down the wide hallway.

"This one's mine," Ronny screamed loudly.

"Fine, then I'll take this one," Mo yelled, "You know I should have the room closer to the bathroom because of Rubén," she said.

"Whatever, you always get what you want anyway so what's the point in arguing," Ronny said and walked out of a large room sulking.

The upstairs had three bathrooms, a European one that included a bidet and two Yemeni bathrooms with the hole in the floor. Mom walked through each and determined she would use the Yemeni bathrooms for storage by placing a piece of plywood over the hole in the ground.

"You'll have to leave one at least for visitors to use," Paps corrected her.

Mom rolled her eyes, "We are not going to have any Yemenis visit us upstairs. They can use one of the Yemeni bathrooms on the first floor."

I stepped into a bathroom and noticed the shower had an electrical outlet right under the showerhead, "Holy smokes, that can't be safe," the entire family rushed over to see what I found.

"Hey this saves time, you can shower and shave all in one Paps," Mo joked.
We began to find ways the outlet might come in handy in the shower.

"Give your enemies a blow-dryer to shower," Ronny said.

"No, you can plug in a reading light while you shower," Mo called out.

"How about a radio in the shower?" I asked.

"Guess we won't be using that shower," Paps broke up the fun.

Chapter 5

A letter from the German ministry of external affairs arrived stating in certain terms that Andreas had an outstanding draft notice to serve an 18-month term in the German Armed Forces. At this time, the family was living a happy and simple life. They had settled in a small village about 50 miles of unpaved gravel and dirt roads away from Guadalajara. Buildings of clay tiles on top of a timber framework and adobe homes speckled these parts of the country.

The family's residence was humble. A tile roof held up by white washed exterior and interior walls. Water colored sunflowers decorated the living room wall; it was Andreas's artistic effort to liven the space. Wooden chairs, crates, and mattresses on the floor made up their furniture. Sofia mopped floors with gasoline to keep critters out. It did not stop small scorpions from crawling into nooks and crannies for protection and reappear at dark. Chloe grew accustomed to the smell of gasoline. When she was a baby, her cribs' bedposts rested in tin cans filled with gasoline to keep the scorpions from crawling into her bed. Their families' most valuable belonging was a VW bug with a rotted out floor that separated front from back seats.

Their life was simple. A small theater, a simple patio with a white bed sheet as a projection screen where people brought their own chairs, was the only formal entertainment in town. Kids played outside until dusk and then the family strolled to the small lake nearby.

Andreas took turns placing the girls on his back as he swam through the small lake with them. Dark cool water rippled and parted to snakes coiling and swimming alongside. A gigantic old tree leaned into the lake from the bank; its massive roots twisted and grasped the ground for permanence. Later, the family landed in Germany with just a few suitcases full of summer clothing. Chloe was seven and Mo three years old. Initially, Andreas opposed moving back to Germany regardless of the generous offers his parents extended. Then, his parents forced his hand by reporting Andreas' whereabouts to the military. Living in the small hamlet of Peppenhoven was only temporary he had promised his family. At 5 foot 11 inches, he appeared taller due to the regal posture in his back and the strut in his walk. A minimalist, Andreas was content wearing the same unmatched clothes, sometimes sleeping in them to save the effort of changing the next day.

For seven years, he traveled with only one set of clothing that he washed at night and sometimes wore damp the next morning allowing his body heat to take the remaining moisture from the cloth. Material things did not matter to him. He was content enjoying the simple things in life without what he called 'bourgeois ambitions'. He hated TV, radio, any form of entertainment. Zen Buddhist existence is what he believed in.

"You can't be creative if you just sit there with the 'do me' attitude," he liked to say.

He played all sorts of instruments, although the violin was his treasure. Every day since he was eight years old he practiced it for hours. His desire to improve was unquenchable.

Patty Smith

His subconscious wish was recognition of his talents and its pursuit drove him to be in a constant state of learning. Reading books, newspapers, memorizing facts from encyclopedias, and playing chess games consumed him. His upbringing was humble.

His parents both worked for the Nazi's during the war. The war left scars, changed people, trained them to always yearn but never have. After the war, his parents built a large home with the intent to live in it with their children. Their unhappiness drove everyone away leaving them in a large home alone. Living through a war had taught them to be frugal. Growing up, Andreas wore the same clothing and pair of shoes for an entire year. His parents always expected more and gave the least amount of praise. It molded Andreas into an overachiever.

He thought he was used to harsh criticism and kept prodding on even when his efforts were unnoticed. He liked to take risks, which is why he did not spend much thought on the details of living in Germany. He knew it was unaffordable and banks did not give out loans. Renting an apartment was also difficult. It was common to find rental ads that requested non-smokers, no pets, and no children as tenants. Having two children would make finding a rental challenging and yet he trusted things would turn out somehow. When his parents promised to help them get on their feet, he first declined the offer. Their large two-family home offered enough space, and so it was that after realizing their minimal options, Andreas accepted the offer.

Once the family moved in, it was difficult for the old German couple to bear the stresses of young children living in their home. They had endured a war, survived the post-war hunger years, and believed they could do something as challenging as share their home. They discovered they could not, perhaps due to a common conflict played out between old and young living together.

Theirs was exacerbated by political views, a language barrier, and most important, Andreas' steadfast refusal to apply to officer cadet training. The family had arrived in the dead of winter and when they stepped outside their skin reacted to the freezing cold with itchy rashes. Andreas had used a single gear Vaterland bike that he had used as a teen to go to the Netherlands on various camping trips as his mode of transportation to go the grocery store.

They balanced on the bike, all four of them, Mo in a basket attached to the front handle bar, Chloe on the back, and pregnant Sofia sat sideways on the crossbar. Chloe gripped her father's coat splitting her legs far out like instructed to keep her feet away from the spokes. She arched her back and curved her neck to twist her face toward the sky as the bike moved the family down the road towards the next small town, Rheinbach. They would pass hefty fields left and right and cross a bridge with the hidden remains of a Roman aqueduct. Snow peppered specks that melted onto her face and cooled her skin.

Their new home was now a small community with only a few farmhouses along a busy street leading in one direction to Bonn, the post-war capital of West Germany, a two millennia old Roman settlement to guard the empire's Western border against the barbaric Teutonic tribes. Ludwig van Beethoven was born there and as a young boy, he played the organ in the local Minorities church. He might have met Solomon the Jewish kid, who established the Oppenheim bank.

The poet of the Lorelai song, Heinrich Heine studied in Bonn and the infamous murderous Nazi doctor, Eduard Krebsbach, was born there. He cruelly killed hundreds of inmates at the concentration camp Mauthausen. Regardless of Bonn's former famous inhabitants, the family saw no happiness there.

Rheinbach was closer, the next bigger town along the street going in the opposite direction, a small place of medieval origin with much of its old buildings and ramparts still standing.

Patty Smith

Charming at first sight and yet it held a sinister history. Many women, even girls, burned at the stake in Rheinbach. At its center, the 'Hexenturm', the witch tower stood tall giving people that knew the history of unfortunate souls who waited for their trial the creeps when looking upon it. Their grandparent's house faced that busy street that led to Bonn and Rheinbach. A long narrow garden undulated into thick growth of forest to the back of the home.

Its gable was long,

making the upstairs interiors have no straight walls. Windows built into the eve allowed light into the spaces and a large balcony wrapped like an apron around the home extending into the branches of a large elm tree to the left. It was the girls' favorite place when they played inside on a rainy day. Sofia often sat out on that balcony from which she could see the forest behind her and the busy street in front. A light snow sprinkled and hugged the road all winter long.

Andreas had fond memories of living in Peppenhoven. He recalled combing the woods with friends and finding arms left over from the war buried in the forest floor right by the three hundred year old water castle. The castle's owner, Baron Max von Boeselager was an old friend and classmate. He thought of the night he spent poaching and burning the neo-Nazi party posters in a big bonfire at three o'clock in the morning and remembered the village farmers who knew the culprits and kept their mouths shut. Regardless of his recollections, he knew that living with his parents was not ideal. The only way to ensure his family's independence while he worked for the military was to move abroad. And so it was, that when opportunities to move to other countries arose, he jumped up and offered himself.

Chapter 6

The afternoon fell silent, stray dogs stopped barking only wielding an occasional growl in response to a car or person passing. Goats bleated, men guffawed, and a sway of cool wind announced the approaching evening. Armed guards with AK-47 Kalashnikovs and the occasional Belgian G-3 sat on the roof of the sheikh's home next door. G3 were rare, although Yemenis loved the hard recoil and heavy weight of the weapon, they thought it was better suited than the light AK 47.

The trouble was that Russian ammo did not work properly with the G3, a shooter had to reload manually after every shot, and dust of the mountains jammed the G-3 sometimes. The men squatted with their weapons across their shoulders centered on the roof. Plastic bags filled with Khat and water bottles to wash down the leaf juice stuffed between their legs. Skillfully, they picked out small tender leaves from larger ones, leaving larger ones on the green branches. They did not contain the substance somewhat similar to Meth, which made the men euphoric, talkative, and most important for their trade, alert for long hours. Cheap Khat came loose inside bags. The better quality kind was lean of insecticide and sold as bundled branches wrapped in plastic. The branched khat was kept fresh with irrigation water. It originated from the Dhahran valley and dusted with volcanic ash instead of chemicals; the Yemeni version of organic food!

The men slung unwanted branches over the wall onto a pile below for goats to consume. The wall, similar with its parapets to the defensive wall of a medieval castle, wrapped the roof so narrow it allowed for easy and vigilant watch up and down the street.

Patty Smith

Yemeni men often entertained themselves by looking down into the patio of the family's home. When they were lucky, they could see Mo sunbathing in the buff, a habit she picked up at the English Garden in Munich. When Andreas was not around, they greeted the women with a licking of lips and a provocative dance that included touching themselves. Sofia, not the least bit daunted, routinely waved her fists at them, only to add to the guard's amusement.

She shouted, "Pendejos," really stretching the 'e' sound at the end and followed her outburst with other Spanish deprecating words.

By now, she had established a morning ritual. Armed with a large plastic bag in hand and equipped with a broom she combed the area in front of her home's large gate for empty water bottles, placed them into the bag along with any trash blown against her wall or stuck in the dry bushes. Using the broom, she pushed away the goats that inquisitively neared her efforts in search of left over Khat branches to eat. When guards stepped outside of the next-door home, she shouted in Spanish and English intermixed and pointed at the trash.

It translated to, "You nasty men eat like goats. Pick up your trash." She waved the filled trash bag in her hand, a disapproving look across her face. She was used to laboring hard to keep things orderly and wished everyone did their part.

"When you grow up poor you take pride in the little you have," Sofia's mother drilled into them as children.

Sofia always completed chores with pride and perfection. Her family often misunderstood her need for perfection. When the family moved to Canada it was the first time they had a large home of their own.

The experience of living in a small apartment prior caused Sofia to take good care of her larger home. She liked to keep things right, perfectly right. She suddenly had an entire house to herself. The beautiful sofa was also her first and the five little cushions to match it.

Her home was flawlessly presentable, just like in the magazine pictures. The girls called the cushions her soldiers. They stood perfectly arranged, stiff, straight, adorning the sofa. It mattered little that the furniture did not actually face the television. That it stood perpendicular to the TV and you had to turn your head over your shoulder to watch a movie. It mattered not, that Sofia had everyone wait so she could remove her soldiers and place them onto a chair to keep them from getting dirty. All four girls lined on top of the sofa in order to watch a movie, and left no room for Andreas. The only good spot was the very right one nearest the TV. Anyone who sat further down had to slightly lean forward to look past the person's head sitting in front. No argument was sufficiently convincing. The sofa stayed where it was until the family moved again. It simply looked the most inviting where she had placed it. Every time she passed the furniture, she fluffed up the cushions, did the karate chop in the center of each one to perk up the corners, and made sure the sofa had not moved back an inch from plopping down into it. Then she brushed the fringe on the rug beneath it. She spent as long as it took to comb out the strings straight with her fingers and ensured that they all separated out nicely.

When she stepped onto the dirt road to pick up trash in the mornings, guards typically smiled shaking their heads. Occasionally, they calmly replied something in Arabic she did not understand. She had left the guards trash inside a filled bag neatly tied in front of the Sheikh's home. It sat there for two hours. The wind blew it over, the knot came undone, and some of the mess spread across the dirt road. Sofia and the girls, in beautiful flowery dresses stepped into the brown Ford Blazer, happy that it was too early for the guards to scrutinize them that morning.

"They must be sleeping off the Khat from last night," Chloe commented eyeing the Sheikh's roof.

Ronny opened the large gate to the surrounding wall of the home. Ever so carefully, Sofia backed out of the narrow opening. She placed the car into park, waited for Ronny to shut the gate and step into the truck.

Sofia drove a few feet and came to a screeching halt.

"What's the matter?" the girls cried in contrapuntal motion. Seeing the trash-bag in the middle of the gravel road rendered Sofia unable to move.

"Ok, you've got to stop the battle with these guys, they don't get it," Mo reasoned.

"I'll pick it up," Chloe sighed.

Chloe jumped out of the truck, her long skirt picked up by the wind and wrapped high around her waist. Laughter filled the truck when she posed to mask her embarrassment. "Mom you're just slightly obsessive," Ronny tapped her Mom lovingly on the shoulder.

Andreas tried to convince the girls to cover up when they went to town. The girls listened but had their own ideas about dress length. After weeks of moving things, assigning everything to a new spot, they were ready to leave the walls of their new home. They had been without entertainment or books to read and afternoons had grown long and dreary. Sofia met someone named Radka when she visited Andreas on the job at the hospital. It would be the first time they drove the truck alone through the city and they had looked forward to the visit for days. When Sofia and Radka met at the hospital, they immediately got along well.

"She is from Bulgaria, but speaks fluent Russian, Arabic, and English and some German," Sofia had a feeling they would become friends, "Radka is trained as an OR nurse and works at the Al-Thawra hospital," she said driving on a dirt road and turned onto a paved one.

"Is she pretty? Old?" Ronny asked.

"She is a tall strong lady with blue eyes and thick dark hair. What does it matter how old she is? She's got a great sense of humor," Sofia said focusing on the traffic chaos, "I hope I remember how to get there."

She visited her house briefly once before with Andreas but feared she may have taken a wrong turn.

Everything looked the same; homes were all made of the identical rock, in the similar color and style. Without street signs to guide them, they could very easily get lost.

"I need your help finding the place," she handed Chloe a piece of paper that Andreas carefully sketched so they could navigate their way.

Unable to convince them to use a driver to prevent them from getting lost in the city, Andreas picked up the phone and dialed the gardener's number "It's for your safety," he had said.

Sofia had pushed the receiver down disconnecting the call, "This little bit of freedom is important to us. It makes us feel independent," she had kissed him on the cheek, the girls had waved, and off they went with the hand sketched map.

"This is just ridiculous," Chloe said frustrated, "We need to start counting the roads after this crossing. I understand that there is no money for street signs. Could they not at least write it on a piece of plywood like it is done in other poor countries? We're going to have to pay attention."

"What do you know about poor countries?" Ronny asked.

"Well I know that in Mexico they spray-paint a name onto a wall when there is no street sign," Chloe said.

"Ok there is the Kntky frrrd Chickn," Mo said.

"The what?" Chloe looked out of the car window in search of what Mo was pointing out.

Ronny, interrupted Mo's attempt to explain: "it means *Kentucky Chicken,*" she pointed to the large sign in Arabic letters, high above the restaurant on the left of the street. Chloe examined the sign. Large letters, red on a yellow background spelled KNTK CHKN.

"They wrote it just like they would write it in Arabic, without using any vowels!" Ronny said with a smirk on her face, as though she just solved a puzzle.

"I knew that," Chloe retorted.

"Well, I did too, that's why I said it first, dummies," Mo, declared.

Patty Smith

"Alright guys, focus please," Sofia said pleadingly, "Hang on, that's got to be it. I recognize it."

The women rejoiced when they arrived at Radka's house in the old part of the city. Homes stood so tight together they held each other up. By presidential decree, all buildings had to have a facade of sandstone and windows topped by an arch of stained glass. Clay homes were only found within the historic center and in the villages outside of Sana'a. Radka's home was not of clay and yet it was small, modest, and narrow-sandwiched at the end of a street. She waited patiently outside for her visitors, timed their trip, and had they not arrived soon, she would have called Andreas at home.

Sofia parked the car in front of her house, right along the black iron fence. Kid's laughter kicking a can down the street, a crying baby next door, and honking cars roused the late morning.

"After we leave here there may be some time to go to the Shamlan House," Sofia said with guarantee in her voice and opened the car door.

A fragrance of fresh baked bread wafted past them when Radka opened the door to her house inviting them inside. She had spent two hours preparing German pretzel buns.

Gloved, she had dipped every one of the raw dough balls into a lye solution for a few seconds before placing them onto her buttered metal tray. They baked golden brown just like the ones found in a German bakery. They circled the large plate inside the kitchen and gawked at the baked goods as if it was the first time they had seen anything like it.

"It's been too long without biting into the soft sour thickness of German bread," Mo laughed in delight stuffing nearly the entire bun into her mouth. Ronny elbowed her, "let her put the plate down first, piggy," she whispered. Mo distorted her face and pushed past.

"Let's get comfortable over there," Radka placed the plate onto the small wooden coffee table.

Heiko, Radka's German shepherd entered knocking his furry tail shifting the plate close to the edge of the table. Radka grabbed a cheap can of beer out of her fridge and placed the can into the German shepherd's mouth.

"It's beer. Just a Heineken, but did you know you can get beer brewed here in Yemen? There is a brewery in Aden," she patted the dog hard on its head. The dog bit into the can and sucked while skillfully dripping very little onto the tile floor, waddled his tail heavy, and disappeared outside back where he came from.

"He is a German dog. That is why he likes to drink beer. I don't always give it to him because he gets easily tipsy, but today is special since you girls are here."
Noticing the puzzled looks, she added, "Do you guys want a beer?"

Sofia shook her head, "too early to drink and we're going to try to make it to the Shamlan house."
"Sure, it's beautiful, you must visit it. It's the one on all the water bottles."

Although Radka was originally from Bulgaria, she had lived in Germany for many years before moving to the Yemen. Her husband was German and worked for the embassy.

"I forcibly learned how to bake and cook German foods being married to Alex," she explained. "I like the food from my country much better, but what can I do, I must feed '*him*,'" she laughed. She ushered the women into the living room and brought everyone a cup of tea to soften the pretzels. For a good hour, they entertained themselves exchanging stories. Sofia and the girls talked about their move and acclimation to the Yemen and Radka shared stories about working at the hospital. At one point Radka leaned in placing her hand up to her mouth as though someone might be able to read her lips and whispered, "There was this girl from Somalia, she was maybe fifteen, did not know her age.

She and her sisters walked for days and days to get out of Somalia.

Her sisters were all younger than she was. They were refugees and escaped to come here, because it is better here. Can you imagine?" she said shaking her black mane, "She came to the hospital because she was cut open, down there."

Radka pointed to her crotch, disdain on her face, "her vagina was sewn shut," she leaned back in her chair, "they do that to make sure the girls stay virgins."

She paused; the room was in complete silence in anticipation of what was to come next. "Some man, he cut her open to rape her. The girl's father made them sew her shut again. She escaped her village after that and walked many miles alone with her sisters."

Radka repositioned herself in her seat as though she could not get comfortable enough, first leaned back and then leaned forward again.

"She came to the hospital because her vagina was infected," she said creasing her nose. Her eyes squinted, she resumed, "You wouldn't believe it, but she walked miles and miles like that. I lifted her dress and it looked like a tennis ball, big, swollen, and smelly down there."

Everyone gasped. Then Radka explained that there were no ambulances or emergency response in the city.

"If anything happens you have to find a way to make it to the hospital on your own." She continued to say, "Just the other day, I was on my way to the Taj Sheba hotel. I wanted to enjoy an afternoon out for a cup of coffee, when suddenly a small child rained down. He landed just feet in front of my car." "Rained down," she clapped her hands, repeated herself in a louder voice.

She had anticipated what was about to happen, slowed her car, stared at the child sitting on the ledge of the open windowsill, up on the second story, as if in slow motion, he fell out, landing right in front of her.

"I thought that child is going to fall. Where is his mother? I asked myself. How could you allow your kid to sit like that? And then boom."

"What are the odds?" Chloe said. "You could help him, right?"

"I stopped the car and banged my fists at the door. Everyone came out to see. The child just lay there on the floor. He was unconscious. Thank goodness, I knew what to do. Men came out of all the homes nearby to help and women peered out of windows," she said.

"Was the boy Ok?" Chloe asked.

She paused to take a sip from the porcelain teacup, and then added, "I checked the kid and decided his spine was not injured. I took him along with his mother to the hospital. The boy was lucky to come away with breaking just a few bones in his legs. They put both his legs in a cast," Radka replied. "People were surprised a doctor was available and attended to their son right away."

With only 20 doctors per 100,000 population, Sana'a had very few doctors to spare. Everyone stepped outside for some fresh air after a few more stories about the difficulties of treating people and the limitations in tools at the hospital. The sun sat low beneath shadier clouds and Radka proclaimed that rainy season might soon be upon the city.

Patty Smith

Chapter 7

I had come to realize that I was unable and unwilling to adapt to my new environment. The Yemen culture was so different from my own. Adapting would include that I cover myself with a Hijab at all times. For now, I decided not to wear revealing dresses in town and avoid a Hijab. Apprehensively I wondered how I was I going to spend my days in this country. School kept my sisters busy. I was not going to return to school, although I probably could have used a formal degree, Sana'a was not the place where I could study. In addition to school, Mo also had her son Rubén. Rubén gave Mo purpose. Ronny and my parents were absorbed with their own doings; Mom with the house, Paps with his job, and Ronny was a teen. Ronny was pretty much self-absorbed and piddled around all the time. It rather left me like a third wheel on a bike within my family.

The other day, Ronny spoke about the American embassy surreptitiously while exchanging gazes with Mo. I wondered what she was unwilling to tell me. I could not bear to watch any more Arabic TV through the home antenna, so I searched for other ways to entertain myself. We sat at the kitchen table when I asked her, "Ronny, what's the deal with the embassy?"

"Well, we can go visit if we are invited," she said, "It's not like we can just show up."

"Is there an invitation on the horizon?" I looked at Ronny who got up from the table and took her plate to the sink.

"Don't know," she said and walked out of the kitchen, unwilling to engage in conversation.

I stayed in the kitchen alone for a good time and sipped my dark strong coffee. My chest was tight as I considered if coming to Yemen may have been a poor decision. My biggest wish was to start my own family. I was ready for a child, a little being of my own looking up to me. Every time I thought of Rubén, envy verged and shuddered my body in dejection. She was a very young and a single Mom at eighteen; forced to grow up. Sadly, Rubén was muddled over who his mother was. Mo was in school all day and Mom essentially raised him in her absence.

He called his grandma "Mama." He suffered from night terrors and Mom checked on him many times a night. Mo just rolled over and slept. I imagine it was challenging to know her son habituated to crawling out of bed in search for grandma. Mo's life was not what I desired. I wanted the perfect scenario. I looked to fall in love with the perfect man, marry, and then have a child, in that order. Since I left Munich, Farris called only once. It was probably safe to say that relationship was over. With multiple prospects, Ronny had a better chance of falling in love than I did. She seemed to like Tanner. Then she also brought this Palestinian friend, Salem, to our house. Salem attended the same school as my sisters and lived in a Palestinian camp. He was a nice young man and Ronny sent clear signals that she liked him. She gave the smallest introduction when they walked in and then she grabbed him by the arm and led him upstairs like a puppy.

I did have a chance to speak to him later; his command of English surprised me. He spoke fluently with a very slight accent. Unlike the Yemeni accent, it was softer, comparable to a French inflection, I thought. I had never met anyone from Palestine. He had attractive facial features. I expected most Arab men to be small like the Egyptians and Yemenis I had seen thus far. Unlike Yemeni men, he was rather tall, probably around six foot, and quite muscular as well. His shirt was tight around his upper arms. In blue sneakers, tight jeans that accentuated his perfectly round bottom, and a t-shirt he strutted into the house.

Patty Smith

The black color of his shirt magnified the onyx sparkle in his eyes. He had perfectly formed bushy eyebrows and his jet-black hair had not a curl out of place. His most striking feature was a square jaw with a small dimple in his chin. He could have passed for a model on an Italian billboard. A smile through quick even toned dizzying speak bestowed him immediate likeability. Salem stayed for a few hours. Given that he was my sister's friend and the manner in which Ronny brought him in the house, I stayed away, alone, downstairs watching TV. In front of me a game of backgammon. I had been trying to teach Mom how to play it. Confused with the fact that my pieces as well as her pieces lined up on her side of the board and frustrated with the rules, she lost interest. I had left the large board open on the floor in hope she might come back after taking a break. In Munich, Farris and I had played backgammon daily. He taught me how to play the odds and make the right decisions focused on moves my opponents take. The board was a parting gift and the only object that reminded me of him.

Approximately half an hour into Salem's visit, he left my sisters upstairs and came down, "looking for the bathroom," he said poking his head into the room with a big smile on his face. I looked up from my book, tried to ignore that my heart skipped a beat, and smiled.

"It's further down the hall. Do you need a European or Arab bathroom?" I asked pointing to the right, "Never mind, we have both one next to the other. You'll see."

"You play backgammon?" he said looking at the board on the floor.

"I do. I have been trying to teach my Mom, but I think she's had enough."

"Do you want to play a game?" he pulled the corners of his lips tight causing the dimple in his chin to rise toward his bottom lip.

"Mm yeah," I said thinking that it was odd he came downstairs after all we also had restrooms upstairs.

"Ok I'll be right back," he said disappearing down the hallway.

We played and I was intrigued with his skill. I will not lie; I was not blind and did enjoy his company. I dismissed the worry about what my sisters may say if they saw the two of us together. My sisters and I had an unspoken agreement about boys. If one of us liked a certain person, we respected that. A necessary rule when there are three girls in the house. It was like staking your ground and marking your territory. Ronny had not said it in so many words but her actions spoke loudly.

"Don't you think you'll be missed upstairs?" I said after we played one game.

"No, they'll be okay without me for a while," he said shaking the dice in his hand and rolling a perfect combination of four and six.

He won the first, I won the second, and third, although I had a strong feeling, he let me win and Ronny came down just as we finished our third game, "Hey, there you are," she said with a forced smile on her face.

"We thought you had fallen into the toilet.

"He jumped to his feet, "It's time for me to go," he put his hands into his pockets and began to walk to the door.

"Okay, I'll walk you to the gate," she said following him. He stopped under the doorframe and leaned sideways, "I'll have to come back and beat you on the next game," he said waving his hand good-bye.

Salem was very cute, but I could not allow myself to like him. I wondered about his age and thought that Ronny was probably too young for him. She was fifteen and he was taking classes with Mo so therefore he must have been closer to eighteen. I would have to figure out a way to get that information out of Mo, not Ronny. Ronny might misinterpret any of my questions about Salem as romantic interest and that was not so, I was simply curious. Thoughts meandered in and out of my mind. The last conscious thought before I slept was determining to get my license.

It was important that I gain some independence and was able to move around the city. Incidentally, the next morning Mo asked me about driving,

"Chloe, we should practice driving Paps jeep."

"That sounds like fun, where is Paps?" I asked jumping to my feet.

"He's in the office."

I washed my cup of coffee and we broached the idea of driving the jeep. Learning how to drive a stick shift was something we both had wanted to do.

"Please Paps, I'll be careful, I promise," I said in a squeaky tone.

"Okay, stop whining. I will agree provided you guys practice around the sand dunes behind our neighborhood," Paps could not deny us anything if we pleaded.

Ronny and Mo hopped into the jeep with me and we slowly made a very jerky drive out of the neighborhood to an open sandy area.

"Hello, now we're talking," Ronny, said excitedly. She always had this kind of happiness about her.

"It's my turn," Mo grabbed the steering wheel before I could hit the gas pedal again.

"You need to stop that. Can you not see I am trying my best not to stall the engine? This thing is heavy," I slapped at her hand.

She rolled her eyes at me, "Really you're going to monopolize the jeep?"

"Fine, if you think you can do a better job, go ahead!" I jumped out of the driver's seat and stomped around to her side. She pushed herself past the stick shift and took control of the car. She jerked the jeep trying to let go of the clutch and simultaneously pushed down the gas pedal. The jeep was a finicky thing, the pedals were stiff, the stick shift hard, and the steering wheel gigantic. This was a car made for soldiers. Mo was happy to take over the driving and continued to struggle with the clutch. She stalled the car a couple of times only moving it a few feet.

"Well, satisfied?" I said, "Now you have to let it sit for a moment before giving it more gas. You probably flooded the carburetor."

"Sounds like you know what to do, smarty-pants," she jumped out and came around to my side of the jeep, "Well are you going to show us your driving skills or what?" she tapped her foot in the sand.

"Alright girls, if none of you can make this sucker move again, I will!" Ronny said giggling.

I took over again and after about an hour, I was feeling confident to drive it out of the sandy hills. Mo was more of a risk taker than I was and said, "Hey, let's take it around the hood," she turned up her portable radio.

"Alright, let's go for it."

I drove it into the neighborhood sticking to the few dirt roads close to our home initially. Our flowery summer dresses flapped around in the wind and our hair waved loose behind us. The jeep had no roof it was wide open. I got more comfortable and took it out of the neighborhood and into the busy streets of Sana'a. My sisters' smiles were generous with pleasure at our newly found independence and at the luring unrest from people who saw us. We waved at incredulous gazes peering through narrow openings in black headscarves and smiled proudly at contorted furious male faces. It felt as though we were aliens inside a UFO. Children chased the Jeep when we stopped to traffic. People pointed at us. We circled around the Taj Sheba hotel, the only area of town I knew well without getting lost. It was our last trip alone in the jeep. Paps stood outside the front gate expecting us with an unwelcoming look on his face.

"You guys are crazy to think you can drive my Jeep around in the city," he said with uneasiness in his voice, "I received a call from the Sheikh next door telling me that I should watch you better."

"Well Paps, what do you want us to do?" I asked.

"Yes, we are bored to death and want to be mobile," Mo said, one of the very few occasions that we agreed.

"We were careful," I said in an attempt to settle him.

"We are getting cabin fever!" Ronny made a good point; we had not left the house for the last few weekends bar for going shopping. My sisters could go to school and socialize with people, but I was going crazy.

"We need some entertainment, there is only so much knitting and crafting we can do," I said.

"I will talk to the Americans and find out if you can go over there to borrow some movies from their library," he said with a calmer demeanor.

A few more boring weeks passed. The highlights of my days were small shopping trips for produce along a dirt road. I worked out on a stationary bike Paps brought home, re-read my book for the third time, and played with Rubén. Finally came the day, the morning rose wrapped in dry sunny mountain weather. Excited I jumped out of bed, it was Friday. I downed a quick coffee with a piece of Arabic flat bread. Then my sisters and I ran frantic through the house getting ourselves ready when I heard a loud knock at our metal gate.

Our gardner had opened the gate and I rushed to the heavy carved wooden door to see outside stood a handsome dark young man. I briefly looked past him; the metal gate still left open, I noticed the old guard stood waiting for a sign to close it. The guard wore Paps' German military parka, the one I borrowed for an entire summer on my trip to Italy. I recognized it by the flag patch on the arm; it had slightly come off on a corner. Troubled that Paps gave it to him knowing how much I liked it had me frown.

"Are you okay?"

"Yea, sure, sorry," I said shaking off the thought and looked past the guard through the open gate in the wall. A dark color Range Rover parked at our street.

"My name is Tanner," the attractive young man introduced himself offering a handshake, "Do you guys want to visit the embassy?" he asked.

I shook his hand and smiled. "Sorry for letting you stand there, come on in please," I said signaling him to come inside the house. Instantly excited, I motioned him into the living area, yelled up the stairs, "Tanner is here to take us to the embassy."

I sprinted down the hall, swung the door to my bedroom open, it bounced back of the wall, then dug through my jeans inside the closet. I wished I had focused on bringing more pants rather than a suitcase full of dresses and skirts that I would never be able to wear in this city. I snatched a pair of jeans ripped at the knees, my favorite ones that I wore all the time in Germany. The material had thinned around my backside. I knew I had little wear left before the bottom gave out. We did not have a scale and so I measured my weight gain by how well these jeans fit. I had gained weight. While I laid flat on the floor, I squeezed into them. They were tight around the waist and my fingers kept slipping off the zipper as I struggled to close it. I was able to zip up the pants by using a hanger to pull on the zipper.

"We won't be eating lunch. We're going to the Marine House," I told Mom who stood in the kitchen fixing lunch.

"You look like a taco, in those jeans," she said when she saw me.

I could always count on Mom telling me the truth. I kissed her and waddled to the Range Rover. We drove through the city, all three of us girls cramped in the back seat. Tanner insisted on keeping the front seat empty, "It is safer to go through checkpoints with all of you guys in the back."

I thought it was because he could not decide who should have the privilege of sitting next to him. With the rumbling of the dirt road beneath us, we drove past a few homes avoiding the inner city. After a windy climb toward the outskirts, we slowed for checkpoints twice where armed guards waved us on before coming to a complete stop. The American embassy truck must have been familiar to them.

A man dressed in traditional wear armed with a rifle signaled us to stop at a third checkpoint by waving his Kalashnikov.

"This is the last check-point," Tanner said. "Let me do the talking. Kev halic?" he greeted the man with a salute. "Your wives?" The man asked as he looked through the glass into the back seat. I dared not meet his gaze suppressing a snicker.

"Yes, these are all my wives," Tanner said without blinking an eye.

The man took a step back, waved his Kalashnikov signaling to move on. Tanner accelerated the truck out of the guard's sight and we burst into loud laughter.

"Who is wife number one Tanner?" I said with a joking grin.

"Hey, you all are."

"Well I think I should be the one, I've got the child," Mo said.

"I thought the oldest is always first?"

"No dummies, it's the first that is the first, so it's me," Ronny whispered so that Tanner could not hear.

The truck pulled up to a massive concrete wall topped with barbed wire, behind it the American embassy. We slowly pulled forward through the gate. A Marine examined the truck through a tilted mirror at the end of a long stick, slowly scanning the undercarriage of the truck for bombs I assumed. Another Marine guard in full uniform leaned in and looked toward the back seat through the open driver's side window, winked, then eyed at Tanner. The two exchanged a greeting. We rolled inside to a parked position. To the left was the embassy, large and majestic, to the right, tucked behind large bushes, was the Marine House. We walked past tennis courts, basketball courts; a long stretched out very green-sloped lawn, and entered the Marine building.

Tanner ushered us straight into a lounge area with pool tables and a fully stocked bar.

"How do you get liquor into the country?" I asked him regarding all the bottles of gin, vodka, wine, and other drinks inside the glass cases.

"Oh there is no shortage of liquor here."
A buff shirtless Marine, in shorts, sweaty body, flushed brown face, introduced himself, "I'm Joe."

Mo jumped forward nearly taking me out to grab his sweaty palm and shake it, "I'm Mo, and these two goofy looking chicks are my sisters, names not important."
He grinned, "Hey Tanner want to shoot some hoops?" he asked.

"Have to watch over these girls."

"We're fine. We don't need watching," I corrected him and felt Ronny's elbow in my ribs.

Tanner winked at her and asked us to follow him into the theater room. An entire wall full of movie tapes and books awaited us. We perused the large movie selection loudly reading titles and synopsis on the back.

"Take as many as you want, they are restocked monthly," Tanner handed us a plastic bag. We filled it with seven movies.

"What do you do with the old ones?" I asked.

"Just store them or give them away."

"Wow, what else do you guys have?" Mo looked around the room.

"Books, food, and booze."

"Cereals for breakfast, real butter, and real milk?" I asked.

"Pretty much."
How I missed the simple things. I had not eaten cereal since we got to the Yemen. The milk sold in some stores was not always pasteurized.

Patty Smith

It could carry harmful bacteria such as Salmonella and E. coli that could potentially make you ill. We received large cans of powdered milk in our shipment from Germany. Drinking it made me feel like an infant and it tasted awful. The only time we enjoyed fresh milk was when we ate at the Thai Sheba hotel.

Yemeni grocery stores did not sell butter either. Butter and cheeses like the ones in Germany were foreign to Yemenis. There was plenty of goat and sheep cheese available, but I could not get past the smell to eat it. I was so happy to find a cream cheese once inside an unassuming convenience store. It was the kind of store, which stocked just about everything from groceries to nails. The small-wedged cheese came wrapped in gold foiled paper. It was the kind sold in Europe. Only normally, the wedges make up one round piece, placed as a whole wheel into one packet.

The storeowner had opened the round packet, taken out the individual cheese wedges, and was selling them separately next to the gum and sweets, as if it was some sort of candy. I saw a person buy one, unwrap the wedge, and eat the cheese alone, without bread or crackers. He bit down half the wedge, left the other half in the wrapper as if he was biting off a piece of chocolate. I wondered if when Arabs traveled to Europe they had the same surreal experience as I did in that moment. We probably did strange things with their foods. I knew they thought it was stupid we ate using both of our hands. Muslims used only their right hand for eating. The other was strictly for using the restroom.

"Who needs butter if you do not have bread to go with it anyway?" I said aloud.

"We get margarine," Tanner said.

Yemeni bread tasted so good butter would ruin it. My favorite bread was the kind they served at the fish and bean restaurant. A place we discovered while driving around the city. We were the only women eating there at the time, but felt comfortable in the company of Paps and his colleague Ernst. It looked like a three-car garage converted into a restaurant.

Yemeni men, sat at long wooden tables and benches, the restaurant's floors covered in peanut shells. Large egg-shaped ceramic ovens in which they cooked stood near the back wall. Freshly caught fish was burned to a charcoal inside them. The cooks slapped pizza-like dough against the hot oven wall and it baked quickly into a delicious naan-like bread, the most amazing I had ever tasted. It was stretchy, full of air pockets, moist, crunchy, some parts burned, others oily. The restaurant only had fish, beans, and bread on the menu. Wrapped in newspaper the fish was black on the outside and incredibly moist on the inside. The entire fish was submerged into the fire with head and tail attached. Then cut open, flattened, and rubbed with spices. The selection of spices created an explosion of sensations in my mouth, my taste buds danced. Who needed bread and butter when you could have this?

For breakfast, I had explored eating papaya with lemon and sprinkled it with chopped dates and pistachios. I had never eaten any of these foods before coming to the Yemen. Surely, we could have found them in Germany but most likely not afford to eat them. The Marines whipped out bags of chips and sodas that did not taste like perfume and we attacked the goods like barracudas. We spent a few hours playing pool, sat at the bar, and chatted. Mo watched a movie in the other room with Joe and came back her hair all messy. We returned with a goodie-bag of snacks and entertainment to last us a week. Charged with the excitement of the day I struggled to focus on a movie we brought back from the Marine house. We had slipped it into the player and sprawled out onto the large leather sectional downstairs. Everyone had a favorite spot on the couch. I liked to sit right in the center where the couch made the L-shape.

Ronny and Mom usually filled in on either side of me. If someone got up, I stretched out. Mo liked to snatch the large matching chair. She turned it toward the TV with its back to the couch to prevent anyone from engaging in conversation with her during a movie. On the other hand, Ronny and I made small side comments all the time. Paps rarely ever watched something with us.

Patty Smith

For one, there was insufficient room for him to sit and the other reason was that he looked forward to reading somewhere without disturbance. Usually he read wherever he happened to be at a particular moment when he happened upon a book. Sometimes we found him standing like a statue by the bookcase reading. A book demanded his attention and he never made it to a comfortable spot. Only half way focusing on the movie, my thoughts wrapped in consideration of my future. If we could go to the Marine House every now and again, it would make living in Sana'a bearable, "Heck, even fun," I said aloud.

"Shhhh," Mo yelled slapping the leather.

The following morning, the Imam did his usual call. I laid half-awake, nuzzled into my pillow. The early sound of his voice echoed off the gravel streets and resonated in the large colorful glass of my bedroom.

In the distance, I heard dogs barking, car horns, and the wind. Overnight, it had picked up a plastic bag and blown it against the corner of my window. The sky was a darker shade of blue. I wondered if it might rain. I carefully examined the plaster around my window while I recalled a conversation I had with Tanner at the Marine House. He told me about some events the Marines had planned. The next large event at Marine house was a party only a week away, and then the Marines planned a yearly ball and a Halloween party the following month.

"The entire expatriate community will be invited to come and hang out," he had said driving us home.

"People contribute to the bar or donate money to buy booze."

I did not care much about drinking. Alcohol had a strange effect on my body. I did my best to stay away from it, however, alcohol attracted people, and that was terrifically exciting. I picked myself out of bed.

Outside my door, I caught the tussling of dishes in the kitchen, most likely Mom was preparing breakfast. I dressed myself in my jeans and a long t-shirt. It was long enough to cover my behind. I felt a little more comfortable when my bottom was not quite showing and knew I would have to increase my exercise.

"Today we are going into the old city," Mom turned to face me. She was drying dishes with a kitchen towel.

"The city center?"

It would be my first time going into the city and I was excited to get out of the house.

"Yes, to exchange some money at the disreputable black market," Paps said peeking over the Arab newspaper. "We get a better exchange rate there than the bank gives us," he was sitting at the small round table that was set up for breakfast.

"Let's have breakfast first. Tell everyone to get ready would you?"

I could not remember the last time everyone sat around a table to eat breakfast. It was an enjoyable moment. My sisters and I had grown apart the last few years, we fought like most siblings did and it became acceptable not to sit together. After breakfast, we piled into the truck and drove to the city. A wind had blown all sorts of trash around overnight. Trees looked like they had given fruit to thin plastic bags that found refuge in branches, empty water bottles and pieces of paper clung to shrubs. Paps swung around to a stop causing everyone inside the car to lose balance and fall on top of each other along the back seat. His driving was horrific since moving to the Yemen.

He turned away from the steering wheel, "Hop out. I'll find a parking space and meet you here."

We were at the mouth of the Souk bazaar. A sea of Yemeni men and wooden carts stocked with produce lined the long steps to the top of a square. Standing around carts and along a row of taxicabs, were huddles of Yemeni men wearing either '*futas*' (ornate woven scarfs they wrapped around to make skirts) or '*thobes* (a white long shirt-like dress).

Their hips embraced by wide belts with 'jambias', curved sharp daggers.

"I'll be right back."

"He couldn't have found a better place to leave us?" I said facetiously looking around the market square.

We spilled out of the truck. First Ronny, then Mo with Rubén on her hip, Mom hopped out of the front seat, then I from the back row. It was a norm to have a car full of people when I was younger. My parents drove a tiny bug in Mexico and when we visited family, everyone pushed inside, even if someone just had a doctor's appointment, or Mom had to run a small errand, the entire family came along. Piling into the truck together to run an errand felt nostalgic. I stepped out last to a crowd of begging children around us.

"Here you go," Mom gave every one of them a small coin, "We better move away from here or more children will come soon," she said.

She was right, as soon as other children further away realized Mom was handing out money they came running towards us.

"I'm sorry, I don't have any more change," she apologized.

Yemeni Men flung Arabic words our way. I turned swiftly to tell Paps to stop the car and let us back inside but only managed to graze the backlight of the truck with my hand.

"Of course, he didn't just hear me shouting and hitting the back of the truck."

Paps was either losing his hearing, his father was hard of hearing, or he was once again inside his head. Lately he seemed distant and always focused on something; you would have to repeat things several times to gain his attention. I pointed to what appeared like an opening further down into the market, a safer spot, and charged ahead through the herd of people.

"Let's wait over there," I said.

Mom and my sisters lagged behind. Protected in the crouch of stone homes we waited for Paps. Some merchants approached us holding baskets with foods, jewelry, and other items. An eternity passed when Paps finally returned.

"Honestly, did you park the truck at home?" Mom asked with irritation in her voice.

We commenced to walk through the market. Narrow streets filled with men erratically twisted around stocked shops. Rarely did I spot a woman; Men did the household shopping in Yemen. When I did, it was behind a counter and unexpected on occasion inside small stores kept with gold or silver and always only in the presence of males.

We walked a maze of sprawling disjointed dirt roads where people haggled hand woven rugs, fruits, nuts, vegetables, live goats, chickens, fresh baked goods, jewelry, and household items. Tailors and repair people sold their services inside small shops. At a T-junction, baskets burst with spices, a dry mist of fine powder hazed the air when a merchant heaved a scoop out of a pile, *ras el hanout*, nutmeg; cumin, saffron, and other novel fragrant spices capriciously filled our nostrils. I sneezed uncontrollably. We reached a labyrinth of organized sections for ornate handiwork; its items confused me of their purpose.

At a juncture,

I stepped into a basket shop and found a wonderful little hand woven plant holder. A small bowl-like basket, woven out of some sort of palm leaf with four long braided strings on its sides; it looked a lot like the flower baskets sold in garden stores back home. Trailing behind me were my sisters. I pointed out how we could hang flowers on the side of the house inside the small baskets, when a dandy old man, eyes closely separated by a thin long nose, clarified out of a black scruffy beard, that they were muzzles for camels (Paps translated). I bought a few anyway with the intent to hang plants inside them.

Patty Smith

I saw a marble plate sparkling, its center raised into a small peak topped with decorative copper. I suggested that it would make a great ashtray, and learned it was an oil lamp. We stepped up to a jewelry shop, only a large counter placed a few feet away from an alcove.

"Salam walikum!"

A man greeted us behind the counter, a slight hump on his back, years of dry weather had rippled his skin like rings in a tree stump, his hands leathery. The display of items he sold exhausted every little space.

A covered wall with *Jambias* made of finely decorated silver or some sort of tin material stood to the right of a glass case. Another wall exhibited belts stitched with curvy curly pattern in gold and silver thread, a third wall wrapped in necklaces, each of big colorful glossy stones among large ornate silver beads. The display case featured oodles of silver bracelets. I bought a bracelet that reminded me of a handcuff. It was large and heavy; opened by pulling at a pin that hooked the two halves together.

"This bracelet is original Jewish handcraft. Very old," the vendor said.

I smirked in disbelief and looked at Paps for confirmation. He shrugged his shoulders. With our backs turned to the small marked street, we stood looking inside the case.

Suddenly I felt a slow but definite touch down my backside, a hand wrapped back up between my legs. I struggled to comprehend what was happening. I looked down, saw a hand appear between my legs, it grabbed my crotch, then slithered back, and disappeared into the crowd behind me. I sought to scream but the shock of being touched like that robbed my voice. I managed to let out a small screeching sound that not even I recognized to be my own. I looked over and Mo had seen the hand between my legs because her face froze into a frown.

Ronny shouted breathlessly, "Dad, someone just touched Chloe between the legs."
Paps was in a daze.

"Paps?" Mo shouted to wake him.

"What? Who touched you?"

"How would I know who?" I said annoyed looking into the crowd for a guilty face but saw none.

Paps ran into the crowd yelling,

"*Kalb*" and other Arabic words, I had no idea what they meant. The crowd parted to reveal someone running in the near distance. Paps rambled behind him. Countless men with sticks came out of the woodwork and shops curious about the commotion. Someone in the distance broke the man's path. The crowd caught up and began to beat him with sticks. The ride home felt like an eternity of bumpy streets and I could not get home fast enough. Once arriving, I jumped into the shower at once to wash the dirty feeling off my body. That afternoon, Paps took all of us out once more.

"You are all buying Hijabs. There is no question about it. You will wear them when you leave the house to go into the city," he ordered.

We searched for the right Hijabs, hoping for some variations, they all looked the same, a black coat-like dress to hide our bodies. In the row of shops next to the Taj Sheba hotel, I bought one that zipped up easily so it felt more like a coat; actually, it reminded me of a graduation gown. The upside to having a Hijab was that we could now wear anything underneath and I looked forward to wearing jeans everywhere.

Patty Smith

Chapter 8

A frosty sheen of sunshine broke through dark clouds; rain had been tapping against the windows all night and well into the morning announcing rainy season. Sofia was a small framed nimble woman in her fifties, olive-brown skin, and an adroitly petite nose that indicated her French roots. Her brown eyes lined in lashes that were too short due to her trimming them when she was a teenager. Her older sister, envious of her long lashes told her that if she trimmed them, they would grow back even longer, they never did. Her hands showed the signs of arthritis. Her finger knuckles swelled up, not always returning to their original state. Regardless how much ice she placed on her joints it was too late for her right wrist, the disease had forced it stiff making it difficult to do things. Sofia rejected capitulation.

She received her diagnosis from a Canadian military doctor nearly twenty years ago. At first, it was a setback. She followed divergent treatment methods, from gold shots to freezing in ice chambers, took anti-inflammatory pain pills, and visualized herself in a wheelchair just as doctors predicted. She felt ulcers growing in her stomach as a result of all the pills she took and her body stiffer with every passing day.

The illness began in her hands, and then progressed to her elbows, and shoulders. Her toe joints popped out in places that made wearing heels a challenge. The dread of waking in pain was overwhelming. It had been impossible to stretch her right arm without agony. With her arm fixed into a ninety-degree angle for months, she was dependent on help to get dressed, climb stairs, and eat.

She had been unable to reach for things across the table or do something simple such as open a jar of jelly.

Then the unthinkable happened, a friend who taught fitness classes at the YMCA insisted that she exercise.

"It's okay Sofia, just move as little as you can," she had said.

Sofia uncovered the key to health and over the next year regained her mobility. She exercised regularly, even ran a marathon, and earned a certification to teach her own classes at the Y. Since moving to Sana'a, she only worked out for an hour or two a day. Every morning she changed into her leotards or shorts. Sometimes she placed weights on her ankles and wrists for a deeper workout. No matter how stiff or how much pain she felt, she moved, stoking the fire in her joints until she felt them smooth again and the pain vanished. She stepped up and down to music, kicked intermittently, heaved her arms in and out, initially slow and painfully, and then with more intensity, pushed through, sweating.

It was not worth the stress it took to get her girls to join her in a workout. They habitually argued over who could stand where or what music played. Her daughters had become less understanding of each other since everyone was back together. It was beyond Sofia's comprehension. She grew up as one of six siblings, four of them girls, all crammed into a small bedroom, not any of the luxuries her daughters enjoyed. Her daughters had their own bedrooms and bathrooms, occasionally a chauffeur, a house cleaner to pick up after them, and yet they complained.

Patty Smith

They made no effort to help around the house. She in turn, grew up with lots of chores to do. Everyone pitched in, mopped floors, helped around the kitchen, cut newspaper, and placed the squares onto the large metal ring to wipe when using the toilet. Chloe protested about the lack of butter. Her girls did not know the struggles of poverty. Sofia had to shred old cotton sheets and line her underwear with them. The pain of wearing a damp lump that stuck to your skin in the heat of the day and the embarrassment of hiding from your brothers to wash your own blood out of the cloth to reuse, she would never forget.

Chores were plenty and yet they walked around complaining of boredom. Whatever memories they formed of first moving to Germany, they had certainly forgotten. Where did their sense of entitlement come from? Sofia was content with the move to Yemen. It allowed the luxuries of a rich life; an experience denied to them had they stayed in Germany. Andreas was a good provider, nonetheless, since moving he had delved intensely into his work, arrived home increasingly later, and did not call to say he might be late. Absent minded, with his head in relentless thought he re-read the same books. He read the entire collection of encyclopedias and always with an Arabic newspaper in his hand. Who read an encyclopedia? She was ready to throw that away. He stacked random facts into the filing system in his brain, like an automaton he walked around with all that information weighing him down.

The incident at the British embassy pool was a prime example. Andreas needed to go home to use the restroom. The restroom situation was always a challenge in Yemen. When they were in close proximity to their house, they always drove back to use the restroom in the comfort of their own home. She expected Andreas to come back straight away and not stay at home reading. Over an hour had passed, she had worried something happened, and then he showed up in a different outfit. He had changed out of his black shorts into a pair of wine colored corduroy pants with a green-mustard tweed suit jacket. Not only was it too hot, he was completely un-matched.

"What the heck took you so long?" she asked him eyeing him from top to bottom.

"Why do you now look like it is middle of winter? I picked out your clothes you had on before. Why did you change?" The tone of her voice raised for the last question.

"I was reading the paper," he whispered expecting her to understand the connection.

"And?" she asked loudly.

He leaned in, placed his hand over his mouth, and muffled, "While using the restroom," he raised his eyebrows and peeled his eyeballs making them pop out of their sockets. She looked at him puzzled. He paused holding the eye peeling, a sign of discontent.

"I realized that I must have forgotten about the time when my legs began to tingle," he said and added, "From deprived blood circulation."

"No," she stretched the 'o', now she could understand the connection. He took so long because he read.

"But why did you change? It's hot!"

"Yes," he paused again.

She was losing her patience. He did this routinely. Say 'yes' and not finish his thought. "Yes, what?" she said annoyed.

Patty Smith

"I jumped up, but my legs gave under my weight. I quickly turned attempting to stop myself from falling and grabbed on to the water-pipe." The water pipe led from the back of the toilet high up the wall to the water tank; it was an old-fashioned toilet.

"I pulled the entire thing of the wall," he said with a smile.

"Did you hurt yourself?" she said in a troubled tone. He ignored the question, "My clothing got soaking wet, the tank came crashing down and missed me as I lay on the floor."

It had shattered into big porcelain pieces next to him. The pipe gushed out buckets of water. He had to shut it off with the key behind the toilet bowl. A solution that came to him slowly enough that the entire bathroom floor had filled like a small pool. Sofia giggled at the memory of Andreas poolside in a tweed suit jacket. She stepped up and down vigorously to one of her favorite eighties songs by the Police. Chloe came out of her room announcing she would work out with her.

"Can I use the ankle weights?" Chloe asked noticing Sofia was not wearing them.

"Sure, they're in my bedroom," Sofia said through a heavy breath.

Chloe rushed into her bedroom to change and returned a moment later in full workout gear. Mo jumped along Sofia with the weights strapped to her ankles.

"Hey, I called the weights earlier" Chloe shouted over the sound of the blaring music.

"Well, I've got them now," Mo screamed continuing to stomp up and down on the plastic board.
"Mom?" Chloe raised her shoulders, wondering why she had let Mo take them.

"Chloe did ask for them first," Sofia said in between huffs.

"Fine!" Mo said unstrapping one of the weights and chucking it at Chloe's face hitting her nose so strongly it bled.

Chloe shrieked in pain clutched the second weight out of Mo's hand while pinching her nose. "Holy smokes, I think you broke my nose. Mom? What the heck?!"

Sofia was not the slightest fazed, "You two need to cool your jets. Separate!" She said remaining impartial. She imagined that Mo was probably struggling with mixed emotions around Rubén. She knew Mo had pent up anger over losing her boyfriend to the justice system. Days before Mo gave birth to Rubén the police had arrested Rubén senior and sentenced him to serving time in jail. Sofia knew he was a skiver, but robbing a bank just days before his son was born, that was a massive surprise to everyone. Mo persuasively moved to the Yemen, she had no alternative and she was probably perplexed at Chloe's decision to move there also. Undoubtedly, she felt threatened by Chloe. Chloe and Mo were quite opposite in their personalities and yet both her daughters. She loved all three of her them just the same despite Mo's accusations that she favored Chloe or Ronny. It was simply untrue. She would usurp the situation, it could not continue in this manner. Andreas not home, girls constantly fighting, and Rubén called her Mom instead of Mo. These issues would be resolved. She had been thinking of a small trip that might help everyone bond and force Andreas out of the hospital.

Clearing her throat with a big gulp of cold water, she called out "Girls how about we take a trip out to the Shamlan House?"

They drove through fifteen kilometers of sandy colored hills with slight green vegetation that occasionally broke the space to arrive at Shamlan village. It was one of the oldest inhabited cities in the world surrounded by mountains of Wadi-Dhaher and plantation farms in an isolated six-kilometer valley. Yet the magnificence of, *Dar Al Hajar*, the Shamlan house, pictured on labels of plastic water bottles sold in every shop in Sana'a, was stunning beyond imagination. A road led around large rock down into the valley. Everyone stepped out of the truck and climbed their way up the small ascent. Circled by a small group, a tour guide stood just outside the palace.

Patty Smith

"*Dar Al Hajar* is this hefty rock palace, originally built in the 18th century, then restored in the 30s by Imam Yahiya who used it as his summer home, it is one of the most popular buildings in all of Yemen. If we had come on a Thursday or Friday, we would most likely see a wedding. Yemenis like to use the site for celebrations," he said in a loud voice.

"Man, we should've come on a Friday," Chloe said listening to the guide, eager to learn about the palace.

Low dense skies surrendered to the strident piercing of sunrays. Andreas knitted his brows looking up at the sky and wondered how much time they had to explore their surroundings before rainfall. Rainy season was upon them and one could nearly set their watch to the predictability of rainfalls, although skies over Shamlan might have had their own temper. The front view of the castle appeared to balance approximately forty feet or more high on top of a large rock, a limestone formation. A three-story building with arched decorative windows framed in white paint and crowned with an ornate wall surrounding the flat roof stood before them. The side view exposed layers of smaller buildings, constructed of the same limestone, cascading down the back of the mountain, marrying the structure into the rock. The girls stepped inside the castle. It was open to the public.

All three together walked past artifacts, not paying attention, up numerous flights of stairs that wrapped their way toward the roof, in ambition for a view. From the roof, they saw a wide road, three rows of traffic, a slowly morphing parking lot that led to a small green oasis of trees and patches of grass amidst dustiness; the village below.

"Wow," Ronny cried out.

"Look at Chloe."
She pointed at her sister standing at the center of the flat roof. Her hair was charged and stuck straight up from her skull. "Chloe, you should see yourself. You look like you've put your finger in a socket."

Mo laughed.

"No, she looks like she's rubbed her head onto a balloon," Ronny corrected.

"Take a picture, already."

"Stand still," Mo said and shot the photo.

Clouds were dark blue with sunlight crusts, the air thick with dampness. Andreas stepped onto the roof uproariously shouting, "Get off the roof, crazies, unless you want to get struck by lightning, come on!"

The sky parted to a flurry of water drops peppering, jarring billows rolled in heavy winds, a large antenna swayed off balance falling onto the floor, loud thunder vibrated the glass windows resonating inside the girls' chests. Wet, they ran back inside the castle, gathered Sofia who was still looking through the first floor holding Rubén at her hip.

"I'll go fetch the car. Be ready," Andreas ran through rain toward the truck.

Light rain turned into sweeps of water buckets thrown sideways against the car lasting the entire ride back to Sana'a.

Streets were under water so deep they feared they might not make it home. Abandoned cars parked along the banks, mounds of trash, plastic bags, water bottles, cardboard, and a small wooden cart traveled buoyantly down the dirt road to their house. When arriving at home, the family found a dark truck parked outside of their home. Chloe jumped out to open the gate. Andreas drove the truck inside the car lot. While Sofia, Ronny, and Mo dashed through puddles into the home, Andreas stepped out to shut the gate and noticed a man dressed in a dark jacket with a small attaché case in hand walked toward him.

"Salam Walakum," he said loudly nodding.

Andreas stepped in front of Chloe ushering her to go into the house, then greeted the man, "Walakum Salam. How can I help you?"

"I have some business to discuss. I am from the Yemen Secret Service. May I come inside?"

"Sure," Andreas led him into the mafraj and offered him tea.

They fell silently, Andreas' attention arrested on the man's face, then realized that he should begin the conversation with small talk, as was custom, before getting to business.

"How are you?" The man asked once more, this time in English.

"Very well, thank you."

"You?" Andreas asked.

"Shukran jazilan, thank you, well. May I ask about your family?" The man said.

"What do you wish to know?"

"You have children?"

"Yes, I have three daughters."

"They all live here with you?"

"They do right now, but one is getting married and leaving soon. The other might leave to go to boarding school in Germany. Not sure yet."

"Do you like it here in Yemen, have you been here long?"

Trying to be inviting and yet reserved, Andreas shared only a few details about his job.

"Do you feel like a Yemeni yet?" The man asked.

The eerie manner in which the man had suddenly invited himself and all of the probing caused Andreas to feel suspicious.

"Do you have a jambiya?" The man asked smirking exposing his yellow teeth, lifted his head, and scanned the bookcase where Sofia displayed all sorts of mementos in addition to books. Then he took a whiff of his tea and said, "Do you own a Kalashnikov, or need a gun?" he sipped the tea, wiped the drops left on his beard with the back of his hand, and added, "I can help you purchase a nice gun or even a Kalashnikov."

"Oh no," Andreas got up and proudly pulled down the Kalashnikov he hid on top of the bookshelf." I have this one, a present from our Ambassador and another. Chinese made."

"Nice," the man examined the gun and placed it down next to him, at this point, Andreas wished he had not kept it loaded. "Let's get to business," he said while gurgling through the last sip of his tea, "I will need to leave this suitcase of money with you," he patted the top of the case.

"Money? For what?" Andreas asked thoroughly confused and wracked his brain to understand the trick the man was playing.

"Yes, I need to leave it in this house. It belongs to the owner of this house."

"Mm," Andreas kept his voice impassive.

The man leaned forward to meet Andreas's gaze, "The owner of your home works for the Police Academy. He will pick this up from you later. Here in this house."

"I do not know what kind of business the owner of this house made with you, the secret service, but I cannot accept this money. Not even just to hold it for a minute," he said firmly, felt alarmed, and knew not to get involved in funny business.

"But the money is not for you, you will be holding it for the owner of this house. This house is his property and so is this money."

"I understand this is his house, but I am renting it from him and so therefore it is my house right now."

Andreas stood up and so did the Yemeni. The man walked toward the front door leaving the case behind. Andreas picked it up and followed him with it. At the door, he pressed it into his arms, "Thank you for visiting," he said with a grin and added, "German law states that I am not allowed to accept any money even if it is not meant for me. I could lose my job. I must insist that you take it with you and find someone else to hold it."

The man looked upset and said goodbye clutching the case. Bewildered Andreas entered the home and put the dead bolt in place. It rained shards of water for days, stopping early mornings long enough to allow glimpses of sun to dry the earth. By mid-day winds picked up and it rained again. The earth was so saturated it could take no more, flooding the city nearly every day.

Chapter 9

Andreas drove like a mad man through the city, pulled up in front of the Taj with a bounce, one tire hopped onto the curb and then plopped back down; the truck came to a parked position. Everyone lost their balance and jostled around on the back seat. Chloe struggled to dislodge the wedged heel of her pump from the grooves within the rubber mat and was last to step out of the truck. A hand reached inside assisting her through the open door, "Ma'am?"

"Oh, thank you," she said kindly gripping his hand and stepped out.

She bunched her dress and raised it to climb the steps leading into the Taj Sheba hotel. Awkwardly, she walked through a flurry of activity inside the wide lobby. It had been glamorously redecorated, special to that night's event. The opulent space felt warmly inviting, fluffy oversized chairs clustered together created intimate seating arrangements. Sofia engaged in conversation with a woman as she waited for Andreas to park the truck.

Past her discerning gaze, Chloe walked to the back of the hotel with a grin. She had made her own dress for the event; it was a beautiful sheer silk gown with velvety flowers strategically placed to conceal her body underneath it. From the front, the dress looked demure reaching high to her collarbone. It exposed a low-sloped cutout at the back and ended just above her sitting bone. Sofia and her sisters had a tailor make their dresses. It was very inexpensive to have a dress sewn and stores in Yemen carried the most gorgeous Indian silks.

Cautiously she stepped over the threshold out to the back patio, wobbling over pavers with care not to catch the heels of her shoes within the gaps of the stone. Red and white lanterns hung like fruit of branches casting prisms of beautiful light beneath them. Eight handsome men in blue uniforms offered white gloved handshakes and welcomed guests with stiff brimmed nods. Gunny, the head marine shook her hand,

"Chloe right?"

"Yes," she said admiring his green eyes.

"Welcome to the Marine Ball, we're glad to have you," he pulled me gently toward the left and pointed to a table, "Your sisters are over at the marine table with Tanner and Joe. There is space for you. You can sit anywhere you like, of course."
"Thank you, I appreciate it. I think I'll get a drink first."

"You can get a seat and a waiter will bring you a drink. There is also an open bar right there," he pointed to a small bar next to a long row of tables.

"Thank you," she said.
Unsure of where to sit, she decided to get a drink at the bar giving her parents time to come outside. The clinking of glasses and chatter of people harmonized with the sounds of the musical ensemble that regaled in the background. Next to the bar along a row of tables rested a spread of lavish international dishes. Waiters perused the crowd balancing silver trays of tiny canapés topped with fresh salmon, finely chopped onion, and capers. A welcoming waiter offered her a bite, "No thank you," she said, "I will grab some food from the buffet."

After her visit to the buffet, she turned to glance over her surroundings with a full plate of tabbouleh salad, hummus, some fresh vegetables, and salmon. Her sisters looked entertained with Joe and Tanner just the four of them.

As she scanned for a place to sit, her eyes caught the gaze of a handsome man dressed in a black tuxedo. He smiled exposing his perfectly white teeth. She grinned back and confidently strutted toward the closest table. Just one couple sat opposite deeply adoring each other as they whispered. She moved one of the chairs. The gentlemen pulled away from his partner and opened his mouth in dissent. She plopped into the chair before he could utter a word. Suddenly someone pulled back the chair beside hers. I turned to discover it was the handsome tuxedo person.

"Hi, are you here on your own?" he asked reaching across the table for a card at the top of her plate, "Mr. Alexopoulos?"

"Hi," she said panicky to see the place card.

"I'm Cian Dawley," his eyes a piercing glass blue with a thin rim of brown. He smiled making the reddish freckles against his light skin dance on the bridge of his nose.

"Ah," she managed to push out a breath of air searching for the right words.

"Your name?" he waited patiently with his hand extended.

"It's Chloe, sorry, I have the wrong table," she said, quickly shook his hand, and jumped to her feet.

"Don't go," he said and referenced the name card once more,

"Mr. Alexopoulos will not mind, I am sure," he pushed the name card to the next spot, "I couldn't imagine he'd contest sitting next to a beautiful girl."

"Thank you," she said, "I really should be sitting with my sisters over there. I just discovered them," she indicated the marine table.

"Oh, so you are here with the American embassy. I work for the British embassy."

"No, not at all. I'm German," I said still standing holding my plate. Realizing that the couple across from us attentively listened to our conversation, I leaned forward and whispered, "It's nice to meet you."

Soon she regretted sitting at the marine's table when she listened to them call Yemenis ragheads, towelheads, and camel jockeys in just about every sentence.

"He's as useful as an ashtray on a motorbike," Tanner said referring to one of the Yemeni's the embassy employed as a driver.

Her sisters laughed highly entertained. The unpleasant conversation had her checking her original table for Cian. He was no longer at his seat. She excused herself to search for her parents and found them in the hotel lobby sitting with another couple. Cian was comfortably in a chair talking on one of the hotel phones. She purposely approached her parents, sat down, and just as she hoped, a minute later Cian was at her table. To her surprise, he greeted Andreas, "Nice to see you here with your family," he turned to look at Chloe.

"Hi Cian, this is my daughter Chloe. She recently joined us."

"Pleasure," he nodded with a big smile.

"Visiting?"

"No, I moved here."

"Well, I hope you enjoy your night. I must be off. Nice to meet you Chloe," he reached out his hand pressing a small piece of paper into her palm, "hopefully we'll run into each other again in the near future."

She crumbled up the note tightly clutching it in her hand and watched him leave the hotel. That night she fell asleep with remorse that she had not taken more time to speak to Cian. The next day Tanner visited, and they sat downstairs to watch the movie he brought with him. The room reminded them of their old living room in Canada. The home offered a vast amount of space and yet they huddled into the smaller room together.

The living room upstairs felt cold and unfriendly with its high ceilings and open floor plan. It made sense to place the TV downstairs where the room had doors that closed for privacy and the sound kept contained if Andreas had visitors. They bunched up like chickens in a coop, one next to the other, side by side on the sectional, Ronny and Tanner, Sofia, and Chloe. Mo sprinted for the big chair. Sofia was able to put Rubén down for his usual naptime.

When she left his room she whispered in relieve, "That boy just would not sleep, but when he does, he sleeps like a log."

She anticipated a long night given that he had not woken up again; his nap was going on two hours. It was nearly six, dark enough to start a good movie. The room needed proper curtains, not something available in stores, rather something large enough to cover the windows and thick so the sun stopped raging through the glass and reflecting onto the TV screen.

In the meantime, they accustomed to waiting for sundown. Chloe played the video and plopped back down onto the couch making everyone else bounce under her clumsiness. Ronny came down with a blanket, covered herself, and offered Tanner to get under it with her. Sofia was unsure how to tell her to leave the blanket upstairs. The two like each other, she did not want to embarrass her.

She was uneasy with both of them underneath it. She would wait for him to leave the room, use the restroom, and address it with her. They waited in anticipation for the movie. Tanner had somehow purchased a pirated copy, from the souk perhaps. The movie began. Then the back of people's heads watching the movie in the theater moved in front of the picture. Someone had unmistakably taped the movie from inside a theater. While watching it, every now and again people's comments were audible, they saw cigarette smoke creep over the screen, and a person stood up. A black silhouette walked out of a row.

Chloe and Ronny cracked jokes about the quality of the video. Sofia was intrigued by the story and wished Andreas were watching it with them. 'Schindler's list' was the title. She had asked Andreas with her most pleading gaze and could not pry him out of the kitchen and away from the book.

"I've seen enough holocaust movies," he said brushing her off.

If she had not been married to him long enough to know otherwise, she would swear he was gay. Most recently, he had not touched her. No interest at all.

"Khat chewing does that to men," Radka had said when they spoke about it, "they lose their sex-drive."

He was sitting in the same position for hours reading, able to shut off the world around him hearing and seeing nothing, rigid like a corpse. He probably had not eaten he was so engrossed with his book. Sofia was not about to ask him if he wanted her to make him something, he could figure it out on his own. She hated treating him that way and usually regretted it. He would get up in the middle of the night hungry, raid the fridge, bite chunks of the imported cheese, and drink the juice straight out of the jug.

Last time she did not feed him because he came home so late, he ate an entire box of 'Mozart kugel' chocolates. Calorie bombs. No wonder he looked heavier. Since moving, he had put on at least a few kilos. Late night feasts, sitting around, chewing, and no exercise will do that to people. In Germany, he rode his bike down the mountain to catch the train to work. Soaked in sweat from riding back up hill still dressed in his uniform he would waited an hour before being able to eat anything at all. Now, there were no opportunities to get exercise, except when she forced him to go to the pool, and then, he comes up with excuses like needing to go home to use the restroom. Crazy that he had to jump in the pool fully clothed, the wintery tweed jacket drenched, when Rubén fell in. That was scary. Sofia thought she should check on Andreas and then thought 'What was that?'

Someone had walked into the house, straight through the hall toward the back rooms.

Entertained by the movie the family sat inside the very first room to the right just after the main copious entrance. The entrance's ceilings high and decorated with white plaster of Paris molding, a large plaster medallion at the center staged a luxurious crystal chandelier. Beyond the main entrance was a long hall with bathrooms further down, a European and an Arabic one, then a mafraj, Chloe's bedroom, master, and kitchen. Large windows topped with colorful concave glass inlays framed in white plaster twinkled cascades of color rays onto the tile floor, a shifting kaleidoscope design as the sun slowly set behind the mountains. The two windows faced the front patio revealing small clay pots filled with green brush and small trees against the grey surrounding wall of the home. The hefty wooden front door opened ever so silently and leisurely. A person entered with light swift cadence, not looking into the living room, passing with a purpose as if knowing where to go, brief, and steady to the very rear of the house.

Patty Smith

Sofia perceived the person, her reaction delayed, her body paralyzed with a rush of terror. She was on her way to check on Andreas in the Kitchen, then fixed in the middle of the living room when she thought she saw a person enter. Incredulous she turned to look at everyone else. Enthralled by the movie they did not notice. Seconds later, inaudible, another person slipped by, then a third, and a fourth. Sofia moved quickly toward the door and saw the men split up, one person climbed upstairs; another poked his head into all the rooms as he moved swiftly down the hallway. She took a deep breath to scream, her mouth wide open, mind racing, what felt like an eternity was only a few seconds, a man grabbed her by the arm and pushed her harshly back inside the living room. A machine gun casually slung over his shoulder. His face covered with a thick wool black facemask, a black and white Arab scarf with tiny white tassels wrapped around his neck. He wore a black jacket and jeans.

Tall and muscular,

his build was not like that of Yemeni men. He grasped the gun of his shoulder and wheeled the machine gun from right to left around the room. He pointed it for a brief second on everyone, first at Mo in the leather chair, then down the couch at Chloe, Ronny, and Tanner. Then pushed the end of the gun at Sofia's chest, she stood solid.

"Don't move," he screamed coldly through the mask in a slightly muffled accent.

Shortly after, two men entered the living room through the hallway back from the direction where the kitchen was. Armed, same masks obscured their faces, one held a machine gun, the other restrained Andreas. He twisted his arm tightly behind Andreas's back while pressing a handgun against his temple.

"Down, on the floor!" he bellowed.

Andreas, had a bewildered look on his face, eyes glazed over from too much reading, the kind of look when startled out of deep thought. His gaze met Sofia's. He recognized she was in fear and wished to comfort her. Andreas hesitated, felt a push on his back, and indecisively lowered down on his knees.

"Down on the floor, lay down, face first!" the man screamed and knocked him in the head with the back of his gun. The family kept rigid silence. Indistinct baby shrieks filled the halls of the house. These were the cries of a baby woken up before his naptime completed. A man said something in Arabic, turned his head swiftly, gestured with his handgun to another, who then left the room. Sofia looked nervously at Mo, a ghostly face drained of blood. The men had missed Rubén. He was snuggled in his crib and covered by blankets. Chloe squirmed on the sofa; she could feel her heart thumping at her ribcage, her own breath heavy. She counted the man's steps toward the babies' room; then heard cries get louder as the man returned with Rubén.

"The blanket, throw it," a man squinted through the slit in his mask pointing the handgun to a spot on the floor.

Ronny and Tanner sat tightly together, blanket over their legs. She pulled it off and threw it on the floor by her feet.

"You," he aimed the gun at Tanner. "On the floor, here."

He swung the gun over to Andreas, who was laying on the floor. His forehead touched the cold tile, strained to roll his eyes up to the corner without turning his head. He worried about the women and yearned to reassure them, tell them all would be all right, but could not catch anyone's gaze.

"Put your hands on your head."
One Arab returned pompously holding Rubén, swung him by an arm, like a fisherman displaying a large catch. The toddler cried loudly, kicked out his legs in rebellion.
"You are hurting him, put him down," Sofia said, fumbled for the word *please* in Arabic "*Min faDlik*" she managed to blunder out the words.

Patty Smith

She looked straight at him for a brief second then swiftly forced her gaze to the floor. They would not like it if she looked them straight in the eyes, a form of disrespect. She remembered the training they received before moving to the Yemen.

"He is yours?" the Arab asked. Rubén arched his back and twisted in anger. His cheeks flushed.

"He is my grandson."

"He's *my* son," Mo bellowed.
The Arab jostled Rubén onto Mo's lap, uncontrollably Rubén cried even louder. The Arab pushed his handgun into Mo's brow.

"Make him stop."

With the gun to her forehead, tranquil, sweet, she whispered into Rubén's ear, softly rocking him back and forth.
Due to the sweat, the skin of her thighs slid on the leather releasing a squeaking sound. Loud screams became sobs, he slowly calmed, clinched to her breast. Sounds of boots running down the stairs broke the tumult. The other two men walked in. One pointed his machine gun toward the couch.

"All woman sit there."

He hissed and looked at Mo: "You, princess."
She hoisted herself up with Rubén attached to her chest and slid back down next to Chloe on the Sofa. Chloe had been irrepressibly sobbing; silent tears ran down her cheeks, triggered by the Arab pointing the gun to Mo's head. Chloe feared for her sister's life and silently sobbed. Then thought the men prepared to shoot all the women as they lined them up on the sofa. One man looked over at Sofia. She still stood ridged.

"What are you waiting for?"

She sat down at the end of the couch and touched Chloe and Ronny's knees, leered at Mo.

"Arms, arms on your back!"

The Arab with the machine gun pushed his boot into Tanner's spine. Tanner turned his head slightly to look over to the couch. The man's foot was heavy on his back, he pressed Tanner's chest tight to the ground. Tanner moaned as the air pressed out of his lungs. The man kneeled, exchanged his foot for a knee. Forced it against the same spot on his back, pulled Tanner's arms behind him, overextending them backward. Tanner worked hard to conceal the pain, pulled against the muscles tightening on his face. A third man entered the room, spoke in Arabic, and handed him a long heavy silvery metal chain. The kneeling man grabbed the chain and quickly wrapped it around Tanner's arms. He dragged his legs backward bending them at the knees and wrapped the chain tightly around his ankles. He heaved his feet closely toward his hands behind his back, and fixed them together in place with a large lock.

Tanner laid unable to move like a hunted down animal. Using the rest of the chain, the man did the same with Andreas fixing his restraints with a second lock. The clang of the metal against the lock was like a timer announcing their death approaching. Slouched inside the couch, the women knew they were only seconds away from dying. Tears ran down their eyes. Mo rocked Rubén, who was calm, but sensed something was wrong. He clung tightly to her breast, did not turn around to see what was happening. His head buried into the clammy warmness of her neck. The man with the handgun took Sofia by the arm and pressed the gun at her chest.

"Take me where the money is," he ordered.

"Walk."

Sofia led him to the bedroom explaining that she did not have a lot of money.

"Shut up!"

He yelled and hit her with the handle of the gun on the back of the head.

"I am telling you the truth. We do not keep much money in the house. Don't hit me again," she said in frustration.

"Give me your jewelry."

Sofia slid the jewelry box toward him across the top of the dresser. It was not much, just a few cheap necklaces and fake earrings. He emptied the contents without examining them, pushed the jewelry into his jacket pockets. Sofia could see two men walking out of the kitchen carrying the microwave and coffee machine.

"Where is the money?"

Sofia pulled a few hundreds, a couple of fifty-dollar bills, and a small stack of Yemeni money amounting to little, out of the closet from in-between her shirts. The Arab grabbed all of the neatly folded shirts in her closet, threw them onto the floor expecting to find more money. All the while, he pointed the gun at Sofia.

"There is nothing else," she said.

Among the pile of clothing on the floor, she saw the family's passports. She attempted to push a shirt over the passports, but they had fallen too far apart. The man noticed, pushed her aside.

"Give me the passports."

She bent down to pick up the passports; he hit her again, so hard she could hear the metal cracking against her skull. She felt nauseous. He pulled her up by the hair.

She grabbed his wrist and dug her nails into his skin. He squealed.

"You are hurting me. Take the money, the passports, everything. Stop hurting me."

"Give them to me."

He yanked them out of her hands, stuffed them into his pockets. Suddenly a resounding Arabic voice entered the home from the outside. The man turned to look out of the bedroom down the hallway.

"Stay here, do not move or I will shoot you," he said resolutely.

Sofia stood, frozen, shocked, unable to move even if she could, even if she wanted to, she could not move. Inside the living room, one of the men pointed the machine gun at the girls.

"You don't need to cry," there was concern in his voice and his eyes had sympathy within them.

Two loud knocks shook the window glass. He stepped backward toward the door, twisted his head to view out into the hall, and kept his gun pointing to the inside of the living room.

"Don't move."

He stepped out of the living room. Chloe, Mo, and Ronny exchanged frightened looks. They waited minutes that felt like infinity. Nobody dared to utter a sound. Where had their mother gone? Complete silence filled the space broken by a faint sound of dogs barking outside, the wind blowing, a tree branch tapped the window.

"I think they are gone," Chloe whispered.

Andreas began to wiggle in his chains.

"Paps don't do that"

Ronny, elbowed Chloe in the ribs with a concerned look on her face.

"I'm going to look out the window."

Chloe slid down the edge of the sofa onto her hands and knees. She slowly crawled her way toward the nearest window overlooking the front patio and saw the gate to the house wide open.

"I think they're gone"

Andreas squirmed himself out of the hold such that the chain was now in front of him. His arms and feet still attached like someone on the chain gang. Tanner did the same. "I'm going outside to check," Chloe announced.

"No, it's too dangerous," Andreas said.

He shouted, but Chloe had already gone to the front door. The men left it wide open.

"The door was open and the coffee machine was sitting on the patio. I don't think they're coming back," she said stepping back into the room. Andreas and Tanner struggled to walk both chained to one another. Sofia was still missing. Chloe frantically ran through the house in search for her mother, found her sitting on the corner of the bed holding the back of her head. Chloe kneeled by Sofia, she gently took her hand; there was blood in Sofia's palm.

"Mom?" Chloe asked with an unmistakable concern in her voice.

"I'm okay."

"Oh my god, they're coming back."
Chloe tugged at Sofia when she heard an Arab calling.

"Quick lets go up on the roof and call for help."
The two climbed the stairs to the roof, carefully looked down over the ledge to the street, and saw no cars below. One of the guards from next door was standing by the metal gate of the house. Andreas and Tanner, chained together, they stepped out to talk to the guards.

"It must have been the guard that scared them away," Sofia concluded.

I n the living room,

Ronny and Mo cried and held each other, in between them Rubén. He laughed, thinking it was a game; he slapped Ronny then slapped Mo. Gasping to speak Sofia entered the room, Chloe behind her.

"Are you guys ok?" she asked.

"Mom you're hurt?" Mo jumped up slung her arms around Sofia and sobbed profusely.

"They have our passports," Sofia said as Andreas returned.

Tanner forcibly trailed closely behind him four guards walked into the room next. It was strange to see the guards who mocked the women step into the room with concern on their faces. Chloe would have hugged anyone that came to rescue them.

"Someone has gone to call the police, well it's more like the military, there is no police here really," Andreas said. Another guard returned with a hacksaw in hand. He worked hard to cut through the metal lock and broke the blade.

"We'll have to wait for the military to get here and take the lock off."
Andreas pulled both arms up toward Sofia's head, gingerly examined the cut with his fingers.

"Let's walk over to the sink to wash out the wound."

Patty Smith

Botschaft der Bundesrepublik Deutschland
Embassy of the Federal Republic of Germany
XI 550.30/3
No.: /93

The Embassy of the Federal Republic of Germany presents its compliments to the Ministry of Foreign Affairs of the Republic of Yemen and has the honor to inform the esteemed Ministry that on 19th February 1993 at 06.15 p.m. the house of first lieutenant Andreas Schneider, head of the German military adviser group in Yemen was attacked by armed robbers in a very brutal way. The wife of first lieutenant Schneider was injured by the criminals. The CID was informed and is investigating the matter.

The Embassy would be very grateful if every effort could be made to recover the stolen goods and for all possible measures to be taken to arrest the criminals and to prevent a recurrence. The Embassy of the Federal Republic of Germany avails itself of this opportunity to renew to the Ministry of Foreign Affairs of the Republic of Yemen the assurances of its highest consideration.
Sanaa, 20th February 1993 BT/--
To the Ministry of Foreign Affaires
Of the Republic of Yemen
S a n a a
2) gespeichert
3) IV for Translation
4) CC Herrn Schneider
5) xdB(Z)
(3007)

Chapter 10

Engaged in conversation with Paps we sat around the kitchen table. Normally, I avoided the draw into lengthy conversations because it usually ended with a recommendation.

"Read this book and then come back to me if you still have questions," he would say not answering my questions.

I suspected that he was unwilling to put forth the effort of simply answering a question due to my lack in background information. He fundamentally believed one needed to know the history of things to understand something deeply. Our incongruent way of thinking often kept us from engaging. Growing up, I avoided asking him for help with homework, a humble math question had the potential of dragging out into an additional hour of homework study. Knowing he had no access to books it felt safe to ask him questions more often.

I stepped into the kitchen, "Hey, any idea if the police have the slightest notion of who committed the robbery?"

"Apparently they don't have a clue," he said.

"They think it may have been Palestinians, based on our description of the men and the weapons they carried."

He briefly pried his glance away from the paper he was reading. I stood still propped up by the doorframe, just in case I needed a quick exit should he make a book suggestion.

"I noticed more boys carrying guns recently. Have you noticed an increase in armed guards as well?" I asked.

Patty Smith

"Well you know that is normal for Yemen. It is one of the most heavily armed countries. It is Yemeni tradition for people to have fully automatic assault rifles and other weapons in general. You are just feeling more hypersensitive due to the robbery. It is kind of, like when you want to buy a red car. All of a sudden, you start seeing red cars everywhere. I think you are paying more attention. It explains why you are seeing teenage boys carry fully automatic assault rifles," he retorted folding his paper into squares.

"It has not bothered me before. It is different now. I find it highly dangerous, especially given that teenagers have such an unpredictable nature. I mean just look at how Ronny acts. Is it just me? It seems as though there are more teenage boys working the checkpoints," I said.

"It is due to a large number in children in this country. Yemen has the highest birth rate among Arab countries. There are around eight births per woman in Yemen, compare that to three globally and you will see much more kids on the streets," his voice was mechanical and he was not getting my point at all. "Only 3% of the population is over sixty years old, life expectancy is around sixty-three. Even though Yemen lacks a strong central state and an effective military, they do have a large military. After the cold war, the Soviets, Russia, lost interest in the Yemen, but left the country with weaponry. The British were here first, after they withdrew from Aden, the Soviets helped the South build a military and infrastructure. It's really much more complicated because Yemen has had an influx of weapons from other countries as well, the Brits, the Chinese," he said sagely placing the folded paper on the table, my signal to leave.

I turned around, "Thanks Paps," and walked out of the kitchen. Sometimes I felt bad about the abrupt manner in which I left our conversations. I needed to stop him or he would begin explaining the manufacture of weapons and hand me a book about the history of the Kalashnikov.

I understood why most of the men carried Kalashnikovs, although I learned that the robbers had Scorpion Machine Guns. I wondered if I imagined that there were more young boys armed at checkpoints and about the city.

Salem walked in.

He had asked to take the school bus home with my sisters, concerned about our wellbeing, when he heard about the robbery. I enjoyed spending time with Salem, he had been visiting us on a regular basis and proven to be immensely helpful. He took us shopping to the souk. A male presence helped to keep Yemeni men at bay. He also translated the haggling of prices for us. We had become close friends. At least once a week we spent time together to play backgammon on the roof of the house or to go for coffee at the Taj. He did not drive and I quite honestly had no idea that it was challenging for him to come to our house. It was an additional fee to ride the school bus. I had a feeling that he walked quite a bit to get to our house and gathered that he did not have much money.

"Are you going to be all right? Were you hurt?" he asked.

I could not help but wonder if he might know the robbers. The military police had determined they were Palestinians. Perhaps Salem had naively shared details about us. It would explain why they seemingly knew the layout of our home. Suspiciously, I listened to him say, "I was concerned about you guys. Is there anything at all I can do?"

"Thanks for offering. We will be alright," I said. "I could give you a ride home," I offered, "Our driver does not work today, but that just means I could take the truck."

"No, really it's okay," he said dismissively and flicked his hand.

"I'll tell my Mom that I am taking you to the Taj so she won't worry. You can catch a cab from there."

"Alright, you can just drop me at the Taj," he whispered.

Patty Smith

Once we got into the truck and I left our neighborhood, I insisted that he tell me how to get to his camp.
He hesitated.

"Really, it is not a problem at all. I could use the chance to get out of the house. Look, I already have the car; it really does not matter if I drive you to the Taj or straight to your place. So tell me where you live," I placed my hand on his shoulder.

He conceded and gave me directions. I quickly realized that I had spoken to hastily, unsure if I would remember my way back. My curiosity superseded my concern and I kept driving. Along the way, I made an effort to memorize markers: Make a left at the intersection, another left at the large tree with a dry broken off branch, a right at the corner store with the goat tied to the door and the chickens in cages lined along the sidewalk, a left at the home with the black gate. Salem talked with ebullience, distracted me, landmarks I memorized fleeted. We arrived at a large place that resembled a compound. Many small homes made up the camp. He pointed to his house. It was as big as our front patio. I tried to mask my surprise by saying how cozy his house looked. I follow his directions for a place to park the car inside the large wall that surrounded the camp. We simultaneously reached backward for his book bag when he nonchalantly kissed me on the corner of my mouth and directly thereafter apologized. "Sorry, I thought you'd be ok with it, I just wanted to say thank you, or goodbye."

Disinterested in a dalliance, I shrugged my shoulders, "It is ok. You know, I would rather we stay good friends. Kisses make things awkward."

"Would you like to come in? I'd like to introduce you to my family," he said opening the truck door.

"Sure, but only for a few minutes," I said happy he was not pushing the kissing issue.

His front door opened into a main room. A small TV sat on top of a little dresser. Unmatched kitchen chairs lined the walls and a coffee table was at the center of the room.

Salem introduced me to a pretty girl, from what I could make out under the headscarf and hidden beneath a wide Hijab.

Demure and pale she greeted me by nodding her head. The wall behind him displayed a large print of an old looking man, a black and white scarf with tassels on his head. A disturbing sensation flushed my body, blood rushed to my head, my face hot as I stared at it.

"That's Yasser Arafat," Salem explained studying my face, "chairman of the PLO."

The heat lay heavy upon my brow and my throat constricted.

"Do you want a cup of water?"

"Yes please" I managed to utter and sat down.

His mother came in, nodded, and shook my hand. We politely exchanged a few uncomfortable words about the weather and then I courteously asked to use the restroom. Happy at first to find a toilet bowl and disenchanted to see puddles of water on the floor. Something I had seen before. The constant water splatters in Farris' bathroom when his parents came to visit from Iran for an entire month. They stayed in his tiny one-bedroom space with just the one bathroom. During that month, I practically spent all my time with Gianna. I am sure his parents figured out I was his girlfriend, I stopped into his restaurant constantly. Once, I surprised him at home. I would like to say that everyone struck a silent compromise to make that visit work. Upon using the restroom, I saw the same water puddles and thought they missed the bowl. When I asked Farris, he produced a canister from inside the sink cabinet.

"They fill this up with water and use it to clean themselves," he said holding the large green plastic can and with a long spout, the kind you would use to water potted flowers. "They travelled with this all the way from Iran."

Farris and I ended up calling it the 'butt-splasher' for lack of better terms. I felt awful knowing that they were keeping the thing hidden and privately brought it out to use the restroom when I visited.

Patty Smith

I dried the seat before using it and stepped out of the restroom to find Salem alone in the living room.

"Hey, would you like to see my workshop?" he asked eagerly and walked to a window. "It's at the back of the house."

"I sort of have to get going," I said anxious that I might have overstayed.

With a disappointed look he said, "Come on, just a few minutes."

"Okay, I suppose I could stay another half hour."
We walked around the outside of the small brick home to the back where there was carport with metal siding. Inside was a dumping ground for all things un-useful. A tire slashed open, pieces of wood slats with nails sticking out of them, different hubcaps, and other car parts. Amidst the metal mess was a small wooden workbench with a stool tucked underneath it. He pulled out the stool and turned over a plastic bucket next to it.

"Come sit down," he tapped the top of the plastic.

"Can I get the stool?"

"Oh, sure sorry," he pushed the stool toward me.
On top of the workbench, an array of tools rested spread out in an organized manner. He lit a burner with a silver lighter by skillfully flicking the lid open and stroking the small wheel igniting a flame in one swoop.

"Whoa, I'm impressed," I said.

"I'm going to show you how I make jewelry," he smiled searching for materials on his workbench.

"This right here is real silver. I melt it down to make things, or pull it to the shape I want," he demonstrated a thin square of silver.

Swiftly, creatively he cut the material into shape, turned and pulled at the piece, cut it some more with his shears, filled the sharp corners soft.

He then melted some of the silver and formed decorations. He handed me a finished ring. He had soldered a letter C on one side and a letter S on the other.

"I love it, my initials," his hidden talent captivated me.

"Well I honestly thought the letter S was for Salem, but you can see it as you like."

I wished I had not said anything. He bent down and pulled a small metal box from underneath his workbench. He kept a stack of photos inside the box and pulled one out after the other. Proudly he showed me the photos pointing to his friends and family.

"Where are they?"

"They live all over the place. Some live in refugee camps." He took a deep breath, "I miss them, but we are fighting for what is ours."

I must have had a perplexed look.

"You know, people say the Palestinians can only throw rocks?"

I nodded although I had never heard anything of the sort before.

"Well, it is not true. I am in training."

"What do you mean?"

"I've been to Italy you know."

"You have? It's beautiful," I said happy to have something in common. We could exchange our experiences of traveling to Italy.

"Well, I didn't spend much time there sightseeing the place. Just in and out. Did my thing and left. Training you know."

"I don't know," I feared he was training to fight and wanted to UN-hear what he had said. I played with the ring around my finger wondering how to kill the subject.

Patty Smith

"What kind of other things do you make?" I said to distract him.

He proceeded and handed me another photo, "You can keep this one if you like."

Afraid he might elaborate I squirmed on top of my stool. It was of Salem in full green camouflage military uniform and black combat boots holding a machine gun with both arms extended over his head, a gigantically victorious smile on his face, and next to him, stood two other young men holding heroic postures.

"I went to Italy to lay a bomb under a car."

"You did what? Why?" I asked shocked. Just the kind of information I wished not to know. This young sweet boy had possibly killed people in Italy. In disbelief, I wondered if he was fabricating that information up to impress me.

"My dad is the head of the PLO here in Yemen," he said proudly.

"Wait, wait, did you kill anyone?"

"When I laid the bomb?"
I silently nodded.

"No. Nobody was hurt when I laid the bomb."
I admittedly knew very little about the PLO. He explained that the photo in their living room was of Yasser Arafat, "The big boss."

"I will give my life so we can have freedom," he said with a glazed and thoughtful look in his eyes.

"Are you serious? Why would you kill yourself for everyone else? Where does that leave you? What about your freedom?" Questions kept rolling off my lips, horrified with his seriousness and stunned by his confidence.

"This is how it is Chloe, this is my destiny," he said firmly.

"What about a family of your own? What if you fall in love with someone and want children? None of these things will happen for you if you do something so stupid."

I had said too much, his smile froze. The beginning of a frown formed across his face then he forced another smile, but his eyes divulged disdain.

"It is anything but stupid."

I desperately searched for the right words to recover. How could I have been so wrong about him? He had amazed me with his kindness. From the first moment we met, he had offered his help, benevolently guided us on shopping sprees, and protected us when we walked the streets in the city. I liked his vigorous content with life and his perpetual smile. He moved freely about without grievance. I realized we had nothing in common and was at a loss of words. Then I realized the time and feared I might not make it back home. My mind had completely wiped off any markers I had memorized to get there.

"Chloe are you alright? I did not mean to make you uncomfortable," he gently pushed my chin up with his finger and said, "I know it is hard for you to understand, for anyone to understand, unless you were in my situation."
The unfathomable faith in his life purpose written across his face, and yet he was suffused with despondency.

"If you think I am unhappy, you're wrong," he said as if he could read my mind.

"But, if you were happy, you wouldn't want to do something so drastically wrong."

"How can you say it is wrong? They wronged us for too long. They have taken our homes. I have the privilege to make things right again," he said with a kind and soft voice taking my hand in his, then pulling it up to his face and kissing the top of my hand softly. "You will only understand if you live what we live."

He exhaled a warm subdued sweet breath. Uneasy I left my hand in his, thinking of how I would make my way home from here.

"You look nervous."

Patty Smith

Leaning toward me, making the space between us smaller, he looked at me deep squeezing my hand and then slowly rubbing his thumb back and forth, the calluses on his fingers rough against my skin.

"No, not really, I am worried about," I paused thinking what would make sense. "The robbery. I worry about our passports floating around. What will happen if the robbers come back for more? They were interrupted, they may come back."

I wavered telling him the truth, telling him that I felt unsafe in his presence, in a Palestinian neighborhood, with him alone behind his house. Nobody knew where I was. We often spent time at the Taj and Mom would not think anything was wrong if it took me a while to get home. Playing Backgammon, we could spend all afternoon together sipping on coffee.

"I have a surprise for you," he said.
He ran his fingertips across my cheek, stopping to pick up a strand of hair and reposition it behind my ear; a spellbinding smile exposed his perfectly straight teeth. My throat was so dry I struggled to swallow. I could still see the photo of Arafat, the black and white scarf with white tassels on his head. Once I saw that photo, I unquestionably knew the robbers were Palestinians.

"Do you have a phone? I think I may need Paps to pick me up and show me home, there is no way I'll find my way back," I said getting up from the stool. I walked out of the carport, and then turned to face him.

"You have a surprise?" I asked.

"It wouldn't be a surprise if I told you, would it?" he pulled his lips into a line, dimples at end.

"Don't worry" he stepped out and stopped to face me, reassuringly he touched my shoulder. "I knew, I would have to drive back with you, I'll take a taxi from the Taj, you know how to get home from there."

The sun had begun to set. A dark blue in the sky parted to pails of water thrown onto the front window of the truck. A small red light flashed on the dashboard.

"Man, I'm running on fumes, can't believe Mom didn't say anything, " Paps hated when I returned the truck with just a few drops in the tank, but Mom and I both loathed going to the gas station.

"There's a gas station at the next intersection, we'll make it."

Salem pointed to a long stream of car lights lining the road leading to the gas station. I pulled into the metal mess and lodged the truck into a scrapheap of old vehicles. Cars, motorcycles, trucks, people on bicycles, and people walking holding gas canisters, everyone under the sun moved slowly toward one open pump. A pickup truck loaded with gas canisters was next in line to fill up. The driver jumped out, filled his gas tank, and then began to fill the canisters from the bed of the truck.

"What the heck is going on?" I asked dumbfounded by the chaos. "I don't have the patience for this, really, it will take hours at this rate," I said annoyed with myself for allowing the truck to get so low on gas.

"I think we can make it, but then you'll be completely out of gas, I'm sure," Salem said.

"All right, let's take a chance. Its dark and my parents are going to worry."

On the way to the Taj Sheba, Salem shared his speculations about the pandemonium. He thought it was due to that particular gas station being the only one inside that area of town.

"That might be true, but my gut is telling me otherwise," as soon as I finished my thought, we came across another gas station. "You see." The same scenario played out there. The street was chock full of cars, open car doors, Yemeni men sat around comfortably chewing khat and smoking cigarettes.

Forced to take an alternative route, Salem shook his head and said, "Sorry, I have not seen this sort of thing happen before. Maybe there is a shortage for some reason."

Patty Smith

I stopped across from the Taj and attempted to slip him a few bills for the cab. He grabbed my hand stopping me from placing the money into his pocket.

"This offends me," he said with an unwavering tone.

"Sorry, I just feel bad because you had to come all the way back here, please allow me to pay for half of the cab ride at least."

He jumped out before I could say another word, swung the truck door shut, blew me a kiss through the window, turned on his heels waving his hand behind his shoulder. Then hopped like a gazelle dodging cars across the busy street. This behavior was not that of a man who would place his friends into a position to be robbed at gunpoint. I still wondered if he might have talked to his Palestinian friends. I snuck into the house without anyone noticing and fell straight to sleep. The next morning I laid awake for an extended period, listened to my sisters arguing and wrestling of plates in the kitchen until Paps knocked on my door.

"Chloe, we've decided to go to Al Khokha, pack your stuff we leave in an hour."

I opened the door to a frantic back and forth. The only person moving slowly was Rubén as he sucked his thumb and carefully climbed the stairs to the second floor. Mom was making sandwiches in the kitchen. Paps filled a cooler with ice and water bottles.

"What's going on?" I asked rubbing dry sleep out of the corners of my eyes.

"Had you been here, you would have known," Ronny said.

"Duh. You are so wise," I kept my back turned toward her.

"I came home and everyone was already in bed," I said looking at Mom. She tended to go to bed around nine. I did not bother looking for my sisters upstairs when I returned.

"So, what's this about Al Khokha?" I stepped closer and kissed my mother's cheek.

"Make your own sandwich," she handed me two flowery flat breads. They were still warm and looked delicious. I filled them with fresh vegetables, peeled the cheese wedges, pressed the cream, and rolled the bread into a burrito.

"The beach right? How long?" I asked feeling distressed that I was left out of the planning.

Sudden decision-making was typical of my parents. Growing up they hitchhiked to Holland and France on the drop of a hat. I slept many nights curled up under tables at friends' homes due to poor planning; lack of funds for a hotel might have had something to do with it as well. "Let's just spend the night. Kids will be okay, they are used to crashing wherever," they would say.

"Where are we sleeping?" I asked.

"Don't worry, it's all under control."

"Really? I would like to know. Will I be crashing on a floor? Should I bring a pillow and blanket?"

"You are sharing a room with us or not?" Ronny said still standing in the doorframe of the kitchen.
"Yes, you will be sharing a room with Ronny, Mo, and Rubén. Paps and I will have our own, and Salem will have his own room."

"Salem?"
I wondered when he managed to finagle coming on a trip with us. He referred to a surprise. It was the trip.

"He brought up the idea to your Dad and offered to be our guide while we are there. He should be here shortly."
I was glad she did not ask me what time I had arrived at home the night before. The phone rang and Mom took the call.

"No problem at all, don't worry, just come by when you can."

She turned, "He will be staying with family and not getting a room at the hotel with us after all. He'll meet us in Al Khokha."

Patty Smith

I wondered if he had the money to pay for a hotel room and imagined that he probably took a bus to get there. Before embarking on our long drive, Paps stopped at a gas station near the city limit. While he filled the tank, Mo jumped out of the back seat with Ruben and walked him about the gas station. Then she approached the truck and positioned Ruben against the half open passenger window while she exchanged a few words with Mom. Ruben placed his little hands onto the edge of the car window and Mom played peekaboo with him through the glass.

Suddenly, Paps jumped into the truck and placed it into drive, the truck advanced slowly while Ruben still hung onto the window for dear life and Mo, Ronny, and I screamed and Mom did so as well, "Andreaaaaas," and Ruben's face was still in a smile thinking it was a game. Hearing his name, Paps only then slammed the breaks shaking Ruben from his hold and causing his to fall into Mo's arms who had chased after the truck. The rest of our trip was uneventful. We spent grueling hours with the sun burning hot through truck windows and the conditioned air dissipating well before reaching our seats in the back having me regret turning down the offer to sit in the front seat to help with my carsickness.

Chapter 11

Windy roads delivered an infinite array of lush green terrace field farms along the hillside bearing crops of barley and wheat. A few years later, Archeologists would uncover ruins of towns built more than 4000 years ago near Dhamar, in this 6500 high plateau. These uncovered ruins existed several hundred years before the trade of frankincense and marked the development of first Arabian towns. These terraces were among the oldest in the world and dated back to 3000 B.C. Flat-roofed square homes tucked into the rock closely together highlighted the traditional elaborate white friezes and windows decorated with intricate design. Wadis (river valleys) used to store rainwater for irrigation, threaten to dry in the approaching summer heat. Al Khokha was a 5-6 hour drive from Sana'a, a small town by the red sea filled with palm trees that gave fruit to large date-clusters where a salty moist scent of sea water lingered in the light breeze. Palm leaves swooshed a delicate song calling Chloe to sit and listen quietly.

Clear cool water, a perfect sapphire blue tapered smoothly to a light turquoise ebbed near the sifted sand. Mellow orange blades tenderly cut spongy waves with the approaching sunset in the distance. Two fishing boats, red and blue paint flaking from the brown, beached, Fishermen dressed in colorful skirts and t-shirts lugged full nets. A group of women in vibrant dresses and head wrappings, filled baskets on their heads and hips counterbalancing, they moved softly over the shoreline, sand flecks stuck to their dark ankles.

A cluster of children, coarse dark hair and golden brown skin, the fishermen's kids, sat closely by the boats, their eyes wide as saucers, their hands covered giggled whispers into each other's ears. The scent of charcoaled fish and sea foam caught in Chloe's nostrils. She agreed to a stroll along the beach. In her bathing suit under a pair of shorts, she gained unwanted attention from the Fishermen and provided entertainment for the children.

"They haven't seen a woman this naked before," Salem explained recognizing Chloe's frustration.

"I figured I would be ok, there is practically no one out here. It is as if we have our own private beach. Besides, I am not naked. You know if I was wearing a skimpy bathing suit or bikini I'd understand, but this thing," she flicked her bathing suit top.

"You look amazing."
He pulled her closely stopping at one of the smaller palm trees, its bushels of orange pre-ripe dates reached low enough to grab.

"I wish I had a camera right now, I would take a picture of you right here. I could have you forever," Salem said.
The family assembled at a large table on the patio of the hotel restaurant. Only one other party occupied the table across, two men engaged in conversation. One man's hands swung as he spoke speedy gurgled sentences among green Khat saliva onto the floor.

"Ugh, we are eating here?" Ronny asked examining the green spit wad drying quickly against the hot concrete floor.

"We can eat somewhere else."

"No Andreas" Sofia disagreed with the constant aim to cater to her children's happiness. "We drove for hours, the last thing we want to do is get back in the car."

"Ok, this is too much" Mo said loudly, "I'm leaving, meet you back in the room."

One of the men facing the table lifted his skirt, exposing himself.

"I'm going over there to say something."

"No Andreas, you can't, you don't know how they'll react, let's just all go and see if we can get a takeout and eat at the beach."

The family took a large grilled fish and fresh baked bread to the beach.

"I wonder where Chloe and Salem are." Ronny said.

"They will show up when they get hungry," Andreas said biting of the bread.

Chloe and Salem continued to walk along the shore, Chloe stopped here and there to pick up small shells to take home, deeply engrossed in conversation. Salem spoke about his call to avenge Palestinian people and shared his struggle with the conflicting contrast between his duty and his desire.

"A nineteen year old should be able to act on his desires," Chloe said. "You are far too young to carry this kind of burden with you. Your entire life is in front of you and you could be anybody, somebody."

"You are driving me crazy," he said.

She was constantly on his mind and he caught himself dreaming about her. She forced him to consider a future. He trained to live for a cause. A future with her was directly challenging his cause. His father, the head of the Fatah in Yemen made it clear that there was too much blood on their hands to have a future. He was going to be a martyr without a future. His purpose was to fight so others could have that opportunity. His father established a training camp in Sana'a. The PLO was a conglomerate of various secular and religious coalitions with an interest in creating a Palestinian State. Arafat was originally the leader of the Fatah movement a coalition under the PLO, then elected leader of the PLO. The PLO's first military terror operation took place on January 1, 1965.

Patty Smith

An employee of the National water corporation detected a small explosive device hidden in an open canal of to the National Water Carrier of Israel. The plan was to blow up the Nahusha water institute near the city of Beit Shemesh. Then a much more horrific act was carried out six days later by a squad of six men, among them Salem's father, resulting in his father's injuries and capture. A military court sentenced his father to death. Thanks to his father's allies, he returned to Lebanon in a POW swap.

After the 1982 occupation of Lebanon, his father immigrated to Yemen, took his family to Sana'a, where he set up a small Fatah training camp. It was where they lived since he could remember. In Sana'a, his father was far from Tunis, where the exiled Fatah leadership resided. Living at such a distance caused his father to feel sidelined and engaged in actions that would force the leadership to see his value. He began to engage in dubious investments with the lush PLO funds he mainly received from Saudi and Kuwaiti sources. His father was not experiencing much luck. The occupation of Kuwait in 1990/91 and PLO's open siding with Saddam Hussein then also caused general funds for the PLO to dry up and pushed his father into financial stress. His latest business venture, the attempt to purchase a large property, went sour due to Yemeni tribal shenanigans. The last time Salem saw his father was on his way out the door and noticed he appeared upset. He had been trying to arrange an inspection of the property he was in the process of purchasing and could not access the land due to a shootout between two tribal groups. Then he discovered that the tribe who owned the land had sold it seventeen times over to different parties. His father would not approve of his involvement with westerners and his interest in a non-Moslem girl.

"I have to tell you something," Chloe stepped away to get some space gaining his attention. "The Yemeni's think it was Palestinians that broke into our house."

"No," he said in a firm tone. "There is no way it was my people. I would have known about that. Your family is under my protection."

He cared for this family, would be horrified to learn that Palestinians robbed his friends.

"I can assure you it was not Palestinians. I can almost swear to it, but will investigate. It sounds more like a setup by the Yemenis. It would not surprise me if there is something else behind this and they used us as a scapegoat."

Chloe was a strong woman, determined like his mother. His mother was a smart woman, although she was spending her time selling handmade cross-stitched cushions for fifty dollars. His Mom was capable of much more. His mother was capable of running the United Nations. His father laughed, but Salem could see her holding an important job working for UN headquarters. There was an immediate attraction between Chloe and Salem. He knew straightaway that he would be in trouble. He found her confidence and quick wit attractive.

"Aren't you wondering about my surprise for you?"

"I thought you coming here was the surprise."

"No, I have another surprise."

"I have arranged for some training for you," he said proudly. "We will train you how to shoot an AK-47."

"Are you kidding me?" Chloe felt excited about the idea of learning how to shoot a gun.

"Who are you referring to with 'we'?"

"A friend will help us," he said unrevealing the fact that it would be with a Fatah trainer as not to scare her. She would learn to load the machine gun quickly, to shoot with accuracy, and most of all, not to be afraid. He would take her out, just the two of them, and the trainer. He held her hand tightly inside his, leaned in closer, and trapped her between the roughness of the palm-tree and the softness of his chest. He whispered warmly in her ear as though it was the biggest secret he ever shared with anyone.

Patty Smith

"I really care about you and want to make sure you can protect yourself."

It troubled Chloe that she desired to kiss him and yet she refused her instinct to turn from his face and leaned in instead. As if not her own, her arms around slung around his neck. Then she tasted his dry warm lips and deeply inhaled his sweet scent. He contoured across her cheeks softly with his lips and down her neck and placed his hands onto her hips, then pulled them against his.

"I really like you a lot," he said.

He read her eyes and waited to hear her say the same, imagined jumping in the ocean with her and with the sunset undress her. Waves broke against the soft sand as the ebb grew leaving seaweed stranded on the beach. Red buoys danced at the end of thick ropes that gripped onto wooden boats. The Fishermen were gone and it was just the two of them as far as the eye could see. Now, both the sun and the moon played among vague stars in a sky completely clear of any clouds. There was still enough light to see and for a brief moment, his deep brown eyes mesmerized her. Their physical chemistry was undeniable and yet it was irresponsible to lead him to believe they could have a relationship. He could not marry, have children, and play house. Living in Yemen for the rest of her life in a wide Hijab was not how she imagined her life. His destiny was clear and his future set for him by his father. She gently stepped back, just sufficiently to escape her trap, and smiled.

"We need to get back. It's getting late."

"What's wrong?"

"Salem, I like you a lot, I told you, as a friend, nothing more."

"But," he scrambled for the right words to say. "Why did you kiss me?"

"See, I told you things would get awkward once we move in that direction. You really want me to answer that question? Let me say this, your lips are irresistible and leave it at that. Anything more and then we'll never talk again," she began to walk away and added, "We better walk back to the hotel now."
Salem jumped to catch up.

"I'm not staying at the hotel with you guys. I am staying with family. I have business here, but I'll meet you back in Sana'a on Monday," he grabbed her hand.
"A kiss is all you can give me, then that will be enough," he said while he held her hand and swung her arm back and forth, "for now."
As much as she liked his friendship, it was the right decision and so she said goodbye at the hotel door before he could lean in for another kiss. Back in Sana'a, Salem visited to deliver his surprise to Chloe as promised. Standing at the front door of her home Salem said, "This is Mahmood; he's really good with guns." He looked at her intensely studying her reaction then quickly added, "He is a friend."
He was ecstatic she was coming out. They drove to the top of the mountains for the following afternoons to shoot at targets. She quickly got intimate with every part of the weapon. That same week, Andreas pulled one of the Kalashnikovs from above the bookcase.
"It will be fully loaded and right here when you need it," as he hung it by the leather strap to the backside of the front door. He then arranged to meet someone to purchase a handgun, somehow miraculously found the man's home tucked in the mountains, without an address or map it had been a gamble to find it.
"He is a reliable trustworthy source," Ernst assured Andreas as they knocked on the wooden door.
The man welcomed them with tea and Khat. Once they performed the typical ritual of formalities, he showed them to a back room where the man pried open the floorboards and exposed a large stash of guns and rifles.

Andreas gazed at Ernst, unsure of what to think of the amount of weapons inside this man's home.

"You buy?" he asked in broken English. "Very good," he said as he modeled one of the heavy guns, and then pointed it at Andreas, who jumped.

"No. Do not worry. I don't shoot you," the man said with a smirk on his face, not able to conceal how funny the German looked.

Andreas purchased the gun and they quickly went on their way home. From then on, Andreas kept the Browning 9mm semi-automatic Pistol next to his bed at all times. The part-time gardener only came twice a week to water the small grassy sections, remove dead leaves from potted plants, and open the door when someone visited for the rest of the day. Andreas increased is position to full time from then on. His job became to guard the home. The old man had been near resigning had it not been for this new full-time offer. He thought of Rubén as a 'devil boy' that had pushed a heavy ceramic plant pot off the small wall that surrounded the roof. The pot came crashing down onto his head knocking the old man unconscious.

From then on, he was reluctant to go anywhere near the wall and continue to take care of the plants. He had taken such good care of all the plants and moved them into the shade only for the wife, Sofia, to move them back right away.

Sofia was happy about the old man's new assignment, "I'll take care of my own plants. He keeps messing with the 'Feng Shui' of my plants and drives me crazy," she had said.

The family felt safer having someone guard the home.

Chapter 12

The note that Cian slipped me in the lobby of the Taj Sheba was an invitation to his house for a barbeque. We encountered each other again at the Marine bar one weekend. I thought I might get to know him better. His preoccupation with drinking and his jumping on the bar to pretend to surf to 'American Pie' made him unapproachable. His eyes were glassy and red. His state deterred me from the desire to talk to him. Everyone was in a drunken stupor that night. I spent of most the evening without enjoyment sipping on the same glass of ginger ale. The quality of conversations declined within the first hour.

I was happy to accept a ride home early with one of the Peace Corps people I met, who also needed to leave promptly. He was going on a trip to Marrib, one of the smaller towns in Yemen, and needed to leave on his trip before dawn the next morning. I did not see Cian again since the Marine House night; we did not frequent the same places, which was a strange phenomenon since there were not many places to go. I regretted not taking the opportunity during the marine ball. After some reflection, I realized that perhaps his strong British accent had intimidated me.

At the Marine house, I purposely avoided him, smiled at him from afar. His work as the counsel for the embassy had me doubt that we had much in common to hold a conversation. Mom and I got into a routine, breakfast, cleaning, workout, shopping for fresh meat and vegetables, cooking, lunch, coffee at the Taj Sheba before dinner, and the same thing over again the next day.

Patty Smith

Sometimes Salem interrupted the daily routine with a visit. He came after school or accompanied us for a dinner out at one of the local restaurants. We stuck to the same scenario every day and were able to cope with the memories of the robbery. We did a good job at pretending everything was okay, although the thought that someone walked around with my passport haunted me, I wondered if someone might be in Germany using my identity. I feared that a terrorist would do awful things, crimes, carrying my passport. Religiously we locked all doors and frequently looked out the windows to make sure the guard was out there. For the most part, he stayed just inside the gate, sat in a lawn chair chewing khat, only disappeared briefly to buy more khat. Paps hired another guard who also became our driver. The previous man had been too comfortable, nonchalantly walked inside our home without announcing himself. Mom was at the sink in her shorts one morning, when he walked inside causing a near heart attack. Paps kindly let him go and we continued to drive ourselves.

Routinely on weekends, we visited the swimming pool at the British embassy during the day and entertained ourselves at the Marine House in the evenings. The expat community in Sana'a was small, making it impossible not to encounter the same people during our small excursions into the city. There were no movie theaters or malls. A small amount of decent restaurants and an even smaller amount of places to spend time were at our disposal. We rotated between the Taj Sheba hotel, the pool at the British embassy, and the Marine Bar at the American embassy. We happened upon thought-provoking conversations and learned about important work in the Yemen. The same small group of Peace Corps people popped up at the Marine House, it was always interesting to hear their stories. I once met a man determined to spread the Christian word of god, in a fundamentally Moslem country, which I thought was either heroic or pure stupidity.

We made acquaintances and received invitations to people's homes. Our tight circle included the Dutch 'odd' couple, she was at least a head and a half taller than her husband, beautiful, blond, big busted, eyes too large and deep set, he was short, stubby, beer-bellied, pudgy faced. They were talkative, gregarious, and loved to entertain.

We attended two events at their home, enjoyed deep-fried donut battered sugar powdered pastries along with the beer that kept pouring out of the gigantic keg imported through the Dutch embassy. We also befriended a couple for a short time. His name was Fibs; he was German and worked for the embassy, his wife from Syria. I watched their two small children a few times and welcomed the cash I earned. Our friendship was one-sided because they never invited us or anyone else to their home. One could count to see them at everyone else's parties. Ernst dating a girl from Ethiopia, his former housekeeper, got her pregnant, and married her. His new wife suddenly showed up with her gaggle of very young looking Ethiopian girls in skimpy dresses to parties. A group of Swedish, Dutch, and British people who worked for Schlumberger and BP Oil companies also counted as regular guests. It was an expectation that everyone take a turn hosting a party. I finally encountered Cian again one afternoon at the Taj. He was in the company of a British visitor and only stopped briefly to talk while he waited for the person to meet him in the lobby. We greeted each other. He looked professional with a nicely pressed shirt, vastly different from the last time I saw him, "It seems that you guys have been getting away with not throwing a party," he said before saying good-bye.

Mom's biggest problem with the idea of having people over to our place was the mess everyone would leave behind. That same afternoon I came home determined to change her mind, "I promise we'll help you clean up. We could have it on top of the roof. Nobody will need to stay inside the house. Come on, Mom, it will be fun," I said in a pleading whiny tone. We had relished a few daytime barbeques at different people's places.

Patty Smith

"You know it really is our turn and I could let everyone know when I go to Cian's place tomorrow."

She agreed and excited I made invitations to hand out the next day. Tanner swung by to drive us to Cian's home for a Volleyball game and barbeque. I learned that Cian had the reputation of a party animal and that his events often ended with people crashing on his floor. We left early, I looked forward to the food, and an opportunity to catch him before all of the drinking began. We arrived at his house and a game of volleyball was already in session. I avoided playing the following game for fear of teasing due to my poor passes and serves.

"Here, you just come and cheer us on," Cian winked at me.

The barbeque raged with delicious meats and people were drinking beer already. Every now and again Cian turned around, smiled, and winking when he scored a point as if to say 'see how good I play'. Relieved not to have to play I comfortably sat in the cool grassy shade and watched with cool lemonade in my hand. I could not handle the feeling when I drank alcohol, the headaches that lingered the entire day and the nauseous jetlagged feeling made it pointless for me to drink regardless of the awkwardness when I walked around with lemonade. In the past I had sampled different cocktails, wines, and beers, all resulting in the same struggles, I gave up. The only drink I could stomach was a Bailey's with added milk and lots of ice to water it down, the balance between the cream and sweetness had to be exact.

I sat contently in the shade of a large shady oak only a foot away from the volleyball game on the lawn, leaned against the rough bark and the branches cast shadows over my bare legs. My skin soaked up the sun as dry skin did water. The days of sun against my legs were far and few between; I relished the opportunity. Two tall Swedish men lunged and hurled themselves at the ball. The strong sun forced then to remove their shirts and reveal their perfect abs.

Games ended and new teams formed. Cian took a break from the next game and walked over to join me under the tree.

"So you like the Swedes?"

He worked hard to keep a smile, the corners of his lips quivered.

"Really? You're a jealous person?"

"Hey, just making an observation."

"Well, to be honest, I was admiring their abs, but I'm not sure if that means I like the Swedes."

"Oh, good, so there is still a chance."

"A chance?" I asked, "For what?"

"A chance to get to know you better."
I leaned in slightly looked straight at him, "are you flirting with me?"

"I guess I am. I have for a while now; I don't smile at any one."

"Well thank goodness for me," I said flicking my hair behind me.

"I've been winking at you as well."

"Did not go unnoticed," I said winking at him, "You do have beautiful eyes."

"Thank you, so do you," the softest pale blue eyes gazed at me.
I felt both warm and tense. For lack of words, I kept silent. I had heard he was quite the playboy, had not seen him flirt with anyone but me so far, but one of the Marines complained about him at the Marine bar the other day.

"He shouldn't be behaving like a drunken idiot, trying to pick up our chicks, he is the British Consul. Like the Brits even know how to surf," Mike had grumbled.

Patty Smith

Mike, the Marine, was upset because Cian dominated the party at the Marine House pretending to surf on the bar and putting on a show for the women.

"Did you not see him stuff an empty water bottle down his pants? That is his favorite. He does this Tom Jones impression and sings Delilah. The women seem to like it; I quite frankly think it's totally uncalled for."
I had missed that spectacle.

"Did you know he calls Americans 'Septic Tanks' because it rimes with 'Yanks'? I heard him say that Americans are living proof that Indians fucked buffaloes," Mike said clenching his jaw, his hands in a fist.

I padded Mike on the back, "You know. He was drunk." A Dutch woman sitting next to us, obviously had been listening to our conversation, added, "People who feel the need to put others down are desperately trying to make themselves look better."

A little skeptic about what Mike told me I said, "You know Mike, the Marine?"
Cian nodded.

"He says you're quite the flirt."

"I know Mike. Mike the bike," he said with a smile, waving his hand, dismissing my statement.
I raised my brows, "What?"

"Mike the bike, because everyone has ridden him. He feels threatened. That is all. Besides, you are a big girl. I'm sure you can form your own opinion of people, right?"

"Good point."

I wondered if he had too much to drink already realizing that I had seen him with a cup in hand since I arrived. I reached into my pocket feeling for my watch, the armband broke, and saw that it was late afternoon. Folks had been busily coming and going for the last four hours. I looked around the back yard.

"Who are you looking for?"

"I am looking for my sisters, Tanner is our ride today, or rather his driver is, and he just calls for a pick-up."

"I'd say, I'd drive you home, but it's my party, I can't leave."

"Oh no, not necessary, I'll figure it out."

"I can fetch you a cab."

I accepted his offer and followed him into the house. Music blared loudly; people were happy under the influence of too much alcohol and took shelter inside from the hot sun. We passed Ronny and Tanner sitting on the sofa kissing heavily. Cian smirked and placed his hand on my shoulder. I shook my head and shrugged off his hand. Ronny was only sixteen, Tanner was twenty-one, Cian must have had the same thought, he tapped Tanner. I would have interrupted myself and told her not to do that, he was too old for her, but I knew it was useless, she was sixteen going on thirty, and she would jump down my throat if I dared to embarrass her. Mo was the only person Ronny trusted and listened to for advice. She idolized her; unfortunately, Mo would think there was nothing wrong with the age difference or the behavior.

Paps was so absorbed in his work he did not notice anything around him and Mom was too naïve. Tanner stopped and pulled his tongue out of my sister's throat.

"I'm leaving," I said looking at Ronny. She grinned and pulled Tanner's face back towards hers.

Cian and I walked into his bedroom, "It's too loud in the kitchen, and we won't hear a thing."

He ordered me a taxi. We strained to chat in the kitchen, music played loudly as we watched out the window for the arrival of the cab. After a while, an old beat up car arrived. Its back bumper and hood covered in stickers, the same John Player and Son's cigarette stickers I had seen on other cabs.

Patty Smith

Yemeni's liked them for their black and white design, the JPS letters were written in cursive black on white, intertwined, this cab driver had placed them side by side upside down and sideways covering the back of the car, never mind one could read them upside-down. I was unaware one could call for cabs, up until then I thought you could only grab them of the street. Cian leaned into the window, handed the driver some bills, opened the back door for me, and gave me a peck on the cheek whispering into my ear, "Is it alright if I call you tomorrow?" I felt his breath warm.

"Sure it is."

"The driver knows where to go."

I reached for his hand and he assisted me into the car. I slid onto the ripped leather seat. He closed the door and waved good-bye. The cab was old, needing to use the restroom, I could feel every little bump in the road, and the car suspension was out. The red leather seat torn from wear, the plastic front panel cracked, likely from too much exposure to the sun.

A red tasseled scarf draped across the back seat of the driver. He kept looking at me with a crooked smile through the rearview mirror. I was uncomfortable wearing a thin flowery summer dress cut too low around the neck, my collarbone exposed. I knit my fingers and placed both my hands under my chin, hiding my skin beneath.

The cab driver toyed with what looked like a hand grenade from his glove compartment, began throwing it in the air like a tennis ball, and juggled it in his right hand while he gave traffic the right of way. My heart beat strong as I contemplated jumping out, then he placed it down and accelerated the cab. Surely, that was just a lighter or something else, not a real hand grenade, although I would not know the difference. The cab came to another stop at an intersection, the man turned around, I hastily grab for the door handle and accidently push down the lock next to the handle.

I fumbled and pulled the handle, at that same moment, the man reached back. I thought he was going to help me with the lock and remove my hand from the handle. To my horror, he grabbed me firmly between the legs his fingers wrapped in my dress. I screamed a terrifying screech, startled myself hearing the pitch I managed to discharge from my lungs. I slapped his arm unable to dislodge his grip on me. Thrusting the door open, I pushed myself across the rough seat. His hand released somewhat as he pulled on the cloth of my dress. I leaned forward and bit his arm, tasting the dirt on his skin, the thick hair on his arm in my mouth. He freed me his grip with a moan.

Somehow landing on my feet in the middle of the street, amidst traffic, cars rushed past much too close, honking horns, I leaped onto the curb, not conscious of how I got there. I ran and ran as fast as my feet would carry me, the sandals straps cut into the flesh between my toes. I kept running, without turning around, straight ahead, down the side of the street. At a small shop on a corner, I stopped to catch my breath. I entered the shop, my breath quick and deep. I offered the vendor money and pointed to his phone. He nodded sensing something was wrong with me. Paps picked up the phone and asked me to pass the phone to the vendor so he could give him directions to his shop. On the way home, he was angry with me, said that Cian should have taken me home, or that I could have waited for the Marine driver to take me, and that I must always call home for a ride.

"So sorry, Paps," told him wiping the snot from my chin, "I keep forgetting about how dangerous this place is, especially for a woman."

"I guess there is no need for me to continue my talk," he said in a kind voice, "You have to promise that you will not take a cab on your own again."
Cian called a few minutes after we arrived at home.

"Are you going to be alright?" he asked and apologized several times after he listened to the details of my experience. "Would it be alright if I come over tomorrow?" he asked.

Chapter 13

Like anyone else, Andreas desired to have his efforts and accomplishments recognized. He reckoned that if he gave it his everything, a hundred percent and above all, of the time, unleashing all he had to offer, credit would be inevitable. Leafy thin branches from the recently planted tree knocked lightly against the bottom of his office window with the early evening breeze reminding him it was time to go home. Andreas had been progressively late going home, worked into early evening hours, and sometimes met with people around work after leaving the hospital. He had recently met some tribal leaders, in conversations they spoke of possible instability in the near future. Tonight he wanted to scout a possible escape route out of the city just in case there would be some unrest. Ernst agreed to go with him, Andreas explained, "We can take my Jeep up the mountains and search for the closest village where we could take shelter."

"You really think that is necessary?"

"Yes, I think we need to be prepared. It would be a safe place from where we could arrange an evacuation or where we could wait out any trouble happening inside the city," Andreas said.

He liked to be prepared and ready for all kinds of situations. His family made fun of him when they moved to Canada and the first thing he did was to equip the Suburban for a survival situation in a Canadian winter, "in case we ever get stuck in the middle of nowhere."

He purchased a large wooden box and placed a first aid kit, towing ropes, snow chains, sleeping bags, granola, nuts, chocolate, water bottles, pieces of wood to place under tires should they be stuck in a snow bank, maps, flashlights, extra batteries, a shovel, and he always had a container with gas. The girls kept sneaking the chocolates and eating them, and he had to secure the box with a lock. This situation was no different; he wanted to prepare for the worst scenario. He got on the phone to let Sofia know he would be late at work again

"Sorry, but it'll be a little later today."

"Again? Why?"

"There is another emergency here at the hospital" Andreas lied about his intention knowing that Sofia would not approve.

"Don't they have doctors at that hospital to deal with emergencies?"

"Sure they do, but they need me to help. We have an issue with a German visiting the country. Don't wait up, you go ahead without me."

Sofia paused and huffed loudly and angrily knocked the phone onto the receiver.

"I will see if I can make it, but just don't know how long it will take me. When you have had enough and are ready to go home just go and I'll meet you at home."

They had planned to go to the Taj Sheba for dinner and dance. Andreas was very content to escape the agony of sitting through an evening of hotel band music. He fetched Ernst out of his office. They packed some bottles of water, stopped at the street corner to buy shawarma sandwiches, and drove the Jeep in search of an escape route through the mountains.

Patty Smith

The Jeep was great for mountainous terrain. Big fluffy clouds with darker edges hung low and winds had picked up. Through the open roof, Andreas examined the sky and thought it would be best to make it back soon. At a junction with some smaller roads, he stopped unsure of which path to take, "What do you think?"

He looked at Ernst in the seat next to him who was busy eating his sandwich.

"I guess we're lost," Ernst stated the obvious.

Andreas knew that arbitrarily taking any one of the paths was taking a big risk, "I don't want to be stuck again riding backward out of a dead end," narrow paths made it impossible to turn the jeep around once you hit a dead end, "what if we can't get back out?"

"Let's ask that guy over there for directions," Ernst pointed to a Yemeni man sitting on a large rock further down another junction.

The man's leathery skin creased deep as he smiled his woven skirt flapped in the chilly mountain air. Andreas leaned out of his window and asked him for the way back into town. "Sure, I know a route back it leads through my village. I could invite you for a cup of tea if you give me a ride," the man slurred through yellow teeth covered in green saliva, remnants of the khat he had been chewing.

"Ok" Andreas said, "Let's give this guy a ride and have a cup of tea. We can see what kind of village this is."

The door released a loud screech when Andreas pushed it open. The man jumped into the back and wedged himself between the backrests of the front seats. Wagging his hand amid the two men, he motioned to drive straight ahead, and gave few directions toward a mountain range thereafter. The dark square outlines of a village appeared in the distance against the deepening sky.

Suddenly, Andreas felt the cold metal of a pistol pressing strongly against the back of his head. The Yemeni ordered Andreas to stop the Jeep.

"I take the car. It will be good for going up and down the mountain."

Andreas contemplated a way out of the situation 'there is no way I am letting him have the jeep'.

"Once we give it up, we will be stranded," Ernst said in German.

"That's the least of my concern; this guy doesn't look like he'll shoot us," Andreas said.

"He has a pistol pointed at us," Ernst reminded him in a low tone.

"What are you speaking?" The Yemeni asked.

"My friend speaks little Arabic," Andreas lied.

"We are Germans. I am just telling him we should let you have the car and you will honor your word and let us go."

"Yes, I will let you go."

Andreas remembered that there was a small inconspicuous key under the dashboard called a "Batteriehauptschalter." It was a small removable I-shaped key that sat right below the ignition and switched the power to the car battery off. Andreas pulled the car keys out of the ignition, turned around to hand them to the Yemeni. Simultaneously, he slid his other hand under the dashboard, turned the battery key to the off position, removed it, and let it drop to the floor.

Steaming with anger, he ran scenarios through his mind of how he could distract him to snatch the pistol out of his hand and perhaps give him a good beating. The Yemeni ordered them to get out of the car "keep your hands up!" he climbed through the center into the front seat while continuously pointing the gun at them. He turned the ignition key, but the battery of the car was completely dead.

"You know, the Jeep has a problem, it doesn't start right. We can give you a push," Andreas said.

His fingers knitted, hands resting atop the crown of his head. The Yemeni looked harshly at Andreas, his forehead folded into endless creases above his brow.

Andreas planned to wrestle the person somehow and pry the gun away from him as he approached the vehicle to give it a push. Unknown to Andreas a secret detachment of troops resided inside a Yemeni army camp tucked away behind the nearby mountain range. They would learn later that President Ali Abdullah Saleh built his presidential palace on this piece of tribal land and that stretched to board the outskirts of Sana'a. The military troops on the other side of the mountain were the President's warriors guarding the presidential palace atop the tribal land.

"Move!" the Yemeni said, waved his gun in the direction he wanted the men to go.

"Don't you want the car?" Andreas asked.

"No, change of plans. It does not run. I am going to turn you over to the tribal warriors. I'll be rewarded well for that," the Yemeni shouted, somewhat afraid to follow through on that plan. The tribal military was fierce and it got dark. Perhaps they would mistake them for a threat and open fire at them. Andreas saw the Yemeni hesitating and possibly contemplating another plan.

"Do you think that's a good idea?" Andreas asked, "These guys shoot at anything that approaches them."
"Shut up" the Yemeni shoots his pistol a couple of times in the air, the loud striking sound of the pistol echoed of the rocks around them "I'm going to get their attention first, have them come to us."

Andreas counted the shots he fired. He counted four bullets left in the chamber. The Yemeni was just a little bit too smart for him. He still had enough bullets in the pistol to kill them.

"You are making a lot of noise."

"Let him," Ernst said in German.

"Speak in Arabic" the man shouted and pulled something that resembled fireworks out of his pocket. It seemed to be some sort of igniter to light explosive loads, Andreas had seen Yemenis carry them. You could light them and release quite a loud sound.

"I don't think that's a good idea."

"I didn't ask you."

"Gee, Andreas, are you trying to help him or us?"
"You keep waddling you tongue in German and I will shoot it off."

Ernst pulled his lips into a tight line and looked to the ground.

The man placed one igniter after the other on a boulder and hit them with a large rock producing very loud successive bangs, all the while he kept his gun pointed at the men with his other hand. The wind increased, roared with a low chill picking up dust and dry shrubs delivering them to new locations. The thick blue horizon exposed various figures shifting larger toward them.

"Here they come," Ernst says with a poignant tone.

"That's it, on your knees, you lose your tongue."

"No" he said, "There, someone is coming," Ernst pointed toward dark silhouettes.

The warriors thought that they are under attack due to all the shooting noises. They geared up, trooped in search for the culprits, and began shooting from about hundred meters. Kalashnikovs make a 'plop' hollow compressed air sound that one hears when the bullets make an impact. Bullets hit the rock feet away from where Andreas and Ernst stood.

"Verdammt!" Ernst shouted.

All three men, Andreas, Ernst, and the Yemeni, hit the ground for cover and wait shortly. The tribal men were close

Patty Smith

enough to hear them, then Andreas shouted, "Don't shoot, please!"

The troops continued shooting until they were nearly on top of them. Twelve men dressed in ragtag uniforms, some in tribal wear, some in military uniforms, armed with Kalashnikov rifles arrived at their location. Four men grab each one of the men; harshly pulled them up from the ground, shouted to keep their hands on their heads. One of them, a nervous young man, a boy really, kept his finger on the trigger while heaving at Ernst, emptied what seemed to be the entire magazine of bullets right before his feet. Andreas wrestled to repress a giggle. He had never seen Ernst move so quickly or jump so high. Ernst was a short chubby person who moved at a very slow pace and required constant motivation to initiate anything. Andreas decided to take charge of the situation and attempted to explain, "This guy tried to rob our jeep. We were just on an excursion, getting to know your beautiful country that is all. We work here, in Sana'a; we do good work with hospitals."

"Amriki?" one of the men asked a large scar across the side of his face. He wore it like a war medal.

"No, no, Almani, we are Germans."

Yemenis had a weak spot for Germans. He told them about their function within the hospital and asked if they would release them.

"We will be on our way quickly and be grateful you helped us get our jeep back," Andreas said.
Miraculously the captain of the group believed him, frowned at the Yemeni, turned to his men, and ordered two of the warriors

"He is a thief, punish him."

The two people stepped forward, and used their guns to beat the man to a pulp.

Leaving the beat man on the ground and the Jeep behind, they marched Andreas and Ernst to their camp. While walking, one of the men assured them they would be taking care of the thief and the Jeep.

"Don't worry," he said with a smile pointing his gun at Andreas' back. Minutes later the captain showed up proudly driving the military Jeep. He figured out the secret battery key.

"Good trick."
He nodded at them.

"I can't let you go right now; we have to get the secret service involved."

"Fine," Andreas mumbled, "We'll wait here."

"Not like ve haff a choice," Ernst said flippantly.

The captain and one of his people in the passenger seat drove away in the Jeep, "watch them" he turned to his deputy swaying his finger. The captain's deputy, who Andreas discovered later was also a captain, was not content with the situation. As soon as the Jeep was out of sight, he gathered his men and talked. Barely perceptible, Andreas heard him say, "They are spies and spies will be shot. You know what to do. Shoot them! We don't need them to tell us what our job is."

Apparently coming to an agreement, he ordered three of his men to line Andreas and Ernst up against a wall.
Ernst emitted an" Oh Scheisse," in lighthearted voice.

Then he added, "On our grave stone it'll say '*these men were shot for pure stupidity.'*"

"We're not dead yet," eyes flickered, Andreas gave Ernst a reassuring smile.

He did not know how he could remain tranquil or where his strength came from; it was just there. He recognized that it was self-defeating to think negatively, to show doubt. It would develop into a downward spiral, lead into a dark hole out of which it would take tremendous energy to climb out again. By no means would he allow himself to surrender to what others called bad luck, for him it is just another opportunity.

Patty Smith

He thought about his Arabic class in Germany. His Palestinian teachers in Cologne, they taught him much more besides the Arabic language, they introduced him to tribal customs, music, and poetry.

He employed one of those poems to get Chloe out of the airport; he learned to recite poetry artfully in Arabic. His teacher was one of the main translators for Yasser Arafat, was often engaged to do translations whenever Yasser had dealings with Germans, he was called upon due to his fluent command in German and his knowledge of Yemeni customs. Andreas remembered learning that tribal people had a law of hospitality, which he learned is much more than just hospitality; it included protection. The original version of the tribal law is as follows:

> 'No matter what you did, say you killed the brother of the guy you are going to seek help from, as soon as he has pitched his tent and you have touched his tent pole with your hand he becomes your companion or host and you are protected under 'Inta rafiki' (Rafiki means companion). 'Inta Rafiki' says that you are under your companion's protection. Your companion is required to feed you for one day. For those twenty-four hours, he cannot kill you, but furthermore he has to defend you with his life against anyone who may want to kill you.'

The twenty-four hour rule was in place because the food you eat a companion's home generally takes twenty-four hours to digest. Andreas recalled discussing this in one of his culture classes. He knew the Yemeni minister of defense, had played chess with him on various occasions.

Their eyes met, "I have just sat together with the Minister of Defense. He fed me and offered me to be his 'rafik'."

The men hesitated. One man's finger jittered on the trigger. The men lowered their rifles. Bewildered and feeling more confident he added, "Ok, you know what is going to happen to you?"

He looked at the deputy captain, his voice barely audible he said in German, "you bloody dogs I've got you now."

Still feeling enraged with his situation he knew he would not be going easy.

"If you want your noses and your ears cut off, just go ahead, shoot us," he restated staring down the armed men.

"The Minister of defense will come and cut your ears and your nose off."

He jubilantly thought he recognized indecisiveness. Ernst later claimed that the deputy captain was drunk, but Andreas was not convinced about that, he knew they did not have much alcohol up in the mountain villages. He thought that simply having an awkward personality could be a plausible explanation for his strange behavior. Two of the three assassins, gabili tribal warriors, lowered their weapons away and pointed them at the deputy-captain. With contempt in their eyes, they led him away. Andreas was pleased that directing his speech right at the shooters might help. He learned that there is a lack of military authority in Yemen.

"If you are a tribal warrior, your boss is just that, another warrior, a clan may agree to have a certain person be the leader and tomorrow the clan may make a new agreement," his teacher in Cologne had said.

"And if you are boss one minute you might find yourself without a function and back as a regular tribal warrior like everyone else the next."

He had witnessed that Yemeni's do not have a lot of reverence to higher person's first hand himself when he met the president. People did not address him as 'Mr. President' they called him 'Ali' a little uneasy he had followed suit calling the president "Hey Ali."

Patty Smith

Eased and apprehensive at the same time, he observed as the two warriors calmed the deputy captain down, and walked him away, then took charge of the situation. Andreas and Ernst still stood as statues glued against the wall, their arms rested heavy upon their heads, and one person was still holding them at gunpoint. The two other men returned from what might have been a difficult conversation with the deputy captain, "you can lower your hands," then asked that they follow them to a room inside "you will have supper with us."

One man unpacked food out of a dirty plastic bag, mostly bread buns that were stone hard, packets of rubbery processed Velveeta cheese, and strawberry jam. They mixed the cheese and jam into a mush spread for the buns inside the bowl. He placed the spread on top of a cloth in the center of the room, "eat."

He pushed the bowl toward Andreas and Ernst. Ernst stomach cramped in revolt and shook his head.

"I vill not eat zis. Zose buns look like you can kill somevone viz zem."

Andreas gripped his arm tight pulled him closer, hissing in German, "This is our life insurance, if we eat the slop, we cannot be killed by them."

Terrified of getting too comfortable with the men, Ernst did not want to share that he was reluctant to sit next to them. Allowing for a friendly supper might open the men to want more, he feared. He had heard that it was a common thing in Yemen that male captives were raped.

"Vat if zey vant us for sex?"

Andreas could not imagine anyone desiring Ernst "You must eat, as you eat you won't be raped either."

Ernst joined the gathering on the floor and ate the food washing every bite down with large gulps of water. Four hours had passed since they left the office, they shared the meal with the gabilis, and the Jeep with two secret service officials and the captain arrived and immediately started the interrogation.

"What were you doing so close to this military installation? Are you spies?"

"We got lost on our way to the next village and were trying to find our way back home and a thief tried to rob our car," Andreas attempted to clarify, "If you allow me to place a call to the German embassy, they will support our story and our credentials."

The secret service granted Andreas one phone call. Given the late hour there would only be an answering machine saying that the embassy was closed. He decided to call Sofia instead.

"You're drunk," Sofia yelled at him.

"No love," he assured her, "I'm not drunk, please get Mr. Schrott from the German embassy, ask him to call back and talk to the Secret Service so they will let us go."

Fuming and shaking her head in disbelief, she slammed the phone onto the receiver. It was around two am in the morning, when the secret service finally determined to let Andreas and Ernst go. They insisted on driving them back to Andreas' home.

"We want to see where you live, see if you are telling us the truth."

Also liking the jeep, they abandoned their own car and jumped into the front seats to drive Andreas and Ernst home. Andreas knew this meant they would be trying to keep it and at this point did not care about it anymore. They had brought two of them into the country. As they approached the home in the wee hours of the morning, Andreas and Ernst in the back seat, the guards on the roof across the street from Andreas' home, got suspicious.

They saw the jeep approach with the secret service people heavily armed and dressed in tribal uniform in the front seats. Andreas had made an agreement with the Sheikh in order to improve the safety of his family. He thought a possible way to keep the Sheikhs' guards away was to ask the Sheikh if they could be under his protection. The Sheikh agreed and the Sheikh's guards kept a watchful eye over his home.

"My guys will take care of you," he had promised that was almost turning out to be deadly. Suspiciously seeing Andreas in the back seat of his own Jeep, they shouted, "What are you doing?"

Without waiting for an answer, an ominous loading sound of Kalashnikovs carried loudly in the morning hours. The pulling back of a Kalashnikov mechanism and its slumming back created a metallic sound. They could hear five or six sequential Kalashnikovs preparing against the quiet night. Upon hearing this, the two secret service officers stopped the Jeep, swung their guns off their shoulders, and aimed them up the Sheikh's wall.

"Let's duck!" Andreas roared. Although he very well knew, there was no sense in ducking. AK 47 bullets could traverse the metal of a car or even 10 inches of a concrete wall.

"We don't want to get shot right here."
Then loudly from behind the back seat, he hollered to the guards, "*Ma itlak*, don't shoot." Andreas shouted, and a silent pause followed.

"These are my friends," he waited for an answer. Nothing.

"I am giving them the car, they can have the car." Still no answer.

"I'll explain to the Sheikh tomorrow."
The guards lowered their weapons.

Andreas said, "Thank you," in a low tone, not feeling genuine gratitude.

Without waiting for an answer, he jumped out of the car, Ernst tight to his heels. They heard the Jeep's engine rev and drive into the distance.

"You're spending the night here."

"Not going to argue with that."

The men tumbled into the home. Andreas swung the door hard into the frame denoting an end to a bizarre experience and locked the deadbolt in place.

"I've got just the thing," he produced a bottle of Don Julio tequila and shot glasses from inside a cabinet, then slid the bottle towards Ernst. They emptied the entire bottle of tequila he had been saving, then staggered to bed. The next morning Andreas shared the story with Sofia, "you had that coming for the stupid excuses about where you are and why you are late coming home."

He did not bother asking about his car.

In the following days and weeks Andreas tried to get his jeep back, after seeing the Secret Service drive it about the city like a souvenir, he understood they intended to keep it. A week later, Ernst received a citation by the German embassy. The Yemeni government had filed a complaint about him. The document had only mentioned Ernst going into a restricted area. Outraged, Ernst said that he was certain the Yemen Secret Service had been behind the robbery of Andreas' home. Meanwhile, Andreas struggled to explain the wild story to his ambassador who decided to bury the citation. The following days, Andreas contemplated Ernst's comment and remembered that one of the robbers kept asking for a second Kalashnikov after finding the first on top of the bookcase and wondered if Ernst was right in his suspicions.

Patty Smith

Chapter 14

His fair skin had him chase the shade. I marveled at the blueness of his eyes and his red sun bathed hair, Irish-Welsh. One of the Marines said being a Brit meant he liked to drink. To me Cian had a ring of a John Cale song and Archer's Bitter Ale.

He suggested it was our turn to host a party, "Nobody will invite you if you do not take a turn," he had said jokingly except I knew he was serious.

That afternoon I floated the idea, "We have tile floors everywhere. I'll mop them for you," I patted Mom on the shoulder.

"I've seen the way you mop," she sneered as she focused on the road ahead, "What about all the dirty dishes?"

"We can use plastic."

"Sure, either way I'll end up cleaning the mess."

"We can hang large trash bags everywhere so people can clean up after themselves," I said pushing my back against the front door as we stepped inside the house.

"People get drunk, then they break things, they get out of control, I've seen it at the Marine House," she said placing shopping bags filled with produce from the market onto the kitchen table.

Paps read at the table, he was like a permanent fixture in the kitchen, "What are you talking about?"

"A party. It is our turn to have one. Mom doesn't want to deal with the mess."

"How about we have it outside? Our yard is too small, but what about the roof?" he offered taking some of the bags off my hands.

A roof party sounded exciting. As far as I knew, nobody had hosted one before and the idea offered an escape out of a no-win discussion with Mom. She was tough to convince and usually right about people's behavior. Then, Paps usually went over-board with any planning. He made sure it was extraordinary; after all, it was his idea to have the party on the roof. He purchased a canvass tarp normally used to cover large trucks and constructed a tent on the roof.

"In case it rains," he said although rainy season was pretty much over.

He asked the Schlumberger workers for some empty oil drums of the field, sawed them in half, drilled a few holes into the bottoms, hoisted them onto bricks, then filled them with wood and charcoal. The drums were a hit. We could have started a booming business; people kept asking where we got them. Guests crowded around the drums like homeless people under a bridge. The Marines brought marshmallows to roast, a novelty to European guests. Paps kept feeding the fires and stoked the flames with an iron rod. One of the Swedes threw the cap of a Vodka bottle into the flames, then emptied it. Soon, his thinking was so impaired that he used his foot to stoke the fire when it threatened to die. His pant leg lit up immediately. He kicked his leg. Instead of putting out the fire, he hopped around and stripped down to his underwear. He continued to party until early morning hours in his tight white bikini and became the target of jokes. Hours later, some people were too drunk to drive home. I was surprised that Cian had maintained his composure and sipped slowly on wine.

Interrupting my conversation with the Dutch couple, he tapped my back lightly and sighed into my ear, "Chloe, could I use your phone?"

"Sure, there is one just downstairs. I'll show you where it is," I said, turned to the couple and added, "Excuse me guys I'll be right back. I'm just going to show him where the phone is."

Patty Smith

We walked inside the house together when he stopped and said, "Sorry, I lied. I do not need to use the phone. It seemed the only way I could talk to you."

"OK," I said puzzled.

"I have been wondering why you are here. What's a young lady doing in a place like this?" a big smile across his face, "Single right?"
"Single," I bobbed my head.

"Well?"

"It's a long story."

"I would love to hear it, I'm intrigued."

"I'm not intriguing, I promise," I said as we walked back up the stairs and onto the roof again, "Let's talk over here away from the crowd," I led him behind the tent into a quiet corner of the roof. It was dark and intimate. We leaned onto the brick wall of the home and looked down to the patio below. "Our guard down there was nearly killed by our toddler," I said, pointing in the direction, and shared the details of the plant pot incident. We laughed until my eyes filled with tears and perhaps the smoke from the oil drums was partly to blame. "Did you know you guys are growing marijuana down there?" he whispered.
"What?"

"Yes, one of your plant pots has a small marijuana plant growing. I noticed it when I approached your front door."
"Oh no, are you kidding? Mom is going to die when she hears that," I wondered how none of us had noticed the plant.

"You know, my Mom has probably been nurturing it this entire time," I laughed so hard I felt my ribs dig into my lungs, "ever since the pot accident with our gardener, she insisted on taking care of the potted plants herself. She is going to be embarrassed when I tell her she is a marijuana farmer.

Paps is always so absorbed with other things he wouldn't notice a marijuana plant if it was right in front of him."

I discovered that we could talk without getting bored for a second. He asked about my move to the Yemen and my life in Germany, then told me how he spends his days, how he liked to swim at the Lion's Club pool, drink coffee at the Taj, and host parties. He complained that he felt unappreciated at the embassy, "like a jack-of-all-trades," he said.

It got chilly without the warmth of the oil drums and a small breeze shivered the trees and my body.

"Are you cold?" he asked and placed his jacket over my shoulders, the sweet woody scent of his aftershave caressed the soft wool collar.

"I could get a sweater from inside," I said slightly twisting myself out of it against my wish to stay in the jacket and sleep it in.

"No, please keep it on."

I felt myself blush. The night's moonlight caught in his eyes, he leaned in to press his lips against mine, and I sunk into his arms. He stopped kissing me to catch air and pointed at the sky. Pressed against his chest, together we looked in awe at the immaculate speckled blanket in the Milky Way.

He pointed out a large K-shaped constellation, "That is Taurus," he said, "and on the shoulder of the bull you can see the Pleiades. The Yemenis have used them since ancient times to know when to plant their crops. Over there somewhere is Kaukaban, the historic mountain village where astronomers told the Queen of Sheba which route to travel to meet King Salomon in Israel and later where camels loaded with incense and gold went on to look for a new king using a bright star as their guide."

Patty Smith

The Police played in the background and I recognized the smooth voice of Sting singing 'Roxanne'. He reached for my face and walked his lips across my eyelids over the bridge of my nose down to meet mine as if drawing a constellation. It was early in the morning and people had dispersed into a few dyad-conversations.

"Could I see you again soon, please?" he asked and donned a curious look.

"Sure I would love to see you," I said.

The American embassy driver offered to take a few people home. Due to the massive amounts of liquor consumption, our remaining guests were unable to walk let alone drive. Cian and Paps scraped the pant-less Swede off the roof floor and hoisted him into Cian's truck. That night, or rather morning, I fell into a deep sleep as soon as I pulled the sheets to my cheek and still smelled the lingering scent of Cian's aftershave.

The following morning yellow sunrays woke me. They beamed tiny twirling dust particles into my room forming a bright oval spot onto the tile floor. Cheerfully, I jumped out of bed. Bare skin landed onto coolness. I ran my foot across the tile under my bed feeling for my furry slippers, kicked them out, and shuffled inside them to my mirrored closet door. Sliding the door slowly open, I gawked at myself in the glass. "You look ravishing," I said aloud mimicking a British accent. Cian's accent once bothered me.

He was Irish and at that point,

I could not tell the difference between an Irish and a British accent. Much later I would be able to distinguish even between inflections of different regions in England. For now, I found his accent a little irritating when he babbled quickly among his friends and could not understand a word.

He slowed down his speech substantially for me so I could understand and he amused me with the things he said, "Stay tuned to this channel, baby," he pretended to brush dust off his shoulder. Others mistook his sense of humor for arrogance. Sharply dressed in brown polished leather shoes, khaki pants, and a freshly ironed light blue shirt he appeared at my doorstep.

"I hope you've cleared your schedule for today," he said with a joking grin holding a bouquet of flowers.

"Sure, let me check my calendar," I said.

"Oi, I'll work my bloody arse off to give you a good time. It's worth canceling all those appointments."

I loved his surprise appearance; it was not as if I had anywhere to go on a Friday, but the Marine House. Fridays was like a Sunday and everything closed in Yemen.

"I've got the whole day planned out."

"Wow, these are beautiful" I smelled the sweet scented petals, "What do I need to bring? Where are we going?"

"Well, I would say you wear whatever you like, but cover it with a Hijab. You do have one don't you?"

"I do, don't like to wear it as you've probably gathered, but okay."

I opened the door wide and led him into the kitchen while I changed. Our day began by going to a Lebanese restaurant for lunch. A large courtyard with a garden patio greeted us where tame peacocks eagerly pecked at crumbs a little boy left, a small pond housed Sulcata tortoises found in the hot dry coastal plains of Yemen, and inside a tall meshed wire cage, a sad looking female monkey swung from branches of a dead tree.

"It's a Hamadryas baboon, they get them from the Bura'a forest," Cian said. "That is half way down the road to Hodeidah, we should go there, it is beautiful!"

Cast iron bistro tables circled the small oasis. We ate exotic renditions of Lebanese foods, meat and pomegranates stuffed pies, and delicious Tabbouleh made with finely chopped parsley.

Patty Smith

The waiter kept referring to me as Cian's wife and then asked that Cian order for me.

"Your wife wants more drink?" he looked at Cian for an answer. Cian turned to me brows raised in signal to give an answer.

"He's being respectful," he murmured.

After lunch, he took me to the Taj Sheba Hotel where we sipped our tea and spoke in interrupted sentences. Twice, people approached our table, greeted him, and engaged in small talk.

I felt both proud of being in the company of a man who obviously was an important member of the expat community but also quite annoyed suspecting he took me there to talk business. He excused himself for a moment to speak to a group of elderly Chinese that looked a bit out of place with their dark business suits. A woman came holding a silver tray with a large bead necklace and a small card on its side. Surprised I regarded the three strains of amber resin beads separated by large triangular silver plaques and a pendant that held a round shaped amulet container at its center. I opened the folded business card.

"Compliments of Mister Mohamed Saleh," the woman said and was about to walk away. Quickly I stopped her, "what's this?" I ran my finger across the silver amulet pendant, "I think you have the wrong person."

"No, Miss Chloe, Mister Saleh sent this to you."

I wondered how she knew my name but I was more interested to know who sent me this expensive gift.

"The gentleman over there," she pointed to a tall young Arab dressed in a thab, the long white shirt-dress, topped with an expensive tailored jacket. A white scarf over his head held in place by a black ring told me he was probably Omani or Saudi. He acknowledged my gaze with a slight nod and a smile.

"He asked me to bring this to you when your friend gets up from the table."

"My friend?"

Suddenly the fear of embarrassment overwhelmed me. Cian should not see me with the expensive gift and the prospect of someone courting me. I moved the tray back across the table, "Sorry, but you'll have to take back the gift."

Cian was already walking back to our table and witnessed the woman picking up the tray.

"Did you order something else?" he asked and dragged the chair to sit down.

"No." I blushed.

"Are you feeling alright?"

"Yes, I'm doing fine, just a little hot in here, don't you think?"

Behind him in the distance, I noticed the woman carried the tray back to the young Arab who appeared unhappy.

"I have a little request," he said reaching for my hand.

"I've been invited to a special event at a Saudi's house. Do you want to go?"

"A Saudi house? Do we take a gift?"

"No gift," Cian said dismissively, "just you if you'll come?"

I remembered that guests did not typically take gifts in Yemen, to do so, bordered on the offensive, and communicated doubt that the host could provide. Paps had to be creative in giving gifts and would leave them unobtrusively in an old newspaper on a windowsill, and on his way out, he might mention that he hoped the little inexpensive item would be useful, even if it had cost him a fortune. Accepting a gift was like accepting a favor with obligation to return the courtesy one day and Paps treated it carefully especially when dealing with high ranking and powerful people.

"I'll go with you but I'm not dressed for the occasion," I looked down at my drab Hijab.

"Of course you are. You can never go wrong in that thing."

We drove empty-handed to a large symmetrically squared house. Oversized windows revealed lovely lit rooms inside. A round driveway led to a regal heavy door that appeared to have inscriptions and decorations carved deeply into the wood. Two men flanked the entrance. One of the men ushered us inside with a hand motion. I clutched Cian's arm as we walked the white lustrous marble floors beneath us. I looked up at the tall fantastically painted ceilings with inscriptions that read 'mashaalah,' God willing.

The hallway spilled into a lush garden. To its right an infinity pool shimmered silver and blue, its walls detailed with tiny gold tile. A long stone table topped with a spread of Arab and Indian foods on gold plates was positioned poolside. Tall bamboo and flowery trees surrounded the perfectly manicured lawn. I held my breath as the host greeted me placing a small box into my palm, "A welcome for Mr. Cian's friend."

"Thank you," I said. Unsure if I should shake his hand I did a small curtsy.

"Some of our women are in one of the back rooms down the hall. You may join them now or later if you like." I squeezed Cian's hand and was happy to hear him say, "Later perhaps."

We enjoyed a generous breeze from the large fan blowing air across the pool toward the table. Indian staff poured water into cups and cleaned off dirty plates. Numerous European and Arab men sat holding what seemed an intense conversation, just one other female guest sat opposite the table. Apparently, we had interrupted the host's attention, one of the men regained his focus by calling his name, "As I was saying, I think tribal law and Yemeni's traditions are vital for the stability of this country. For centuries, this country has resolved conflicts from fights between families, clans, and tribes over water rights and market access."

Cian jumped right into the discussion, "I agree with that, the Yemeni people have depended on tribal traditions which have been used to establish justice, and regulated conflict for centuries."

He turned to face me and completely caught me off guard when he voiced my name, "Chloe's Dad will argue that tribal leaders play an important part in keeping the country from facing political conflict; I have had conversations with him about it. He has worked closely with tribal leaders."
I was not aware Cian and Paps had conversations at all.

"Well, this is a good point," the host said stuffing a small wine-leaf stuffed roll into his mouth.

"It is something that people should consider when planning their interventions in the Yemen; one must understand tribal function, traditions."

Yemen had seen its fair share of interventions: the Ethiopians, Romans, Turks, and recently in the sixties, both the British and the Egyptians played a large role in the civil war. I was sure there was more beyond my knowledge. I strained to understand the conversation and remembered a similar discussion about the conflict between the traditional tribal way of life and Western expectations between a nurse and an engineer at the Marine bar one night. The engineer was in charge of a project to enhance the infrastructure in the country, "I feel like we're moving one-step forward and two steps back," he had said in a frustrated tone. He often found his projects in pieces. Important parts, such as the bolts to hold the bridges together were often missing only days into a built.

"People are selling the parts in the market then they buy Khat with the money."

"Sounds like they don't need the bridge and have you thought of welding the bolts in place?" I had asked thinking that somehow, people had managed for hundreds of years without metal bridges and obviously wanted the money more.

A nurse jumped into the conversation, "In Somalia, we gave people condoms, travelled the villages, and trained both men and women how to use them. We passed around loads of contraceptives only to find them as decorations hanging from the roofs of their ramshackle corrugated iron huts," she had said. Then she added with a shrewd smile, "Maybe the custom of the Danakil nomads is still alive?

They used to cut off the penis of their enemy killed in battle and display the shriveled up member as a trophy on their doorframe. From afar, the condoms looked shockingly similar."

Traditions were hard to break and difficult for us to understand. A blue-eyed grey haired man sitting at the other end of the table opposite our host leaned in, "We need to prevent the escalation of violence. There is immediate need for national reconciliation."

The host nodded, "Western politicians should recognize that we, a tribal society, try to limit the influence of radical groups."

I attempted to follow the dialog,

I thought the Yemen had reunited to become one country, was thoroughly confused, people at the table spoke as though the country was divided. One man, his last name was something "H", did not catch his first name, said that he believed in peace. He was part of the BY group, the Believing Youth group, he explained, "We have run summer camps for the last couple of years to promote a Zaidi revival."

Cian tilted toward me and whispered, "Zaydis are almost like Sunnis but not quite the same."

The conversation did not seem to take a shift away from politics. Anxious to see the content of the small package, I excused myself to use the restroom; it was an opulently decorated room with shiny gold fixtures and a gold plated flush lever. I opened the package revealing a gold Raymond Weil women's watch. I returned to the table and slightly opened the box to show Cian the watch.

"You can't accept that," he looked sternly at me.

"But, why?" The watch looked expensive and I later discovered that it was worth a few thousands of dollars.

"I am a diplomat. It is unethical to accept a gift of that expense, could be considered a bribe."

"This is a gift for me." I wanted to argue to keep it, knew I would not convince him, but sought to try.

"Yes and you are *my* girlfriend."

This was not something we had discussed, but I liked hearing the word girlfriend. Reluctantly I handed over the box. He would know how to return the gift gracefully.

I got up again, "I'll go join the ladies."

Uninterested in more conversation, I left the table in search for the other room the host had mentioned. I walked through the wide airy cold stone hallways, stopped to regard a large painting of a white and two brown running horses inside a gold gesso frame. If it had not been for the ornate frame the painting would actually seem all right. A faint sound of music led me down the hall and I walked toward a large wooden door.

The vibration of strings similar to a guitar laced with the light tickles of a flute and the thudding sound of a large Madiff drums and fast rhythmic beats of Darbukas. Echoes of percussion juxtaposed to a slow howling. The singer's voice rose and her pitch deviated from the instruments and then regained perfect harmony.

I had heard Arabic music before inside cabs, stores, and the Taj Sheba hotel, it usually played in a sharp register. This music however, was hypnotic, happy, and dichotomously sad. I stood closely, pretended to look at another extravagant painting of a large palm tree with coconuts looking strangely phallic while I enjoyed the sounds around me. The handle on the door moved and a small woman, all in black only her eyes peered out of the narrow slits, glided out. Unable to ascertain if she was smiling or frowning, I directed my stare back at the painting. She moved through the hall and disappeared into another room. Uncomfortably, I turned around to make my way back outside when the door opened once more.

"You are welcome. Come in," a small voice said.

"But," I hesitantly looked over my shoulder.

"Please join us," an uncovered black shiny mane over big wide charcoal framed eyes poked out of the cracked door.

"Ok," I said and approached her.

Her arm swung around the door, grabbed, and tugged me into the room. Big windows heavily draped in white and black velvet and a chandelier the kind that belonged into a hotel lobby hung low shining hues of blue and yellow. A stereo played somewhere; I searched for the music source and found the speakers inconspicuously installed inside the wall. Women dressed in modern clothing occupied plush chairs. Two gestured a welcome then talked amongst each other. Stretched across a chaise lounge, a woman relaxed. Her décolletage was adorned with henna design. I watched as the artist worked across her skin in sections, first deposited a thin wet amount, allowed it to dye the skin, then wiped of the henna revealing the intricate lace design.

Generous amounts of gold bangles jangled as they waved their arms when they spoke. A new happier song played and a young girl, stood up from her chair, loomed toward me, and took a tight hold of my hand, "What do you have under this?" she clutched and tugged at my Hijab.

"I didn't know," I said apologetic, I was wearing my jeans and shirt under the Hijab given that Cian said it did not matter. All the women were dressed as if they were going to a major event.

"Don't worry," she said rolling the 'r' softly, "You don't need this," she jerked on my Hijab again.
I contently unzipped the robe and handed it to a woman that reached out for it. The ghostly woman I saw exit the room earlier entered with a tray full of finger foods. Women danced to the new song and awkwardly I mimicked their moves. Dancing in that manner was new territory, "You all look so nice," I said.

"Do your husbands see you this way?"

"We dress for ourselves and to look good for our friends," she said taking hold of my hands and moving her hips rhythmically to the song.

She demonstrated some moves I failed to copy.

Cian knocked on the door to my relief, "Hey, it's time to go. Are you ready?" he called from behind door.

I shook the girls hand and followed Cian to his car. It was midnight when I arrived at home. Slowly I turned the knob to the house after kissing Cian good night, tiptoed into the house, and was startled to find Mom still awake sitting in the living room with a book.

"Your father is still not home; I'm staying up for him," she placed the book on her lap upside down.

"Where is he now?"

"He said he would be late because he was going to help the pilots from the cargo plane unload and then have a quick drink with them at the Taj. That was at eight."

Every so many months a German TRANSALL cargo plane arrived full of medical and electronic supplies for Paps' project, sometimes an odd amount of razor wire for the embassy, and always a shopping list Mom submitted that included German sausages, Haribo sweets, and a good amount of Bitburger Pilsener for Paps. The way she sat, Mom looked sunken into her body. With her delicate small nose and smooth olive skin, Mom had always seemed at least ten years younger than her age, now she appeared tired and vexed.

"Mom, I'm sure he's ok. Let's go to bed."

Chapter 15

Sunlight wrapped the mountain range behind the city in bright orange and purple where both the moon and the sun appeared against the sky and the wind was still as if in anticipation. Radka sat at the kitchen table. She wore her favorite dress. It was a rare opportunity to make herself up and go out without the black Hijab that covered her any other time. Shorn of hiding her hair - she had almost forgotten what it was like to wear it loose. She had washed and styled it with care. Nobody would take notice and so it did not matter any other time when she kept it tight at the nape of her neck tucked inside the dark headscarf. It was a distinct feeling when she carried it loose, made her feel incredibly extravagant. The elastic band to hold it had been part of her and left split broken strands where it usually rubbed around the ponytail that she then tucked into a bun.

"Can I pour you another cup of coffee?" Sofia pushed her chair back scratching the chair legs across the tile floor releasing a long screech.

"Radka, you have the most beautiful hair."

"Thanks Sofia, I am so glad not to wear the cloth on my head."

"Thanks for bringing the delicious pretzels again."

"Hey, if you only knew how easy they are to bake," Radka smiled, "I gave you the recipe. You should try to make them."

Andreas shuffled into the kitchen, "Hi Radka. Hi Alex." He grasped a bun off the plate and filled his mouth with it.

"Andreas, please use a plate," Sofia slid a plate across the table.

Chloe right behind him, "I heard you brought pretzels?"

"Yes, help yourself," Radka offered and pushed her chair to make room for another person.

"I'm not really hungry right now, but I'm going to take one anyway," she wrapped it into a napkin and placed it into the fridge, "for later."

"You better call your sister down."

Ronny was upstairs alone. Lately she spent much of her time in her room and everyone dismissed her new behavior for doing homework. Chloe inhaled deeply and yelled over her shoulder, "Ronny, come down, Radka is here."

"Really? I could have yelled myself," Sofia said peeved. Chloe shrugged her shoulders, "You were saying?" Chloe turned to Radka, who continued to speak. The women leaned in close to listen to the latest stories about the Hospital. Ronny walked into the kitchen, rested her lower back against the counter, and took the last pretzel bun off the plate. Andreas and Alex engaged in dialog across the table that progressively increased in volume. A faint burst sounded in the distance like a tire blowing. Conversations stopped, Ronny pushed herself away from the counter and stood rigid with both her feet firmly rooted as if prepared for the ground to shake. A loud ear-splitting blow quickly followed the initial burst, vibrated the glass windows, and echoed through the walls of the home. Everyone braced and held their breath and looked at Andreas. Andreas looked out the window. Succeeding smaller quick pops like small firecrackers filled the space.

"What the heck?" Chloe whispered.

Loud reverberations of sound and jolting strikes shook the thick brick walls of the house.

Stunned, Sofia stiffened her jaw, "What is that?" she asked through her clenched teeth.

"That sounds like guns," Andreas said in a flat tone and his face solid in a scowl.

Patty Smith

After he paused to think he said, "The large blow could have been a tank." He stood up. "It's very close probably moving this way," he said forebodingly.

There was no use in looking out of windows. The wall blocked any view to the outside from the first floor. He motioned everybody out of the kitchen, "Quick we have to take shelter," he ran up the stairs for a view.

"Where should we go?" Chloe yelled after him.

"The hallway," he was already half-way up the staircase and Alex charted behind him. They arrived at the door to the roof when Andreas hesitated to open it.

On the first floor of the house, Chloe grabbed her mother by the hand, her expression pale, "Come on you guys. Let's go!"

The women huddled down into the long narrow hallway and silently listened to the sounds outside the home. Chloe struggled to calm her heartbeat, leaned against the cold plaster wall, her bare knees bent tightly against her chest. She hugged her thighs by wrapping her arms underneath them, her prickly calves on her forearms and wished she had taken the time to shower and shave that morning. Sometimes she put off a shower to late afternoon, especially when it was a hair-washing day. She skipped hair washing to an every other day affair. The climate in Yemen was dry and all the blow-drying made her hair feel brittle. Her mind wandered, she urged for a long hot shower and smooth legs and clean fresh hair.

"I have to use the restroom," she announced and left the hallway. Dazed she stepped into the shower and released a long sigh when warm water ran down her back.

"Is that the shower running?"

"I think so," Ronny looked at her mother and rolled her eyes, "It's Chloe of course not thinking much further than herself."

The shower drowned out any sounds of guns. Chloe lathered in lavender smelling soap. Cian brought it as a gift from England; it was from a new place called the Body Shop. This might be her last shower, the only time she washed her hair, and she wanted to look her very best. She cleaned off the small hand razor and ran it over her soapy calves, feeling remorse about her choice to move. If only she had waited, been patient with Farris, or if she had gone to the technical drawing school like Gianna. Gianna had the courage to do something with art. Competition was too great and she had no patience to make the time investment. It was years ago when she had first considered it and now she had nothing. Soon after she left for Yemen, Gianna entered art school. She would be half way through her program and could work as a designer when she finished. Quickly she wrapped herself in a towel and rubbed her hair inside another one. Then she parted her hair into thin strands and pulled each slowly over a thick round brush against the hot air of the blow-dryer from roots to the ends.

"Chloe, it's not safe," Andreas knocked on the bathroom door, "You need to stop blow-drying your hair and take shelter with us."

"There are no windows in here."

"I know. It's still unsafe."

"Ok, ok, I'll only be a minute," she said knowing that blow-drying her hair was at least a thirty-minute ordeal.

In the hallway, Radka laid her head onto her knees.

Overwhelmed by worry she thought of her dog, he was alone at home, "I'm going to rest my eyes for a few minutes." Sofia looked across the tile, a small fine dust layer rested on the floor like fine ash. The multiple strands of glass beads glistened and the bulbs casted a hue of blue and yellow across the marble floor. Sofia tried to remember when she last mopped.

Patty Smith

The house was much too large for her to clean it alone. Her hands could simply not take the repetitive motion of mopping that many square feet of tile. When she was young, she cleaned the floors all the time, one of her assigned chores. The floors of her childhood home always gleamed with cleanliness after she was done.

This big house required a schedule for mopping: Mondays she did the kitchen, living room, hallway and Tuesday's the mafraj, master, Chloe's bedroom, bathrooms downstairs and Wednesday's the upstairs bedrooms and Thursday's the upstairs bathrooms, upstairs living room and finally on Friday's she took a break from mopping. She dusted and washed everyone's laundry on Fridays. The girls were old enough to wash their own clothes. Sofia liked to take care of it for them and wanted it done right. She had stopped ironing Andrea's socks and underwear and that helped. The floors looked like they needed more mopping. The city was too dusty and sand always flew in through a brief crack in the door. She thought of Rubén who always left the front door ajar and she thought of Mo.

Mo was in the United States at a funeral. Joe's best friend had passed. The two would be looking for a home while they were in Joe's hometown, Abilene. His deployment was nearly over and he asked for Mo's hand in marriage. Sofia was happy for her daughter and she would miss Rubén. It would be challenging not to have him run around anymore and she had looked forward to raising him and watching him grow into a handsome young man. She had gotten used to that little boy.

A week ago, she was unsure how she would fill her days without him and now she did not know how she had found the time to take care of a baby with all the cleaning. Her life had reduced to cleaning a fresh blanket of dust that continuously settled down.

Bursts of bright sparked high, consecutive pops overpowered tranquility and the perfume of antagonism devoured the morning. Andreas reemerged downstairs his breath was quick and heavy. He knocked on Chloe's door. Calmly she continued to dry her hair, dressed, and stepped into the hall. "Without a basement, the hallway is the safest place," Andreas said pacing the hallway then stopped to face everyone lined against the wall.

"We don't want to be near any windows to the outside. We had to go to the roof of the house to get a good view. It seems there is a tank just down the road, a block or so away not much more than that. Not sure, what it is shooting at. In order for the tank to shoot at something thousands of yards away, the shell has to travel at a high speed. We are hearing the sound of the shell blowing off," he muttered holding their attention, "I actually think we are very safe being so close to the tank."

Sofia and Ronny had not moved, they sat on the cold tile floor and rested their backs against the wall. More sounds of gunshots rang in their ears and Radka jolted to her feet, "I have to get Rex, he's not safe, and he must be scared," she said loudly, then hastily walked to the front door. Her husband clutched her arm and pulled her backward. She lost her step and nearly fell, "He's going to be fine, and for right now we have to stay put, wait, and see what happens.

The shooting may stop soon," Alex placed his arm around her and walked her back to the protections of the wall. Andreas jerked the home phone out of the kitchen as far as the cord would reach into the hallway and placed calls to the German embassy, the American embassy, the Brits, the hospital, and Ernst. After fruitless attempts to speak to anyone, he realized the amount of anxiety it brought and pushed into one of the bathrooms and continued to make calls. Alex, Radka, and Chloe pulled the mattress cushions of the mufraj and positioned them along the wall of the hallway. Chloe crawled into her bedroom for pillows and blankets feeling like she was in a very surreal situation. They spent the entire night on top of the mattresses inside and slept hunched up like sardines in a can.

Patty Smith

Shooting ceased for a few hours and started up again before dawn. The next morning Sofia and Radka tiptoed into the kitchen and whispered while they brought back bread, hummus, and vegetables.

"The electricity must have been cut off overnight, the fridge isn't running," Sofia announced.

The entire day, Andreas was on the phone. They told jokes and stories and played backgammon to pass time. Toward late afternoon, the shooting ceased once more.

"I guess they have to take a break for prayer and khat chewing" Chloe said annoyed.

Radka took the opportunity, lunged to the front door, and proclaimed she was going home, "Rex is going to be so scared. I have to feed him," Alex ran after her, turned around briefly, "I'll call you if I can, don't worry, we'll be OK. We'll go to the German embassy once we have Rex," they walked out slamming the door behind them.

"Really, I can't believe what people do for their pets," Ronny said and shook her head.

The city lay in distress without electricity and running water. Foods threatened to rot. They planned to open the fridge as little as possible to conserve the temperature inside it. Toilet tanks ran out of water and Andreas designated the upstairs toilet to use multiple times before flushing it once. He snuck behind the house and Sofia was upset with him. She shouted that it was too dangerous and banged her palm against the bedroom window facing the small strip of grass while Andreas fumbled to zip-up. By the second day, an offensive smell of urine creeped out of the upstairs bathroom and Andreas relieved himself outside again. The narrow hallway space smelled of sour body odor one could only perceive when entering from outside. It now seemed ridiculous that only a few months ago Chloe's biggest problem was finding a suitable person to date. She needed to stretch her legs and said that she was going to use a bathroom.

"Just be careful to stay away from the windows," Andreas replied and placed the phone onto the receiver.

The shooting ceased for some time and yet they anticipated the pulsing blows to continue passionately. Upstairs on the second floor Chloe walked past the bathroom and continued up the stairs to the roof of the house. She yearned for fresh air. There she stood looking from where the tank parked and over the horizon and thought of drawing back the curtains for the first time and transporting into early centuries. Immediately the Yemen had taken hold of her. A country stuck in the dark ages appealed to her: people's naïve thinking, the simple and yet breathtaking architecture, both unaffected by the passing of time and people's unwavering values strong as the walls of their homes.

Upon her arrival, she realized that Sana'a was the physical manifestation of her imagination when her grandfather read stories of Brothers Grimm's Aladdin and One Thousand and One Nights at her bedside when she was a child. Sana'a was where she found love and respect and understanding and how esoteric that she found herself. Here she felt happy and safe irrespective of the challenges as a woman. On all fours, she carefully and lightly placed each palm on the ground in front of her feeling for small pebbles and glass, and then shifted her weight between her hands. The rough concrete floor dug into her knees. Yemen collapsed.

She moved toward the closest corner of the wall and watched with astonishment and horror. Above the mountains, a sequence of lights popped and lit the sky like a New Year's Eve fireworks show. She remembered the roof party. They held hands at this very spot, beneath this sky they kissed. A complicated emotion overcame her that she could not explain: fear, love, anxiety, anger, disappointment, all rolled into a hurricane, hot and cold meet and shudder her body. She had been in a forbidding situation before, in Italy. Within minutes of leaving the car parked on the streets of Naples it was stolen.

Patty Smith

To make matters worse, when she and her friend walked across the street to the train station in search for a payphone, a police officer arrested them. Admittedly, she had just left the disco dressed in skimpy clothing and it was three o'clock in the morning. It was the first time she was without her passport in a foreign country. A few hours only, she spent inside a holding cell while the officer vetted her for information. Those few hours were excruciatingly long. The memory evoked laughter, how insignificant that situation now seemed. She shrugged off her concern and gained control of her thoughts. Cumbersomely she crawled along the wall to another point to assess the state of homes around. Her knees pressed on something sharp and she exhaled a loud yelp. A small silver metal piece dug into her knee, she removed it from her skin where it left an indentation. It had melted and broken off something larger, a shell with Russian letters engraved along the side.

She was at a good observation point and wanted to find a way to spend time there at night. A heavy smell of war-breeze swayed strands of hair onto her face. She sat down leaned against the wall and scanned the roof. Big oil-drums still stood on bricks left over from the party. The large tarp under which people had talked together held onto metal poles, motionless and sturdily and the afternoons her sisters sunbathed behind the small house of the staircase hiding from the guards next door, all would have been missed. She caught a glimpse of bright glow for a second and it quenched; shots in the distance.

Chapter 16

It was late afternoon; wind swept up dirt and broke the grimy heat over the tarmac of the Sana'a airport. Stowed warmness radiantly hovered below the knees. Sanaa's desert climate and temperatures gradually rose to highs of eighty degrees during the day and lows around fifties at night. Andreas waved his hands rushed since there was not much sunlight left, "We need to un-load quickly."

The city enjoyed longer days as the sun increasingly set later in the afternoons. It was already five fifty and Andreas saw the sky turn purple-orange. He welcomed the cooler gust upon his sweaty neck. Most of his afternoon he spent helping the pilots of the dark green TRANSALL C-160 Medium-Lift transport aircraft heave boxes out of the voluminous interior and load the cargo onto the bed of a large truck parked alongside the tail fin of the plane.

"Thank goodness," he huffed wiping his brow with the back of his hand, "This had to be the largest load in a while."

It was increasingly more difficult to import his contraband that included two barrels of Bitburger Pilsener. Fundamentalists had taken over the majority of the custom officer positions. In order to get the two barrels of beer through customs, Andreas had asked that the barrels be painted olive green and labeled with 'MACHINE OIL'. The loading master forgot about the camouflage.

When Mohammed, the long bearded customs officer, crossed the tarmac to check on the cargo, Andreas quickly grabbed the flight manifest on the oversized clipboard, and placed it onto the stacked barrels, "we can use this," he said and motioned an invitation the improvised table.

Mohammed meticulously checked every item on the list walked between the cargo bay and the flight manifest without once looking at the barrels. With pockets full of candy to which he first said, "no, I will not take a bribe," and Andreas answered, "It is not for you it is for your children," Mohammed contently walked away with a formal goodbye: "Ma' assalama."

Andreas answered with the same words and quickly the barrels were loaded and covered with cargo nets. One of the pilots dusted his jacket off in the wind, threw it back over his flight suit, drew his arm through the sleeve, raised the cuff to his face, and pulled a dirt line across his forehead. They loaded all the goods into the truck, drove to the German embassy to drop a few items off there and took the rest home.

"I can drop you off at the hotel," Andreas offered and agreed to a drink before heading home.

The pilots spent the night at the Taj Sheba hotel before returning to Germany early the next morning. The three men sat at a table inside the restaurant and chatted the usual pleasantries. Upon finishing his drink, Andreas scooted his chair back, thanked the pilots once more, and handed them a piece of paper with his number, "Just in case you need anything."

On his way out the door, the first secretary of the German embassy stopped him, "Andreas, fancy finding you here. I just got my order of cigars, would you like to join me for one on the terrace before you leave?"

"Sure, I would love to," he accepted the cigar although he did not smoke and did not even like the taste of cigars.

The two men chitchatted, sucked in and puffed out the sweet smell of Cuban tobacco, and gaped at the swathe of city lights. Suddenly, with one swoop, as if someone flipped a switch, the city was cloaked in darkness that revealed the interweave of stars.

"Oh, that's not a good sign," Andreas mumbled and lifted his face at the sky for a moment.

"Don't worry, we know everything that is going on in the area, nothing is going to happen," the first secretary said and fixed his collar and took another deep breath from his cigar. As quick as the light extinguished, it came back on and the secretary would be wrong in his comment.

The next morning, surprising everyone, the war broke out. Andreas had sustained the noise of belligerent shooting the entire day. Huddled on a thin mafraj mattress without much sleep, he had only managed to close an eye for a few minutes although the hallway had been pitch dark and one could have slept with eyes open. He relieved himself in the yard, his stomach rumbled in protest of the tuna he ate out of a can. It was now the second day of war and the shooting had not calmed down in the slightest. He grew increasingly anxious and needed to find a way out of the city.

Happy to have escaped the constraints of his job in Germany and enjoying the liberties of his work in Yemen, he hoped to ride out the unrest. He had known that a civil war was on the books. His perfect world had prevented him from recognizing the warning signs and the timing of the outbreak surprised him. The first day most of the city laid in absolute blackness, the family played cards under the flicker of candlelight, squinted to count the dots on the dice to the backgammon game, and told stories in an effort to retain confidence. Not knowing how long he might have a working phone, Andreas ran to the phone immediately when hearing the first shots.

His first calls were fruitless;

people had other concerns than answering a phone. He discovered that everyone had limited connections, "We can't call out," the first secretary had said, "Since you can still make calls out can you call around and assess the situation with the other embassies?"

Andreas rented the home from an officer of the military police academy. Luck would have it, that his phone connected to the police network, and therefore, it had not been limited like other lines in Sana'a. Fated to have one of the few phones with the ability to make outgoing calls, he dialed the Dutch, British, Russian, American, Italian, and all the other embassies. Everyone was limited to only receiving calls. It was without question that Andreas link communication, receive, and transfer information between embassies and families. He rested flat against the floor of the small storage room to evade any shots that might fly through the low window and continued to place call after call, took copious notes, relayed strategies, informed, and offered advice. People needed him and he would muster all his energy to help. A southern army elite battalion was camped a block and a half away to the right of his home and to the left, northerners shot through buildings to cut corners. A large tank only a block away rattled the windows every time it fired and with every passing blow, he thought the next one might shoot through his window. He placed the phone back onto the receiver.

"Could I call Cian please?" Chloe asked with a small voice.

"If you catch him, find out what plans the Brits have," he said.

Chloe dialed the numbers "Hey, how's it going over there?" she paused, looked out of the corner of her eyes, Andreas still stood at the door.

"Will I be seeing you again? Really? Do you think that is a good idea? I miss you, too," she whispered.

She disconnected the call and turned to her father, "He was told to go to the embassy before his phone was shut off like everyone else's."

"Ok, he'll be fine, don't worry," Andreas climbed the stairs to the roof of the home to assess the surrounding situation.

Another dry cold breeze blew gently upon his skin reminding him that only forty-eight hours ago he had helped with the unloading of goods from the truck at the airport. Shots fired at a satellite above his home.

Yemenis seemed to shoot at everything they could not discern: birds, satellites, specks of dust floating in the air, anything that moved the slightest in the clouds became a target. He pivoted his weight heavy on his knees and swiveled his head back and forth, they had converted the mosque behind his home into an antiaircraft position. Confused he heard the sound of small stones falling; shells from the mosque landed upon his roof. He picked one up to see the caliber and confirmed his assumption when he had heard the slow firing rate marked every second with a thudding rhythm. He had seen long barreled S-60 guns towed by slow moving URAL trucks and wondered if Yemenis would use them how the German Afrika Korps did when destroying British Matilda tanks with the Flak 88 in the battle of Tobruk where his Dad had fought. He hoped that airplanes refrained from bombing it given its proximity. He clutched the edge of the wall with his fingertips and pulled himself up just sufficiently to look at the mountains in the distance. The presidential palace was the target of shots a mile further up from the home. A dark point marked its location in the distance and he wondered about his Jeep.

The family looked comfortably playing cards when he returned. Another night of shooting was ahead of them and they sat waiting like a rubber ducks at a shooting range, "I am going outside to assess the situation."

"Really? Are you now leaving the house? You were just on the roof. Could you not see enough from there? Why do you always have to go to the extreme?" Sofia said her voice sounding squeaky.

"Mom, is right, it's too dangerous Paps," Ronny chimed.

"It'll be alright. Its dark now, the shooting is slowing down for the night, and they will not be able to see me in the dark. I will be right back. I promise."

"Do you want to borrow my Hijab as camo?" Chloe asked.

Patty Smith

He did not reply, was already out the door. Even though airplanes attacked during daylight, they could not identify their targets in the pitch darkness of the city, and danger was still very high.

Guards around the city were armed and nervously shot at anyone approaching. Half-blind, he walked along the greyness of the evening toward where he suspected the tank stood. His eyes slowly adjusted to darkness and fuzziness became clearer. The silence and emptiness of the streets felt eerie. The tank had not shot in a while. Finally, he neared the metal beast and knocked lightly on the metal. A lid atop opened with a dull sound and a man's white bandaged head poked out. Andreas expected to see a helmet, but was not surprised that the man's head was wrapped in a headscarf instead. His eyes were big and piercing like those of a hawk ready to peck at its prey.

"I am German and that is my house," he pointed to his home, "I am respectfully asking that you not shoot through my home, as I have wife and children sitting there and we are peaceful and take no sides in this disagreement. Perhaps if you do need to use my home as a shooting path, would you please tell me now, so we can get out?"

As Andreas babbled on the man's gaze softened as he thought of his own family at home and then leaned out of the tank to see exactly where Andreas pointed.

"Don't worry, you can stay in your house," he said.

Relieved, Andreas thanked the man and walked slowly toward his home. Carefully. He felt the man's stare burn holes into his back. His was now clear and he panicked when he noticed that soldiers used the home opposite his own to camouflage themselves. Once a beautiful new construction, like his own, solid brick, now had broken windows. Everything in the shooting path inside the home destroyed and only unrecognizable rubble material left. Earlier in the day, shooting was heavy.

The home was empty now and he imagined the inhabitants had made it out safely. It reminded him of when he spoke with someone at the Italian embassy. He thought the secretary on the other end of the phone was a little scandalous. He had screamed so loudly Andreas held the phone a few inches away from his ear.

"Oh my god, oh my god, they are shooting at us," the man had said in a strong Italian accent and followed it with numerous Italian words that sounded like the names of delicious dishes, "I am all alone up here."

"Where is everyone else?" Andreas had asked. "They are all hiding in the basement. The tank is destroying the building. They are trying to shoot through our windows," the Italian had shouted.

"You should take cover in the basement with everyone else."

"Get us out of here," the Italian had yelled.

"Are you crazy? They are shooting at your building, how do you suppose we get you out? We have no tanks to get you out of there. You're going to have to hunker down and we'll keep a beer cool for you."

Next, he had called the hotel to get a count of how many foreigners were taking shelter there. One of the German pilots of the cargo plane took his call, "We tried to get to the airport, but there was heavy fighting, we barely made it back to the hotel. Armed guards at checkpoints challenged us on our way back to the hotel. We heard that our plane got hit at the airport," the pilot had said exasperated with his situation.

Andreas had called the airport and learned that the German plane now looked like Swiss cheese with seventeen bullet holes. Along with the German embassy, he had strategized a plan to gain permission for an evacuation and offered to negotiate with the minister of defense, given that he knew him well enough, he felt confident about a positive response. The Germans requested that he go directly through the President's office instead.

After succeeding pleading calls to the President, he finally agreed and extended free conduct of expat populations. A second later, for some unknown reason, he changed his mind.

"Another day lost!" Andreas had shouted and slammed the phone against the receiver repeatedly furiously.

He arrived safely at his front door and turned to look down the dusky road. The tank still stood solidly with its gun pointed away from his home.

He opened the front door to pitch darkness. Candles had burned out. Heavy breath and even a snore was a pleasant sign that his family was finding much needed rest. Gently he tapped Sofia out of a light sleep. He hated waking her up but needed to leave the house again, this time with the car.

"I can't believe you are going to risk your life in order to help a complete stranger," Sofia whispered gripping his arm.

"It is necessary that I get out there and see exactly what our situation is so we can get out," he pushed himself up from beside her, propped his weight onto his knees to kiss her, and left against her gripe.

He jumped into the seat of his truck and in his mind charted the drive into the city. An earlier plea to help the French embassy had him leave again, "There is a lady who needs her dialysis desperately. She needs a ride to the hospital and then back home," the French ambassador had said in a desperate tone. For a brief second, he switched his truck lights on and knew that it would give him away as a possible target; he left the lights on just sufficiently enough to see where he was going, turned the lights back off for about twenty to thirty seconds and gradually drove blindly praying not to hit anything along the way. He repeated the scenario of lights on and off all the way to the French embassy and then all the way to the hospital in hope that they had electricity for her dialysis.

He waited for the woman's treatment to end and at two in the morning he dropped her back off at the French embassy. Relieved to have made the scary drive and thankful to be back near his home he took a shortcut through the back of his neighborhood past the mosque. Bullets ricocheted off the street right next to his car originating from the anti-aircraft station inside the mosque. Harshly he pressed the gas pedal to the floor. Skittish, his legs soft, palms clammy, he reached his home.

Without bothering to park the car inside the driveway, he leaped out, sprinted through the open gate to his front door, and banged loudly onto the wood. Sounds of rebounding bullets against the wall startled him. It was too much. He turned, shook his fist into the obscurity, and yelled all the nasty Arabic words he could remember. Impressing the snipers, they stopped shooting. Chloe heard the loud banging and bemused she dragged the door open and stumbled like a zombie back to her sleeping spot on the mafraj.

Chapter 17

I ploughed through a crowd of bearded skirted men and pushed aside a gathering of cloaked women. With a determined stare, I focused on the ship in the distance, it yawed heavy amidst the waves and pushed off without me. Feverishly, I ran, soft white sand pushed through my naked toes, waves whipped harshly against the shore. A flood of men hurried behind me, punished the wind with long slender sticks. A gathering of black ghosted women hovered around the piers' mouth. They toddled their tongues rhythmically.

A high-pitched strident cry released "lalalalala," in unison. I boarded the pier, sea water splashed angry onto my ankles. Salty mist upon my lips.

Paps sat behind a desk at the pier's end. He craned his neck long above a stack of papers and a phone to his temple, "Sorry about the bureaucratic inertia of it all, you have to fill out this form," he pushed a piece of paper into my chest and stopped me from jumping after the ship. I woke up with my throat dry and a sore back. I had rolled off the thin mattress during the night, felt the hard floor cold on my naked calves, and then had pushed myself back onto the dusty velvet of the mafraj mattress. It was early morning. Sunrays worked hard to push through underneath the crack of the bathroom door.

I heard Paps on the phone: "We will have to arrange an evacuation out of both areas. Yes, yes, a ship out of Aden."

He hung up the phone, noticed that I watched him attentively, and explained that the civil war was between the North and the South and therefore he was arranging for people's evacuation in both areas.

"I've been on the phone all morning," he said with a smile, his skin looked grey, and his eyes bloodshot.

"Paps, did you get any sleep?" I asked my voice cracked.

"I can sleep when I'm dead," he said, "Let's hope that's not here in Yemen."

"Don't say that," I sneered.

"Just kidding, I'll make sure we all live a while longer."

"We have very many people gathered at the German consulate in Aden already and it is getting a bit dangerous down there with a battle going on the coast just east of the city," he said.

The German consulate was a large compound and all the non-governmental organization workers from the GTZ (Deutsche Gesellschaft für Technische Zusammenarbeit) had gathered there while they waited for an evacuation out of the country.

"It is an agency that channels international aid from the Federal German Government to developing countries."

He took note of my puzzled look, "A whole bunch of small organizations and tourists are caught in the country, and hundreds of people are waiting there."

I propped myself up against the wall. Mom miraculously conjured some coffee and heated Malawah flat bread over a gas flame on her treasured cast iron Comal that had traveled all the way from Mexico to Yemen.

"I just got off the phone with an elderly tourist couple in their seventies. They had flown to Yemen and were driving from Hodaida to Sana'a, were stuck in some village along their way because of the shooting they wanted to turn back to Aden. Going back to Aden would have been impossible because they would have had to cross the front lines.

Patty Smith

Luckily, I could talk them out of it. Somehow, they made it to Sana'a. The gall to demand *'you have to save us, we are here and we are Germans,'"* He mimicked the person's voice and added, "Excuse me; I told them, first of all you came here at your own risk against the advice of the German Government not to travel into this country as a tourist.

We are here for everybody not just for you. Therefore, you are not going to receive special treatment. Just try to hang tight and do as we tell you," he continued, "They wanted to sleep in the ambassador's bed and have a private plane out of the country."

Hassled, Paps spent most of his day on the phone rounding people up for evacuation. He struggled to convince a selective few to leave their homes.

"I cannot believe folks need to be dragged out heels digging and that people are actually refusing to go. Bullets are flying over their heads and they're saying that it is not going to get that bad," his voice was hoarse.

Unaware of time or weather changing inside the narrow hall, I thought about my inchoate relationship with Cian and wished we had more time together. Tense, I listened to Paps negotiations and watched him closely when he hung up the receiver. The upside to limited phone capability was that I could call Cian whenever I wanted without waiting for his call and minding the usual phone etiquette. Paps monopolized the line and so it was difficult to get the phone for even a minute.

"I can't believe I finally get to call you," I said, "How are you?"

Cian was staying at the British embassy, as many other British people who found themselves stranded as tourists in the country.

"You should be proud of your dad. He really is doing an important job," he said when I whined about the annoyance of Paps' calls.

"I know, I should not complain. It is hard to pry the phone away from him. I swear the phone feels warm! What are you doing?"

"You won't believe what I am doing right now."

"Tell me, I want to know how you spend your time over there. At least you are not stuck in a narrow hallway staring at walls," I whispered so Ronny would not hear as she also waited to use the phone.

"I have a job to do here. I have to work and keep a straight face, project confidence. Do you know how hard it is to calm people? They look at you for answers; I do not have specific answers to give. That is not easy. My job does not end; it is a twenty-four hour job, around the clock."

"Mm, I had not thought of it that way. You are right, I am so sorry, that has to be tough. So what are you doing right now?"

"I am sitting here with a blow-dryer."

"A blow-dryer? How? You do not have electricity. What are you doing with a blow-dryer? Can I borrow it, would love to wash my hair right now," I snickered my stomach prickled; chatting with Cian had me feeling so much better. "Well, we have a generator, and I am thawing a dead body."

"A dead body? What?"

My mind raced, "Why are you sitting with a dead body?"

"Well, let's just say she got a little too cold and we didn't think about putting the body into the coffin in time."

"Are you saying what I think you're saying?"

"Yes, you are hearing me right."

I remembered our conversation on the roof; he really was a jack-of-all-trades, seeing that his duties now included that of a mortician. Once a tourist, an overweight English woman had died from heart failure. The paperwork for transport, took a few days; meanwhile her body placed into a freezer at the morgue of the Al-Thawra hospital.

Patty Smith

The lady would have stayed in the freezer until the end of the war and nobody would have moved a finger to send her body back to England had Cian not already initiated her transport before the war began and obtained a permit, arranged transport, with a flight leaving the next day. The day the war broke out. Two things went wrong. Due to the war, the hospital staff forgot to take her out of the freezer and not secured her body into an appropriate position.

As a result,

Cian found a spread-eagled frozen corps that did not fit into the zinc coffin with the screw down top. Like most anything frozen, the limbs would simply break off when forcing them. Cian had spent an entire night with a hair dryer unfreezing the body on the embassy lawn while drinking a bottle of Glenmorangie single malt Scotch. Everything turned out fine in the end, the woman fit into her travel cask and transported out of the country on an evacuation flight and nobody noticed anything unusual save for an aromatic smell of lingering highland spirits.

"So sorry. I wish you were here, I would comfort you right now, hold your hand, kiss you," I pressed the receiver to my mouth.

"Me too. I love you," Cian whispered and hung up the phone.

My jaw dropped. I held the phone to me ear with the dead ring tone vibration and the echo of his last few important words. Not knowing if we would have the chance to see each other again changed courting rules. Cian had important work that kept him busy and yet he found the time to speak on phone. Like vultures, Ronny and I watched for Paps to hang up, and then lunged for the phone elbowing each other out of the way. Paps got so angry that he would have pulled the phone off the wall had he not needed it himself. I passed the receiver to Ronny who waited to call Tanner and clutched it distorting her face.

It was their last call together. The Marines were active in securing the embassy that was converted into a full-blown military command center with encrypted communication to CENTCOM in Florida. If Tanner had talked to Ronnie again after that call for even one second he would have breached COMSEC. Mom checked in with Radka next. She hoped to receive a call from Mo since we were not able to make international calls. Mo did not call. Out of boredom, Ronny and I switched up the rules to our card games, did sit-ups and copied Mom in her yoga exercises. Mom stopped demonstrating positions when we fell into a laugh-attack during downward dog. We counted gun fire which was a challenge given that it was highly irregular, most of it was bursts of small arms fire with a rate of 600 shots per minute for AK-47 it was 10 shots per second, really impossible to count and so we estimated. At night, aerial attacks intensified and anti-aircraft batteries began their deadly concert. Paps would not allow us onto the roof and yet, behind his back, we snuck up for brief moments of reconnaissance and stargazing.

"The BBC announced that every foreigner would be rescued by the French fleet and that it would dock to an assembly location at the beach of Little Aden east toward a small harbor town," Paps said cantankerously, "Yes, just east of Aden," he bobbed his head in between words as if the person on the other end could see him. He continued, "I guess that would have been sensible if it were not for the current circumstances."

Everyone listened intently.

"I know from my contact that fighting is happening at Al Mukalla beach. Yes, right at the point where they asked for everyone to gather for evacuation," he said, "It is a main battle area," he reiterated in a calm tone.

His idea was to have the French fleet go straight to Aden's harbor area instead, an unexpected move, and people could board the ship from there. An artillery battalion from the North had managed to break through and move toward Aden and had shot precisely at the area of evacuation.

Patty Smith

For some time, there was real danger. To have a thousand people drive to the harbor town with a French fleet amidst the shooting attempting to evacuate would have been mayhem. The South worked diligently at destroying the Northern artillery battalion. This bought him time and he hoped to coordinate the evacuation from Aden before the battalion broke through.

"To coordinate this plan, the radio message from BBC needs to be changed," he uttered a few more words, hung up the phone, and released a deep sigh.

"What's the matter now?" Mom asked.

"Don't ask me how this could be possible, but somehow the German embassy's iridium satellite telephone is out of commission."

"How is this your problem to fix?" Sofia asked," You cannot fix their phone."

"I know that, but the embassy cannot contact the German Government and without the satellite phone we cannot get in touch with the BBC either."

"The BBC?" Mom raised her brows.

"The BBC is sending out the wrong evacuation location, if we don't change the location, we'll have a potential massacre."

Mom huffed loudly pulling down the corners of her mouth.

"I am going to have to ask the American's if I can borrow their satellite phone."

Ronny and I kept silent. Our silly interaction had the potential of aggravating the situation.

Mom looked to the floor, "I guess there is nothing we can say. I just do not understand why there is nobody else that can do these things. Do their cars not work either?" He silently blew her a kiss, "Ok Maus," and hurried out the door.

Chapter 18

Through sloping roads Andreas drove, down and back up a lonely hill and past rubble and damaged homes. He arrived at the American embassy. Nobody was there to receive him at the front gate, although he was expected, and so he simply made his way inside. He used the American's satellite phone to call Germany and connected with the main person in charge, the German chancellor, who ran the crisis center in Bonn.

The chancellor prodded him with questions and asked for details on the situation in Al Mukalla where the original evacuation for South of Yemen was to take place. Patiently Andreas answered with precision and then requested permission to change the BBC's outgoing message from the evacuating point at Al Mukalla beach to a new evacuation point at Aden harbor. Then he asked for the frequency of the French fleet to make direct contact with the ship. Upon ending his conversation with Germany, he would contact the French fleet. In return for the use of the phone, he promised the Americans a six-pack of beer as soon as he could get his hands on one. They thanked him, although they had plenty of alcohol and most times provided Andreas with liquor when he needed some to barter.

The Americans offered him connections to people with short-wave radios with the ability to relay a message to the ship's captain. Two Americans that worked for Hunt Oil, one in the Sana'a office the other in Aden, agreed to relay a message via their radio to the French fleet.

In emergencies, people knew to listen to their short-wave radio for recommendations. More precisely, they listened to the BBC channel for updates.

Andreas never met the Hunt Oil person on the other side of the phone, who sat under duress near Aden while bullets shot past his head and nevertheless agreed to remain under fire until he successfully passed on the message. Andreas promised him a bottle of black label and would never learn the man's identity and thus not fulfill his promise. The message caught the French fleet commander by surprise.

He was unsure if he should follow a request from a complete stranger and then thankfully changed his mind and course for his ship to the new evacuation location at Aden harbor. As a result, he successfully picked up nearly a thousand people, among them Ernst. He had been working at the Aden military hospital at the time the war broke out and was unable to make it back to his home in Sana'a. Later, when southerners conquered Aden, they ransacked all the embassy buildings, including the German consulate. Much later, upon returning to Aden when it was safe, Andreas asked to supervise the reconstruction of the German embassy and consulate. While going through the destroyed buildings he discovered that the Yemenis had taken special interest in a safe inside the consulate. The safe was covered in dents from Kalashnikov bullets fired at its door, unsuccessful with that strategy, Yemenis opened the safe by shooting at it with a rocket-propelled grenade instead and found it only contained the keys to people's cars.

Southern Yemen had six scud missiles, tactical ballistic missiles developed by the Soviet Union during the Cold War. The first scuds landed right inside the city of Sana'a and others hit the presidential palace. Both South Yemen separatists and government forces began to fire Scuds. The Scuds were notoriously inaccurate. They fired them from a distance of about three hundred kilometers without exactly knowing where they would hit and typically laid everything to waste. They had about a ten-kilometer radius of chance.

"The city was quiet during the evacuation, but as you know there was reported fighting on the outskirts," Andreas reported on the phone.

Nearly a thousand people had assembled for pickup by the naval ship Jules Verne. From there the ship took them to Djibouti, where representatives of respective embassies had prepared to meet evacuees.

"Yes, fighting was reported a few miles from the southern port of Aden but the evacuation was smooth," Andreas paused his heart relieved a little, "Yes, I heard that northern troops shot down seven southern warplanes during battles in the south," he listened in silence and then said, "We are hearing scuds overhead. It is time for us to go as well."

Scuds had nearly a ton of explosives and could level an entire block at once, quite a few of them had landed right in Sana'a and left carnage. It was time to get his family out. The next morning he would do it. That night Andreas had a much-needed deep sleep and recharged his tired mind. Sunrays struggled to push through the early morning skies and everyone slept soundly when the noise of crickets roused Sofia. She rolled over and poked Andreas in the ribs, "Can you hear the crickets?" she whispered in a sleepy haze resisting the urge to use the restroom.

"You're dreaming, those aren't crickets, they're gun shots," he said and tasted the sourness of his last meal, "wake up the girls, I have to run and prep the evacuation," he pushed himself onto his feet fully dressed.

Standing there, he brushed his teeth with a dry toothbrush and a dab of paste, and squirted warm water from a bottle into his mouth and spat the foamy slush into an empty cup from the scotch he drank the night before, his sleep aid. He smoothed his pants and donned a fresh shirt. With remains in the water bottle in hand, he skipped out the door.

"Chloe, wake up. It is time, we are evacuating," Sofia shook Chloe's shoulder softly and then crawled over to where Ronny lay.

"Finally, we are out of here!" Ronny was already awake.

"Yes." Sofia shook Chloe once more.

"Stop it, I'm awake," Chloe barked out of a yawn.

"It is time to pack a few things. We can only take the bare minimum. A small bag each. Strict orders," Sofia said adjusting herself.

"How are we getting out? How long will we be gone? Why can I not take more stuff? What about all my clothes?" Chloe rattled quickly.

"I don't have the answers to that."

"Where is Paps?" Chloe asked.

"He is dealing with the details of the evacuation."

"Can we call him? We need to ask him what to pack. Where are we going? What do we need?" Ronny's enthusiasm to leave temporarily stifled by the details of packing her belongings into one single bag.

"Listen, this is not a vacation. Just pack the minimum, like a pair of jeans, some shirts, and underwear. We need to hurry and make it over to the German embassy quickly," Sofia knitted her brows.

Chloe pushed herself off the mattress, rolled up her blanket into a corner, just as she had done every morning for the past days. Both girls disbursed into their rooms to pack.

"Please be careful, crawl while you're in your rooms," Sofia shouted and entered her own bedroom to pack a few things.

Inside the bathroom,

Chloe opened the faucet to find that miraculously cold water flowed. Quickly she ran water over her head, closed the faucet, shampooed her hair, opened the faucet, and placed her soapy head under the slowly flowing water and it stopped flowing.

"Dang it," she shouted.

"What's the matter?" Sofia asked seeing her step out with a towel around her head and soapiness dripping down her neck and temples.

"I thought the water was back on, but it must have been just what was left in the pipes."

"Jeez, Chloe, that is not important right now. Did you pack your clothes?"

"Yes, but I can't go with soap all over my head. I am already beginning to itch."

Sofia grabbed a big jug of water out of her makeshift pantry that used to be an Arab bathroom and where once they found mice hiding in the squat toilet underneath the ply wood that made Sofia have nightmares for days. She shuttered at the thought of seeing only a mouse's tail trapped beneath the metal spring after Andreas placed them into the room and they moved all the foods out except the water jugs.

"I guess conserving doesn't matter anymore at this point," she walked to the sink, "I'll help you wash the soap out."

"Are we waiting for Paps to get us?" Ronny was ready by the door with her tightly packed small bag.

"No, Cian is picking us up and taking us to the embassy."

"Really? He didn't tell me that," Chloe said, water onto her shirt.

"He arranged it with your father last night."
A knocking on the door announced Cian's arrival, "Quick, we have to go."

With their bags over their heads to shelter them from light rain, they ran to his car and piled into the back seats. For the time in days they stepped foot outside the home. Cian had left the engine running. He quickly drove toward the German embassy past torn streets and destroyed buildings up empty sloping roads, a car here and there and the girls jostled in the seats and Cian's heart raced. The town was ghostly empty.

Patty Smith

Entering the German embassy, they came upon a large gathering of people and Andreas amidst the crowd spoke loudly through a horn: "We apologize, but at this moment we are giving preference to pregnant women, and mothers with small children. We can only hold about sixty passengers at this time, but more planes are on their way."

"How many more?" Someone shouted from the crowd.

"We are expecting about four to five more planes all capable of transporting a hundred passengers," his head spun due to the effects of the night before when he allowed himself the scotch. It did not help that he had skipped breakfast.

"Why only sixty in this plane, then?" Another voice asked.

"Sorry, we have to get moving, we only have a short window for the plane to take off."

Andreas saw his family behind the crowd, walked over and said, "change of plans, you guys will have to go back home."

"No. You can't be serious," Chloe whined, ready as ever, her hair washed, freshly showered, and her most valuable clothes pushed into her bag.

Cian took Chloe's hand, "Don't' worry, everything's going to be hunky-dory, and before you know it you are back in Germany," he said.

"What's going on?" Sofia asked.

"Look, I don't have time to explain right now, you just have to trust me. I will get you out of here 'safely'," Andreas swiveled on his heels and walked back toward the crowd of people.

"Wow, he really thinks he's important right now," Ronny said facetiously.

"Don't be rude," Sofia, corrected her with a frown. She turned to Cian, "can you drive us back home?"

"Sure, it's not a problem," he said confidently, "I will have to come straight back and help with the evacuation of British citizens."

"Are you sure you can take us?" Chloe looked up at Cian's eyes. She had not anticipated the relief she felt. Now she could spend more time in the same country as Cian.

"Don't be daft; of course I'll take you back."

For the past hour, it had been silent. In order to evacuate safely, Yemenis struck an agreement to cease the shooting for a short window of time. Back at home, Sofia called Radka. She did not seen her at the embassy and wondered if she had heard about the evacuation.

"I am scared to death, Sofia," Radka sobbed, "your husband said to wait until tomorrow and then come out, but they will not evacuate my dog. What should I do?" Andreas had told Sofia that people turned acutely strange during emergencies and that he had struggled to convince people to leave their homes. Radka looked for an excuse to stay. Sofia took a deep breath in search for the right words, "how should I say this, Radka? You have to come without your dog. He will be okay."

"But, he will die without me," Radka's voice crackled snorting mucus into her throat.

"I'll talk to Andreas, he has someone lined up to watch our home for us, and maybe they can go by your house and feed your dog."

"I am so scared to stay here, the shooting sounds really heavy." Ceased-fire only lasted a few hours, now, Yemenis fervently terrorized each other again.

"Why don't you come, bring your dog, and we and figure things out tonight when Andreas gets back," Sofia said in a gentle voice.

"Alright, I'll do that." Moments later Radka arrived with her dog and husband.

Meanwhile, Andreas had called saying that he would be coming home late and wanted to take care of things in preparation for the following day evacuations.

The hot tarmac summoned the memory of the TRANSALL plane. It had landed in Africa successfully although Andreas had worried it would not make it off the ground in one piece. The compromised cargo-plane was in a shaky technical state when he and the pilot drove to the airport to inspect it just that morning. The day prior to the full-fledged war breaking out, Yemenis shot at the plane adorning it with seventeen holes.

"Fuck, I can't believe they did this. A bullet-storm must have attacked us," the pilot said scrutinizing the damage. He stuck his index finger through one of the holes and ran it over the sharp metal edge.

"Let's not fret now, can you start the engine?" Andreas asked.

The pilot started the plane's engines and was able to keep them running for about two hours then decided, "It seems to do alright. It's a miracle no vital parts were hit."

The tall German pilot produced a roll of metallic colored duct tape from a small case, "this is part of our tool kit," he used his teeth to tear off strips and began to patch the holes.

"Good, hand me some, I'll help you out," Andreas said smiling.

"Purely cosmetic you know, don't want people to freak out," the pilot studied his masterpiece, "this shall do it," and deemed it airworthy.

Afterward, Andreas had nervously watched the plane take off successfully and disappear into the evening sky. He now debated how he would get the remaining people and his family out of the country. More planes were in Djibouti, however fighting was now particularly heavy over the Red Sea.

He called Yemen air command once more to get another cease-fire, "yes, approximately two hours should do it."

Haughty, he jumped into the truck and began the drive back to the city and with the two-way radio from the embassy he continued his plan, "Ok, you guys need to connect with Djibouti, tell them the planes can't take off for another hour at least," he said.

"An hour? We have already given them the Okay," the German said on the other end.

"You have done what?" Infuriated, he punched the dashboard of his truck, "Ah," he sighed dropping the radio onto the passenger seat.

He fastened his seatbelt with one hand while steering with the other and heard the muffled voice on the seat speak. Swerving the jeep he reached for the radio, "What did you say?"

"*Die sind schon auf dem Weg.* They are already on their way," the voice shouted in German.

"Put the radio to the phone and call Djibouti," Andreas said firmly.
"Jawohl."

The embassy's secretary placed the receiver near the radio. For days, the iridium network was overloaded and acquiring a connection was problematic. The embassy secretary who could not endure failure continued to try and when he established a connection, he refused to let it go. Once inside the network, one could retain a connection for however long although it was pricey and cost somewhere around the order of ten dollars per minute. The embassy footed the bill to keep the connection day and night for fear they would not have it when it became critical.

"What do you think you guys are doing? You are sending an unarmed military cargo plane into a warzone without coordination with the war parties. Do you want to lose your airplanes?" Andreas asked enraged that his planning was for nothing and sabotaged by someone making a hasty decision on the other end.

"Don't we have permission?" a voice questioned in a leisure tone, "well either way it's too late the plane is on its way."

Patty Smith

"No, we don't have permission at this moment, but we will have it in two hours. Who is your boss? Let me talk to him, I am not dealing with you," Andreas demanded and nearly drove the truck into a ditch. These were pressing circumstances, he wanted to climb through the radio and shake the person or perhaps wring his neck instead.

After a short wait, a three-star General introduced himself, "Calm down, I relieved him from his operation of command. He does not know what he is doing. Now let's talk business."

Two hours was all they had to bring the planes in, refuel, board passengers, and then take off again. He met the planes at the airport, refueled them, and informed the embassy, "ready for evacuation."

It was important not to have everyone gather at the airport unless planes were ready to go. Having hundreds of people standing around on an unsheltered tarmac was highly dangerous. The drive to the airport was risky as well and so timing had to be just right. Andreas practically singlehandedly coordinated the evacuations. The Americans on the other hand had an army to plan and execute their own evacuation. They had a plane outfitted with AWACS (Airborne Warning and Control System) and a couple of fighter planes that circled in the air. It took a Marine Corps detachment and about a hundred soldiers and ten officers and about three to four hours to get their evacuation off the ground.

The Egyptians coordinated their own evacuation as well. Their production proved to be a bit smarter and a bit bolder. They did not ask anyone for permission to bring an airplane into the country and just did it. Extraordinarily amidst fighting, the Egyptians landed an empty commercial airliner while they dodged bullets. Sanaa's air defense aimed to take it down and hit one of its wings. Upon landing, they frantically loaded all the evacuees who had waited for hours on the tarmac and then flew off into freedom. The entire ordeal lasted less than a couple of hours. Quite a stunt.

The fact that they evacuated two days before any else, helped. Andreas had heard reports from people who evacuated on the Egyptian plane that it had taken off with double capacity and passengers were scared to death. The German planes were good for sixty soldiers. Andreas figured if the Egyptians could do it, then so could he. He would board about one-hundred and ten people onto each plane. He had kept the Swiss-cheese plane at capacity. The German embassy was the meeting point for everyone the next day. Amidst everything, some people asked to leave their cars in the safety of their own homes instead of driving them to the embassy or leaving them parked at the airport. They took tires off their cars to prevent theft while they were gone and asked to take a cab or carpool to the German embassy.

Transporting hundreds of people from the embassy to the airport proposed yet another layer of difficulty for Andreas. Most gasoline stations had run out of gas and cabs were scarce. The only vehicles left with gas were public transport buses. People stopped riding them for obvious reasons. Before driving home, he detoured through the city in search of buses to line up at the embassy the next morning. He rounded up about fifteen buses, paid them a first installment right then, and asked them to show up at the embassy promptly in the morning.

He promised a second installment the next day once people made it to the airport. Andreas paid the bus drivers about a weekly salary to do the special airport run and they happily accepted the job. The next morning, rickety blue and white buses with undercarriages that showed the signs of rust, some with missing doors or windows, and most had few seats that were still intact, lined the front wall of the embassy. Like a scene out of a Mad Max movie, people stuffed into them each with a small case, until an indistinguishable mass of limbs and heads hung halfway out of windows.

Patty Smith

Chapter 19

Insanely, he charted empty streets toward the airport.

Cian's eyes darted at the road in front with an insistent obligation to protect us. A checkpoint appeared in the distance and instead of approaching it carefully; he sped up and zipped right through it. A once bustling and often nauseatingly loud city was now silent of happiness and cried evidence of war. The rain from the night before left the stench of wet dogs and rotten foods. I sat in my seat, clutched the dashboard, and pushed my feet into the floor at every turn. Most checkpoints were abandoned, then ahead stood a child-soldier with a rifle. A wiry boy in a camouflage jacket over a woolen skirt with the usual belt and knife, and additionally around his shoulder, he carried a machine-gun, which he quickly buttressed against his chest aiming it at our car.

"Brace yourselves, we won't be stopping," Cian said.

"No way, he'll shoot at us," I shouted, my nerves pulled my stomach into a tight ball.

"Duck," Cian yelled.

A strange wretched sound puffed out of my chest as I threw myself under the dashboard for protection. My head between my knees, I could smell the dusty red velvet cloth of my seat. It reeked of stale smoke. This moment was not what I imagined to be my last.

"You're crazy," I shouted and held my breath.

In the back seat, Mom mouthed a prayer and crossed herself, "this needs to stop. God, help us."

"If we stop, he could still shoot us and we may never make it," Cian said, hitting the gas pedal hard.

I reached between the seats for Mom's hand. We interlaced them and squeezed tight. Cian shot the truck through the checkpoint and the boy did not shoot.

"Thank you!" Ronny sighed from the back seat.

"Let's hope there won't be another," Radka said. She, her husband, Mom, and Ronny sat tight in the back row. As soon as the boy was out of sight behind us, I popped back up and patted Cian's thigh, "thanks Cian, good job." Minutes later, we arrived. Large gates locked the entrance to the airport and an armed Yemeni man guarded the gate. He tipped into the driver's window with a questioning expression.

Cian rolled the window down to a strong smell of carnosine and a roar of plane engines, "we're here for the evacuation," he said and smiled.

"You are late," the Yemeni slurred nonchalantly through a scruffy beard.

"No, that is impossible," Cian leaned out of his window to get a better view of the tarmac. "There, everyone is waiting to get on the planes," he pointed out of the window to where crowds of frayed looking people filled the expanse.

"We need to get them over there. They are the family of Mr. Andreas," Cian was a figure of reverence for me, the way he remained collected when I was near screaming. I watched his lips move and thought about our kiss, the softness of them on mine, and I continued to think about feeling them the entire day.

The Yemeni tented his brow and inceptively peaked through the back windows, "the German?"

"Yes."

"You cannot drive inside, you must walk," he motioned his gun signaling to get out of the truck.

"Quick," I said, "we can do this."

I jumped out of the car with my small bag that I had packed and repacked and still had not fit all my clothes until I rolled every item into a tight taco and only then managed to fit an additional six tops. The Yemeni swung the unchained gate open and we ran toward the four planes parked side by side on the tarmac of the airport. People were amidst boarding one gigantic green cargo aircraft through a wide ramp leading to the vast interior of its belly.

"There you are," Paps waved us over; "I love you guys. Will see you soon. You must go now," he said his voice clogged while he looked at Mom in a way that I had not seen him do for far too long.

"Andreas?" Mom strained to comprehend, "You are not staying!" Tears collected in her eyes, "don't tell me you are staying Andreas."

"I must." He hugged her tightly lifting her feet off the ground, "I am in charge. I will leave when the last person is out."

He gently placed her down, hugged Ronny, and nudged us toward the ramp, "get on. We don't have that much time," he raised his sweaty brow.

"This is not what we discussed, I have your clothes," Mom took hold of his hand.

"Do not worry. Everything is going to be fine. Call the General when you get to Frankfurt. I'll take the clothes," he wiggled out of her grip.

"Come on Mom," Ronny slung her arm around her and led her toward the ramp.

I scanned the area for Cian,

he had respectfully distanced himself while we said our farewells, "I'll see you soon, promise," he said and waved.

"You're not going to kiss me goodbye?" I said approaching him and kissed him fighting back tears, then swiveled on the heels of my shoes and boarded the large plane.

Due to the one-bag rule, I had donned several layers of clothing, thinking I had outsmarted everyone else, and felt them constrain my breath. Feeling myself sweat, I wondered if I would survive the flight without stripping out of the jacket and at least a few tops. It would be much colder in Germany and I did not want to be without sufficient clothing once we got there. The plane was empty of seats; we entered a large flat metal platform with a few narrow benches running along the sides. A German soldier directed everyone to sit: older people on the benches, younger ones on the floor. Mom, Radka, and Alex, sat on a bench, Ronny and I sat on the floor in front of them.

"There are straps on the floor for you to hold onto," the soldier shouted through his cupped hands.

"If you need to use the restroom during flight, let me know and I will help you," he pointed to what looked like a shower curtain that hung in a circle from the ceiling in the center of the plane.

"Oh my god," Radka murmured," I have to use the restroom."

"Go." Mom said.

"Are you kidding?"

"Well then, you are going to have to pee in your pants. You better go before the plane takes off," Mom hushed into her ear.

"No, I think I can hold it," Radka spoke in a whisper. She pressed her thighs and rocked herself on the bench. People filed into the space, one hundred and ten of them. Once everyone struggled for comfort, Radka made up her mind that she needed to go after all. She got up, tiptoed around the tight spaces on the floor, and asked the soldier, who still stood rigid at the center, if she could use the restroom.

The soldier held the curtain shut while Radka's legs with pants wrapped around her ankles protruded below the drape. The large metal door creaked shut and locked into place with a big thump rendering the inside void of any light. The plane moved slowly, the engines hummed loudly, and we shifted onto each other as the earth's gravity pulled against the aircraft's ascent. I was happy that once we reached a cruising altitude the temperature inside the vessel dropped tremendously. After some time it got very chilly and even I with all my layers of clothing froze. We huddled closely together for warmth. The engines rumbled so tremendously loud I could not hear my own thoughts and no one attempted to speak a word in respect to people's silent prayers.

Chapter 20

Blackness engulfed the plane's interior, after some time, the features that belonged to Mom's face became clear. She looked sad. She extracted bottles of water from her small bag and handed them to Ronny and I. The obscurity of our location made us restless and anxious, for all we knew the plane could have been circling over the city. We could only guess that we safely made it over the mountains and were out of shooting range. The engines vibrated loudly. Initially, we strained to hear each other as we screamed and then gave up talking and communicated with hand movements and reassuring facial expressions. After what felt like an eternity, the plane began its descent into a jerky and bumpy landing welcoming us to Africa.

"He is a military pilot and not used to flying a cargo plane filled with passengers," was Mom's explanation for the horrific landing.

Refusing to eat anything before leaving, caused the water I emptied into my stomach to slush around, and had made me nauseous. I normally did not struggle with motion sickness when flying. Driving was a different story, especially if I sat in the backseat of a car. I could not put my finger on what made me feel so sick, the lack of food, or the bumpy landing. The gigantic airplane door opened slowly. It reminded me of the scene from the ET movie. The one when ET boarded his spaceship to go home and the camera panned to everyone standing outside the ship as the door slowly closed.

Our plane slowly opened to a cloud of hot humid air that gushed inside the fuselage and fogged up people's glasses. People stood and waited outside the plane as a blanket of moisture showered us.

Patty Smith

My hair stuck wet to my neck and puckered into its natural state of something not quite curly or straight. My multiple layers of clothing shrunk tight against my skin. I suffocated and shed my coat. Then I took off a long-sleeved-shirt and the other one under that and my last t-shirt still felt like too much. My feet sloshed sweaty inside my boots. For the first time since the war Mom joked, "My feet feel like tamales," she said and we laughed.

I skirted the edges of the crowd moving in slow motion down the ramp. Scorching heat radiated and the tar of the tarmac felt soft. I was losing consciousness and saw black with flecks of light before my eyes. My tongue tingled. Numb. I propped myself against Ronny. She pushed me aside. I strained to regain balance, stopped, and recovered. With the crowd, I walked another step, a few more, until we lined up outside. We had landed in the republic of Djibouti, located in the horn of Africa. The country's official languages were Arabic and French.

Paps had warned, "You will have to be prepared for extreme heat. Djibouti practically does not have seasons, and temperatures reach over a hundred degrees with a humidity around the eighties."

"In other words it is always dang hot and miserable!" I had said with a grin ignoring his advice not having an idea it would feel like stepping into a sauna fully clothed.

French soldiers wearing khaki shorts and shirts welcomed everyone and offered to carry our bags toward large tents only a short distance from the airport. We entered a tent filled with rows of cots, a hundred or so crammed side by side with little room to get into them. Rolls of grey blankets neatly lay at the end of each bed. It summoned memories of war movies and injured soldiers. Sunlight faded and yet it remained uncomfortably stuffy and hot all night long. I laid awake for hours listening first to the sound of birds, then crickets. The buzzing of hungry mosquitoes outside the net around my cot and nearing my ears loudly had me adjust, and readjust my net.

I tucked it under my pillow and legs.

The next morning after inspecting myself for bites and taking a birdbath by a sink, I searched for coffee. Soldiers hurdled us in a friendly manner to long tables with a simple breakfast of dry croissants, coffee, and orange juice. Before too long they asked us to pack up. A Lufthansa plane waited. It would fly to Frankfurt and from there people could fly onto other destinations. I collapsed into my seat and hoped to shut an eye.

Flight attendants offered cups of water and food from a cart and one handed me a pair of headphones and a blanket. I wiggled the plugs into my ears, began to watch the inflight movie, and sleep pulled my eyelids shut. I squinted at Mom slumped deeply into her seat and at Ronny who slept with swollen rings under her eyes and dozed off. I worked the scenes of the movie into my dreams and woke up to the sirens of a police chase and a stiff neck. I nibbled on the peanut residues inside the small bag. A wide blanket of clouds pierced by sunrays above a quilt of green and brown fields, snaked roads, dotted by squared buildings told me we neared our destination. Upon our arrival in Frankfurt, an agent ushered us into separate lines to enter the country. Ronny and I crossed together and when I turned to check on Mom, she had disappeared into the crowds. Nervously we pressed our faces into the glass until we spotted someone leading her through a side door. A few minutes later, she reappeared with a scowl.

"What happened?" Ronny asked when she cleared customs.

"Well, they pulled me aside," she said pushing her back and added, "keep walking."

"Why? Did you not give them the letter?" I said.

"Of course I did. It did not stop them from asking me my name, where I was born, where I was coming from. Like they didn't know we all came from Yemen."

Patty Smith

"Oh, no, Mom, so sorry," Ronny said and hugged Mom who waved a piece of paper in her left hand.

"They looked at the letter and didn't believe me when I said I had family in Germany. Then they finally let me through."

We carried an official letter from the German embassy to replace our stolen passports.

"Jeez. That's not the kind of welcome you needed," I said.

"I know," she said and waved her had dismissively, "We have other things to worry about now. Where are we going to stay? I do not want to go to your grandparents' house."

"Didn't Paps tell you we should call the General in Munich? Maybe the military can help us out?" Ronny asked.

"Thank goodness Mo is in the States and it is just the three of us," Mom said as she walked toward a phone booth. Ronny and I trailed behind carrying all the bags. Mom called the General in Munich who was in charge of Paps project in Yemen. His response was so loud Mom held the phone away from her ear.

"Oh my god, you do not have to worry about anything, you just come here with your daughters, and you can stay here. You can stay in the officer's' quarters."

We purchased tickets at the airport and took the train to Munich's main train station. From there, we grabbed the subway to Olympia Park and then a taxi to the military base. It felt as though we had travelled around the world when we arrived and the cab driver unloaded our meager belongings from the trunk onto a curb before the entrance to the barracks. A tall man in a German uniform stepped out of the narrow guardhouse and greeted us. Minutes after he stepped back in and made a call, two more soldiers arrived and respectfully walked us into the large concrete compound.

We looked like death warmed over when the General met us at the bottom of a building; our sleeping quarters. He ordered the soldiers to carry our bags and led us to our rooms that he said were, 'the Officer's' quarters'.

With a firm handshake exchange between us all he said, "And let me know if something is amiss." Sensing our exhaustion, he refrained from asking too many questions. The men plopped our bags onto the floor of the small apartment and Mom quickly divvied up the sleeping arrangements. One after the other we showered and without too many words immediately fell into a solid sleep.

Patty Smith

Chapter 21

Chloe tried to shake off her drowsiness; she had slept close to twelve hours. She stepped out of the steamy shower smelling of stale military soap.

"Please give me all of your dirty clothes. The General is sending a maid to the room to pick up and wash our laundry," Sofia said with a happy quality in her voice, "He also invited us to have lunch with him in the Officer's lounge. Get ready it is nearly twelve."

"I swear, the soap makes me itchy," Chloe scratched her left arm with her right.

Behind the open closet door, Ronny dressed and collected her hair into a ponytail that left a wet mark on the back of her shirt. They walked down the grey stone staircase that spilled into a large unmarked concrete area that resembled a parking lot, which they crossed and then zig zagged through a perfectly maintained grassy lawn with the sign that read, "do not walk on grass," past the medical tank monuments of the first war to the eating hall where the General waited at a table. He was a friendly grey haired man with piercing greyish-green eyes that told the story of his battles with alcohol. Stiffly he sat in his anthracite pants, light-blue shirt, and light-grey dinner jacket, colorful pins adorned the lapel. He was well known for wearing a dinner jacket, as so many Generals do, he always dressed up. 'Napoleon' was his nickname, earned due to his small statue. He was content taking a break from his day that started many hours ago with a cup of black coffee that he drank through a flawlessly combed mustache.

He was now sipping on his second cup,

"Spain? Italy? France? Where would you like to go?" he asked dabbing the wet drops that left yellow stains on the white cloth napkin, "don't worry all expenses will be paid of course." He folded his hands and leaned forward, "So, tell me, why is your husband not here with you? Why are you here alone? Why didn't he come with you guys?" A deep crease formed between his brows.

"Well," Sofia paused.

The General was not aware that Andreas meddled with all sorts of activities not part of his job description and meanwhile had coordinated an entire evacuation. Uncomfortably, Sofia squarely faced him trying to seem confident. She searched for a way to explain what happened without placing Andreas into an unfavorable position.
"He is supervising the evacuation."

"Who told him to do that?" he asked with a disdain in his voice.
"The German embassy?" Sofia replied softly.
The General inspected the coffee ring in the bottom of his cup, and then respectfully excused himself leaving Sofia wondering if she had said too much. Inside his office, he called Sana'a and ordered Andreas onto the next possible flight out of the country, "I expect you here with a full report."
Meanwhile, Mo was in the US with her now fiancé Joe as the two searched for a new home. Back in the room, Sofia called to let her know everyone was all right. Mid conversation, Joe took the phone, "Sofia, you know your family is welcome to stay here in the US with us. Mi casa es su casa." Joe was counting on a decline. Mo and Joe's visit had already overcrowded the home.

Patty Smith

"We really appreciate your offer Joe, but we have found accommodations here in Munich. We might also visit Andreas's parents in Peppenhoven. They are getting old and they will probably appreciate a visit."

She hung up and turned toward Chloe and Ronny who sat comfortably on the small couch. A queen size bed, couch, and TV furnished the small room. The only sink was in the restroom. There was no microwave or coffee machine to make a cup of coffee in the mornings. Sofia was getting tired of needing to wait for the girls to get dressed in order to get a cup of coffee. They took forever. She had always been an early riser and wanted to get her day going as soon as she woke up. Perhaps taking the train to Peppenhoven was not such a bad idea, "What do you guys think if we visit your grandparents?" she asked.

Chloe looked puzzled at her mother, "Did I just hear you say grandparents? I don't think I'll be going with you," she said contemplating imposing on friends.

"You should call them first," Ronny said without turning her attention away from the television, "You know how they are. You have to make an appointment. God forbid we drop in unannounced."

"Of course, I'll call them first," Sofia looked through a small notebook for the number.

Chloe would stay with Gianna. Her grandparents were the last people she wanted to visit. It would be problematic now that she was less tolerant of their snide remarks and age amplified their atrocious character. That afternoon, when Sofia and Ronny boarded the train to Peppenhoven, Ronny looked up with a plea in her eyes and Chloe felt wretched saying goodbye. Chloe rang the doorbell to Gianna's apartment, the door swung open, and Gianna pulled her into a tight squeeze. They had breakfast together and picked up as if years of time had not passed between them.

"You just brought a few things. Please pick something in my closet to wear. You always did that in the past," Gianna said.

Chloe stood before the large closet and moved hangers back and forth on the rod regarding the multicolored wardrobe. Gianna's closet smelled of expensive perfumes and fresh laundry detergent.

"I have nothing to trade. I was only able to bring one little bag with just a few tops, that is all," Chloe said holding a white top up to her chest examining herself in the mirrored door.

"Look, you are welcome to go through my closet. Especially since you do not have much with you. You must be bored already of wearing those same tops."

It was a Déjà vu. Gianna pulled out a few tops and laid them onto her bed, "Here. Pick out what you want," she pointed to a new garment with the tag still attached, "This is going to look so cute on you, try it on."

Contently, Chloe slipped on the new silk top tugging the material into over her waist. She felt strange. The war had occupied her and she had not considered why she was feeling off. The large bulb above the mirror flickered warning it was on the tail end of its life lighting the bathroom just sufficiently. She scrutinized the white blouse and concluded it looked good. Her stomach gurgled up sourness. She flung the toilet lid open and hurled out a vial liquid of egg and bacon breakfast. A few timid knocks followed by the door opening just a small crack, "are you alright?"

Chloe wadded up toilet paper and wiped her mouth, "Mm…yes."

"Do you need help? A glass of water?"

"No, I'm okay, going to brush my teeth."
Gianna squeezed inside the bathroom, "Sorry, do you think it was the food?"

Through toothpaste foam, "No, something is wrong with my stomach. I've been feeling off for a while now," Chloe said. "Vomiting?"

"Sometimes. More like feeling queasy, like I'm going to faint, can't describe it."

"Chloe is there something you haven't told me about?"

Patty Smith

"What, no…do you think?"

"Yes, I think you may be pregnant."

"Holy smokes, that makes sense. I have been very irregular. I thought it was the stress from the war."
"Get ready, we're going to buy a pregnancy test."
They took the subway downtown, strolled the streets of the *'Fussgaengerzone'* (the pedestrian zone), had another coffee inside a small coffee shop, and perused boutiques. Not the least bit happy with the orders of the General, Andreas re-packed just a few items in preparation for the visit with his parents in Peppenhoven. He had settled into the small room inside the military compound in Munich just for the night and hoped to gain permission to return soon. The fighting in Yemen had ceased. Although he had done everything he could to evacuate people out of the war, there was much more work left to do on readying the hospitals. Relaxed inside the leather chair he looked through some information he received from a friend in the Yemen while he simultaneously listened to CNN anticipating an update on the situation. Within the stack of papers, he found an article that read:

> *The north and the south of Yemen unified on May 22nd 1990.*
> *Integration of the divided north and south sides of the country was slow. It was two separate countries, the Yemen Arab Republic (YAR) in the north and the People's Democratic Republic of Yemen (PDRY) in the south.*
>
> *The two sides agreed to unify and create the Republic of Yemen. Southerners were unhappy about political and economic sneering by the government in Sanaa.*

Yemen's stability was a negotiated agreement between the government and the regional tribes that was strengthened by the vast arsenal of small arms in their possession.

On May 4th, 1994 an outbreak of open fighting between the two Yemeni armies began with an attack on Southern forces and northern troops who escaped capture and formed the advance guard of the northern assault.

The country erupted into a full-scale civil war fought by the regular armies of each former state with some tribal support on each side. President, Saleh, recruited Afghan veterans from across the Arab world to wage a victorious jihad against the Soviet-backed socialists of South Yemen resulting in proliferation of weapons, the south fell to the north, vast Soviet stockpiles of small arms 'disappeared' when Northern tribes looted entire stockpiles of the former southern army.

At one time, the Islamist network had its own school system, ministries, and governorates including Hadramawt (the Bin Laden ancestral home); however, it changed after the fall of the socialists in the south. Islamists replaced the vacuum with their own quasi-Taliban rule. The Yemen holds strategic importance it holds a narrow waterway that links the Red Sea and the Gulf of Aden, the Bab al-Mandab strait, much of the world's oil shipments pass through it. In the near future, it will ignite a regional power struggle between Shia-ruled Iran and Sunni-ruled Saudi Arabia who share a border with Yemen having an impact on the rest of the world.

Patty Smith

He turned the page and surprised to discover a

contract written in Russian between a Russian arms trader and a small German enterprise. At first glance, he thought it looked fake. Then he discovered registration records declaring that the small enterprise was registered in Berlin. (Much later, he discovered through hearsay that the enterprise was really a certain Mr. Schreiber living in Canada wanted in Germany for illegal arms trade).

The contract was signed in the Moldova's capital, Chisinau, for the purchase of Mikoyan MiG-29 twin-engine jets, the best fighter aircrafts the Russians had on their program.

South Yemen Airlines was shown to be the receiving party for the planes; it acted as a fake front. This confirmed his suspicions. The South of Yemen and Russia still had close dealings. Southern Yemen ensured the support of the Saudis, who financed billions of US dollars to the South in support against the North of Yemen. Taking a large sip of breath, he leaned back in his chair. Silver moonlight filled the small room and casted shimmers across computer screen. The phone rang. The German Secret Service invited him for breakfast the next morning.

"We will give you the details in person," a strong voice said on the other end of the phone.

"How will I know who you are?"

"Just look for two guys dressed in black leather jackets. We will be carrying a newspaper of the Frankfurter Allgemeine under our arm. We will meet you in the front lobby of the hotel."

Thrilled, Andreas hung up the call and made another to Peppenhoven. He asked Sofia and Ronny to return to Munich at once.

The German Federal Intelligence Service was the agency that worked to alert the government of threats from abroad by gathering military and civil intelligence.

Unsure of their agenda, he did not know how to prepare for the appointment, but he suspected that they would ask him about the details of the war. They would meet over a fancy breakfast at the Vier Jahreszeiten Hotel.

A gorgeous Munich morning unfolded the next day.

The family had re-joined, Sofia and Ronny arrived early in a taxi from the train station, and Chloe had walked the two-mile distance from the subway. Crisp air under light blue-grey skies and a hint of recent rain lay in the cracks between the cobblestones. The rain had washed the walkways cleaner than they already were.

Chloe loved the rhythm of the city, the hustle of suits orderly waiting in lines for the subway doors to open. People patiently waited for passengers to disembark before pushing through to find a seat on the U-Bahn. She had missed the pedestrian zones bordered with beautiful boutiques and the flood of tourists standing below the gothic town hall gawking up at the Glockenspiel; a twelve-minute display of artistic engineering, whereby eighteen figures danced around the sounding of several bells. She never tired of walking past Frauenkirche, St. Peter's Church, and all the architecture Munich offered and always discovered new details among the intricate design of the buildings.

Normally she hated the smell rain left, the smell of wet dog and urine. She loathed it anywhere else except in Munich. Munich was so clean that not even rain brought forth dirt and grime as it did in other cities. If there was an unwanted graffiti drawing upon a wall, workers wiped it clean within minutes. She often wondered where the special cleaning unit was that patrolled the city constantly.

Patty Smith

She saw something in the morning on her way to work by the end of work on her way home it was no longer there. The familiar sound of the subway was comforting and she watched as her father attempted to read another passenger's paper on the bench opposite his through the reflection of the window. The subway came to a stop and people hurried toward the open doors. She planned to continue for a few more stops to Farris' restaurant and surprise him. Her parents stood up from their seats, they had arrived at Marienplatz Station.

"So we'll meet you here in two hours?" Chloe asked before the subway's door slid shut.

"At the statue upstairs," Sofia confirmed their earlier agreement.

Out of the hazy window, Chloe watched her parents ascend the stairs to the plaza; from there they would each go their own way. Sofia wanted to shop and Andreas had his meeting nearby.

"Yes, I should be done in two hours," Andreas kissed Sofia on the forehead and walked toward the Vier Jahreszeiten Hotel.

The men were easily identifiable: they looked very secret service typical; black leather jackets, dark shades, and clutched the identifying newspaper under their armpits. One of the men's forearms rested upon the glass tabletop, he reached for the stein mug of Hefeweizen and drank the golden liquid in big gulps.

"We want to catch the right hand of the Carlos Terror Group," one of the men said removing his sunglasses from the bridge of his long narrow nose that rendered his eyes to look undersized and deep in their sockets. He drew more attention wearing the dark shades inside the faint lit room.

Andreas knew of Johannes Weinrich and Carlos. The terrorist group was widely known for breaking into OPEC, the Organization of the Petroleum Exporting Countries meeting in Vienna.

Carlos 'the Jackal' was a notorious Venezuelan terrorist. His right hand and main hitch man was Johannes Weinrich, a German left-wing political militant and terrorist. In fact, Andreas once knew his girlfriend. He lived in Berlin around the late sixties, the same time as Johannes Weinrich. Coincidently, he had met Johannes' girlfriend and dated her in Berlin for a short while. Magdalena Kopp was her name; she went by the nickname of Maggie. The two had dated a short while. At the time, Maggie worked in Berlin as a photographer. Her strong broad German dialect was annoying to him. She was originally from Ulm and people from Ulm spoke strangely, Schwaebisch, which was difficult to understand, even for fluent German speakers not from that region.

Her singsong and heavy 'r' rolling drove Andreas crazy and he split up with her because of it. During her spare time, she engaged in the leftist revolutionary scene and initially dragged Andreas into that milieu. Together they had participated in some wild demonstrations, broke a few windows and so forth. After an arrest, they even spent an uncomfortable night in jail. Andreas's parents had saved all the newspaper clippings, like trophies. He once made it to the front page of the Bonner General newspaper. The photo captured him throwing rocks at Police officers breaking up the crowds. His Mom had recognized him due to the scarf he had pinched from her to disguise his face.

Andreas's revolutionary anti-establishment movement craze was nothing out of the ordinary; everyone who lived in Berlin during that time was into that sort of thing, only he had moved on with his life, while others got fanatical about it. Surely, the Secret Service did not think that he was the right person for the job because of his former acquaintance to Maggie.

The men handed him a photo of Maggie. He had not seen her for years and now she was staring back at him with her usual smile. He tried to conceal that he recognized her. Before this meeting, he had no knowledge that she was now the girlfriend of Johannes Weinrich the terrorist.

Patty Smith

"Johannes is quite a violent guy. He did a lot of killing," one of the men explained handing Andreas another photo, this one of Johannes. It was an old picture.

"We need your help in finding him. We have good reason to believe that he is currently hiding in Yemen."

Andreas held the printed photo and turned it over to scrutinize the face. It was at least fifteen years old, altered using a computer program that generated a prediction of what someone might look like many years later.

"This guy is really good at keeping himself hidden. We do not have any recent photos of him at all, but this should be very close. This is what he should look like now, if he has not had any work done on himself, of course. We have had some recent sightings in Damascus that confirm he looked very closely to this photo not too long ago."

Andreas burned the image into his memory.

He agreed to help the Secret Service, really had no choice but to agree. Helping to catch Johannes would ensure his return to the Yemen. He left the hotel with a laptop, a floppy disc, and a promise that he would fly back to Sana'a in a few days.

Chapter 22

At Goetheplatz station, I disembarked the subway and walked through the wicker chairs on the patio of Café Goethe, Farris' restaurant. Poised and feeling self-assured, I approached the entrance to the restaurant. Farris and I stayed in touch, exchanged several letters, he also called a couple of times during my first year in Yemen, and then the calls stopped. For a while, he sent me a card here and there the next year then a complete silence followed last year. When we spoke on the phone, our conversations increasingly turned one-sided, filled with my reports on life in Yemen. When I asked him about Munich, his answer was the same, "The usual." I tapped him on the shoulder; his back turned away from one of the waiters to find me standing there, paused, and then he swung both arms around my waist tightly lifting me up in the air.

"What the heck," he said through a permanent smile. I smiled hard as well, my cheeks hurt, struck by how handsome he looked.

"Take over," he turned to the worker, placed me back down carefully.

"Shoot, I truly have just a little while, getting ready for the lunch crowd, but I really want to spend some time with you. What are you doing here?"

"I thought I'd surprise you."

"What a surprise for sure. You are the last person I thought I would see again. Can we meet tonight? After work?"

I hesitated, wrinkled my forehead, unsure if I wanted to come out all the way to Goetheplatz from Olympia Park on the subway that late at night. Nothing had changed; he still worked ungodly hours. I felt embarrassed about our quarters inside the military base and imagined the discomfort if he stopped by to visit.

"I am only here for another two days," I said remembering how much I missed his smile. I felt happy to see him again and anxious that I was leaving back to the Yemen soon.

"That can't be, why are you here? Why didn't you tell me you were coming?"

"We were evacuated; there was a civil war in the Yemen. You didn't hear about it?"

"You know I don't have time for TV."

"Ok, you are putting me in a very difficult position here."

"I am? Sorry. I didn't think you'd be too happy to know I was in Munich without saying 'Hi.'"

"Listen, can you just give me a half hour, just a half hour please? Sit down. Stay here. What do you want to drink? Eat?" he appeared nervous.

"All right. I am not hungry, but I'll have a coffee, I suppose."

He turned and snapped his fingers at one of the waiters. I hated when he did that, it made him seem so bossy and he was probably the kindest manager I knew, always rolled up his sleeves, and helped where he could.

"A coffee for my friend please," he shouted to a server balancing a tray with empty glasses, bent down moved my hair away from my ear and whispered, "I won't be long, promise, don't go anywhere."

My coffee arrived and I sipped it slowly as I watched people come up the subway exit and others run down in a hurry. Half-hour later, I was growing impatient, had not seen him even once come out on the patio, I prepared to leave. Clutching my purse and pushing my chair from the table, I caught a glimpse of him behind the counter through the open door of the restaurant. Soon after, he finally reemerged outside and approached my table.

"I was ready to leave. I have to be back in a while, am meeting my parents at Marienplatz."

"I just made time. You have to stay now. Come on, let's go for a walk," he offered his hand and helped me onto my feet.

We walked side by side with our shoulders touching, he clasped my hand tightly, and I left it in his as we strolled to the end of the sidewalk. He turned, pulled me closely, swung his arm around my shoulder, and looked at me deeply, "You know, I really struggled with telling you that I really liked you in the past, I mean loved you," he said in a soft tone.

"You loved me?"

"No, I mean, I love you, still, love you, loved you in the past and struggled telling you. I love you now, haven't stopped."

Stunned, I pulled out of his hold, stopped, and looked to the ground. His words were unexpected and yet what I had hoped to hear for the longest time. Now that I heard him say he loved me, I was unsure how I felt. I was going back to Sana'a. I could not stop thinking that it was too late.

He nervously reached into his pocket and proudly produced a small black box. My stomach grew tight and my palms felt clammy. For a brief moment, my good senses abandoned me; I nearly jumped up in happiness. It took me a minute to process what was happening. I took a deep breath, opened my mouth: "Ah…"

"Wait, before you say anything, open the box," he placed the black velvety cube into my palm.

"Open it," he reassuringly nodded.

"You did not know I was coming. When did you get this?"

"The half hour I needed?"

I hesitated feeling its softness.

"Please, it's not what you think."

Patty Smith

I opened the lid to find a gold necklace pinned to a small cushion. A relief and simultaneous disappointment overcame me, "Farris, sorry, I can't accept this. I am going back to the Yemen. In a couple of days. Don't know when I'll be back again," I pushed the gift back into his hand and rearranged the strap to my leather purse high on my shoulder.

His face and heart dropped. He stuffed the box deep into the inside pocket of his vest. Too afraid to commit, it must have been his way of saying he wanted me to stay in Munich. Despite my heart pouncing against my chest, I filled the walk back with awkwardly light talk that ended with an uncomfortable silence at the entrance to the U-Bahn. We hugged far too briefly. His scent was intoxicating making me want to linger in his arms. Too afraid to kiss him, I allowed him to give me a peck on both cheeks followed with an impersonal, "See ya."

I quickly turned and walked down the stairs fighting back an overwhelming sensation to cry.

"Keep in touch," he shouted after me.

Without turning around, I yelled "Ciao."

I needed to plug up the courage to tell my parents that I was pregnant. Three times the test came up positive. It was no mistake. A few days later, I said goodbye to Gianna at the passenger drop off area of the airport. She borrowed her Mom's car to give me a ride. We had parked it in a short-term lot leaving us with a few minutes to say goodbye.

"Gosh these have been crappy good-byes," I said hugging her.

She was making her best attempt not to tear up, "Don't worry, everything is going to be fine!" She said with a cracked voice, "If you change your mind, you know you can move in with me," in a serious tone.

"You're too sweet," I winked and turned to catch up with my family. I had spent my last night at Gianna's and arranged to meet them at the gate. Once more, I turned around to see she grumbled something under her breath and blew me a kiss, "Call me, and write."

"Okay," I said stepping off the escalator.

"This time don't let too much time pass," she yelled after me.

At the bottom, I could see the check-in counter. It would be a lot faster getting through then the last time I took this flight. I spotted my parents; they had already checked-in and waited down the hall.

"There you are. We were getting worried," Paps said, waving.

"Told you I would make it. Plenty of time," I pointed to my watch. The same stiff Lufthansa agent stood at the counter, the odds. Her hand stretched out, I reached for the boarding pass and joined my parents. We entered the once again crowded flight to Egypt.

Patty Smith

Chapter 23

'The jackals said so,' chattered the monkeys. 'And how did the jackals find this out?' 'The hares told us,' yelped the jackals. 'And how do the hares know?

- **Jan Parker And Jan Stimpson, Raising Happy Children**

Upon his return to the Yemen, Andreas instantly had so much on his hands and felt quite overwhelmed. The German Secret Service did not only expect him to find Johannes, they also asked that he perform full time spy work. He was to submit frequent reports on who were doing what, troop movements, and activities inside the Presidential Palace. The only way he could imagine gaining that kind of information was to contract a few additional trusted men to help him. Ironically, among one of the people he hired was the son of the former south Yemen Secret Service head. During the civil war, the son lost his father, their family home, and became sort of an outcast.

When Andreas asked him to help retrieve information, the man happily agreed and provided Andreas with much useful material. To catch Johannes however, would be a tougher challenge. Andreas decided to meet with Mr. Wagner. Wagner was married to a Syrian woman and worked for the German embassy. Andreas did not particularly like dealing with Wagner. He was self-absorbed. Like some sort of comic character out of a movie, Wagner drove a Harley Davidson while wearing a leather coat with a machine gun around his shoulder. Andreas knew that Johannes had spent some time in Damascus, and so had Wagner, he had worked for the German embassy there prior to his station in Sana'a. Andreas entered the office, closed the door behind him, and moved toward Wagner stopping a foot away from his desk, "Ok, you can give me away or not, but here it is. I am looking for Johannes Weinrich," he said his feet rooted firmly to the ground.

Wagner turned pale blending into the white wall behind him, "I have to sit."

"What is wrong? This is official business."

"No, you don't know," he said, "I've met him. Are you saying he is here?"

Wagner was close to fainting.

"Maybe I should leave the country?" he asked, and then anxiously added, "He threatened to shoot me right away if he should see me again," he said and added, "I made the stupid mistake to recognize him loudly during a meeting in Damascus," he told Andreas. "He pulled me aside and threatened me," his complexion had now turned to a bright red.

Wagner was on Johannes' hit list, he feared for his life, requested an immediately transfer, and received the Yemen as his next post.

"Johannes is a short fused violent guy," Andreas recalled the words of the German Secret Service during his meeting in Munich, "he shot an entire family, Mom, Dad and two children when he suspected they had recognized him."

Patty Smith

That information had convinced him to take a real interest in catching this terrorist and he had promised: "This guy doesn't deserve to be arrested. I am going to shoot him when I find him. I'll shoot him and will send his little finger to Pullach." The German Secret Service had naturally refused his plan, "We're happy to know you are passionate about catching him," they had said, "he is much more valuable alive than dead. We are hoping that he will sing and confess who he is cooperating with."

Andreas left Wagner's office in disappointment. He did not get any useful information out of him except the confirmation that Johannes was a dangerous man. He created an entire network of people that provided him with information and worked up relationships with a variety of sources by helping them out. He created a useful relationship with a Lebanese arms trader by providing him a Christmas tree. He was Christian and his family yearned to celebrate the holiday in proper fashion. Andreas ordered a tree filled it with ornaments from Germany and secretly dropped it off at their door. The family rented the home next door to where Andreas suspected Johannes lived. He plopped the tree down and said, "Now I need a favor."

"Sure anything for you."

"Tell me about your neighbor."

His method was not to chase the terrorist and place himself in danger by showing photos to everyone; he wanted to be more inconspicuous. Through his visit with the Lebanese, he discovered some of Johannes' habits, found out when he typically came home, what restaurants he liked, and who frequented his house. Andreas sat back in his office chair and swiveled it to face the window. It was getting late, he should have made his way home, but it was wonderfully quiet and he was alone with his thoughts.

Now that he was almost certain he found Johannes, he would need to involve the Yemeni President. The only useful piece of information he gathered by speaking to Wagner was that Johannes might be under the protection of the Syrian government. Surely, Johannes was now under the protection of the Yemeni government. He could not just raid his home and kidnap him, or have him arrested, as you saw in the movies.

Messing with government affairs was not a bright idea. From one second to the next, they could make Andreas disappear or something else not very pretty. It made more sense to go to the top person, the President, and gain his allegiance. Indirectly, he had access to the Yemeni President, via the President's mistress. He knew the mistress' cousin, a Jew from the Jumblouds family, a very powerful Lebanese family with a close-knit community. Her name was Halal Jumbloud. She used another name of course, owned a magazine in Lebanon or Syria, and was one of the mistresses of Ali Abdulla Saleh. The President's budget administrator was her cousin. After all, the Yemeni President was one of the richest men in the Middle East and needed places to hide his money. The Jumbloud family managed some of his hidden money in Cypress. Andreas had met the cousin while he was in Yemen for business and discovered through his sources that he had dealings with the Russian ex-KGB agents. Andreas befriended him, as much as one could.

"That's the answer," he burst out and jumped to his feet. It was time to go home and begin his plan. He would have to recruit Halal's cousin to act as a go-between until he could recruit Halal directly.

An hour later, he made the call. The cousin agreed to act as a go-between, "Halal is refusing to meet you in person. It is too dangerous for her," the cousin said returning Andreas initial phone call.

"If I can call you weekly over a secure line, would you agree to relay the information to Halal?" Andreas asked.

"Yes, sure, I will do you that favor. Friends help each other."

Patty Smith

Over the next week, the Secret Service asked Andreas to collect more information on Johannes Weinrich to be certain that he was in fact living in the Yemen. By now, Andreas had received several reports that positively identified Johannes, sightings of him at his favorite restaurant and other places. He was still unsure how he would gather the demanded evidence. Johannes was smart and made sure any indications of him disappeared when he ate out. Andreas followed him to a Lebanese restaurant, waited for him to leave, and then approached Johannes' table. He could not retrieve a single fingerprint. Johannes gave strict orders to clear everything as soon as he left. He followed him along a road in hope he dropped his cigarette, but Johannes carefully collected his buds inside an empty can he carried.

> *'Struggling to retrieve anything with a fingerprint. He gives staff strict orders to wash everything immediately. What to do?'*

Andreas typed in his report. He communicated via the large black laptop the Secret Service had handed him at the hotel in Munich.

"This is only a one-way communication method," one of the men had explained and had proceeded to place a floppy disc inside the machine, "You write something and it is immediately encrypted. You must encrypt everything you write. You cannot use this machine for personal writing," the other person had added, tapping his finger on the table.

"Clear," Andreas had affirmed.

"This software," the grey-toned person said with a scorn, "it contains the encrypting program. It cannot get into the hands of Yemenis."

Andreas encrypted the message and it simultaneously whipped everything on the laptop clean. Not even the draft was there. The message automatically sent via 'tunneling', a direct point-point communication method through a modem.

Then the message made a handshake with an electronic mailbox in Germany upon arrival.

The phone rang; "I've got it," Chloe screamed and attacked the phone, "Hello?" she asked.

"Yes, who is speaking please?" A dark voice asked.

"This is Chloe. Who is this?"

"I would like to speak to Aunt Angela. I am hanging up, calling again in a minute."

She heard a dead-ring-tone on the other end. Chloe hung up the receiver confused.

"Who was that?" Sofia asked.

"Some weirdo asking to speak to Aunt Angela, wrong number."

"What exactly did they say?" Andreas perked up.

"I am telling you, it was a wrong number. The strange thing is that they spoke in English with a German accent. Asked for Aunt Angela. Then they hung up, said they'd call back in a minute."

"Ok, thanks," Andreas entered his home office and placed his hand on the receiver, ready to pick up the phone as soon as it rang. "Don't pick it up when it rings," he shouted back through the open door.

His code name was 'Tante Angela' Aunt Angela, which he thought was ridiculous, why had they not named him Uncle something else? The phone rang and Andreas hurriedly grabbed the receiver, "Yes?"

"Aunt Angela?"

"Yes."

"Aunt Angela should go to Dubai, shopping, and stop by the lobby of the Marriot hotel at 9am. In four days."

A ring tone followed.

Patty Smith

The Secret Service was reluctant to go visit the Yemen. The country had an unfavorable reputation. Andreas needed to fly to Dubai to meet the Secret Service and had no idea how he would manage to get a visa so quickly. This was the only communication he had received since his return to the Yemen. His work with the Secret Service was completely against the rules of the Military and the law of the German Government. Working for the military, his job was not to cross with any work of other government agencies. Engaging with the Secret Service was a problem that had already nearly cost him his job. He had gotten into hot water with the German ambassador.

Andreas was unaware that the ambassador's brother worked for the Secret Service. Suspiciously, she had approached Andreas and demanded to know what other work he was doing already knowing through her brother that he was doing some sort of spy work. He initially considered saying that she knew whom he worked for, the military. Then he quickly rationalized that she would not be asking, if she did not already know something, "I hold you in high esteem and this is why I trust you with this information. I work for the German Secret Service," he had said.

She was a tall broad shouldered woman,

who had only recently come to her position as an ambassador. It was her first posting abroad; she took her new job very seriously. Her demeanor had changed to a pleasant smile, "Good for you, if you would have lied to me, tomorrow you would be sitting in a plane back to Germany. But for now, continue what you're doing just give me a copy of the reports you're writing."

What at first might have been a tricky situation had turned in his favor. Now he was able to ask her for support.

He drove to the German embassy, requested to speak to the ambassador in private, and within minutes he entered her office, "I need a letter so I can get into the United Arab Emirates embassy."

"What's the purpose of your visit to the Emirates?" she knew he would not share, but it did not hurt to ask.

"You know I can't tell you. You just have to trust that it is vital I go. I have to be there in four days."

"You normally require a sponsor, someone in the Emirates, in order to visit the country."

"Yes, I am aware of that." Andreas was not fond of the idea of a sponsor, it meant that he would probably end up with someone watching him very carefully.

"I don't want any attention drawn to me."

"Well, especially knowing that you are German military, you probably do not want to have a tail on you?"

"Right."

"Okay, let me think about this and type up a letter for you to take to the Emirate embassy. You'll have it this afternoon."

Andreas had limited time, as soon as the letter was ready he drove to the Emirates embassy, only to have his request for entry into the country denied.

"I would like to speak to the ambassador."

Hours later, a man ushered him into the ambassador's office. It was a room of remarkable dimensions with six-meter high ceilings and oversized colorful windows. All the fixtures bathed in gold and a marble floor that reflected the light of the opulent chandelier. There he sat in an adorned chair dressed in traditional white Arab wear. On his right hand atop a brown leather glove sat a glorious Falcon, "You were told you cannot have a visa into our country?"

"That's correct."

"And you disagree?"

"I very much thank you for the audience, Mr. Ambassador," Andreas approached the carved wooden desk, pulled one of the two chairs back, "may I sit?"

"Of course, please." The ambassador motioned with a flick of his wrist, "I read your letter," he said as he rose from his chair and moved the piece of paper toward Andreas on his desk.

"The way we work here is: You will be an official guest of the United Arab government."

Andreas was happy to hear him say that and yet braised himself for the catch. The ambassador paused and walked with his falcon toward a window, "But we are doing this on our time, it takes five to six weeks to process."

"I need to have it for this week, for tomorrow preferably," Andreas pushed forward to the edge of his seat, "is there a way around that?"

"No this is impossible," he transferred his pet to a stand near a window, "When you have it, you will have a limousine waiting at the airport. You will be our guest, no expenses. You will be happy."

Feeling uncomfortable sitting while the ambassador now moved behind his chair, Andreas stood up as well, "There is a small issue," he stepped out of the cramped space between the chair and the large desk, "My wife really wants to go shopping in Dubai and she wants to go shopping now."

Andreas had Sofia's passport. Going shopping in Dubai was his cover, a completely plausible one, many people shopped in Dubai. It was a desired destination, a dream with duty free shopping, the latest trends in clothing, and newest available technology. He stretched out his and Sofia's passports in his hand.

"No, I cannot do this," the ambassador said unwilling to accept the two passports.

At that point,

Andreas dreaded taking the next step. He had thought out different scenarios and this next solution was usually a secure way out of situations in the past. It was a big risk, the ambassador might even make an official complaint about him, and then he would be 'persona non grata', go back to Germany. He looked at the ambassadors red nose and determined it was worth a shot, "Maybe we can make a deal?"

"What do you mean?"

"I have a case of Johnny Walker Black Label," he worked to disguise his discomfort.
"What do you mean you have a case of Black Label?"

"Yes, I have a case of Black Label, if you want it, you can have it," Andreas said shifting himself away from blades of sunlight breaking red and green through the glass causing him to squint.
The ambassador breathed deeply, "You know what, we are not allowed to drink alcohol, but I have a couple of foreign friends that I entertain and Black Label is actually very hard to get. You really have a case of Black Label or are you just talking?"
"Yes, I have one."

He did not have a case, but was positive he knew how to get one.
"Alright, but I need to have it this afternoon."
"Okay."
"Tomorrow morning you can pick up your visas, but you cannot use your diplomatic passport, don't you have a civilian one?"
"Sure we have both."

Sofia had both a German diplomatic passport and a Mexican Civilian one, being that she was Mexican.

The irony though was that she could travel everywhere with her German diplomatic passport except for Mexico. Andreas rushed home and made a call to Joe at the embassy.

"You want to marry my daughter?"

"What do you need, Sir?"

"I need a case of Black Label."

"Well, the Gunny Sergeant is not here, and I happen to have the keys, but you have to replace it."

"No problem, I'll replace it."

Andreas called Cian next.

"I need a favor," Cian owed him one; "I need you to go, pick up a case of Johnny Walker at the Marine house and drop it off to the Emirate's embassy."

"Mm…I am guessing I can't ask why?"

"It's a matter of life and death."

Chapter 24

Once in Sana'a I picked up the phone immediately and called Cian. I had tried to reach him from Germany, his line sounded busy all the time. I assumed that his phone was still out of order from the war. Now that I called from inside the country I expected to get through, instead it still sounded busy. Then I placed a call to the British embassy, "I would like to speak to the Consul," I requested.

"Sorry, but he is not here, could I take a message?"

"No thank you," I hung up the phone.

I had not seen a doctor while in Germany in fear my parents would discover the purpose for my visit, after all I would have had to use Pap's insurance information. I figured that I would find a good moment to speak to them once we returned to Sana'a. I knew I had to speak to Cian first. My calculations placed me at roughly three months of pregnancy. Too late for an abortion, not that I was going to have one, although the thought had crossed my mind for some brief seconds. I announced that I was going to the Taj Sheba to meet a friend for coffee and asked the cab driver to take me to Cian's house. I paced back and forth like a caged animal in front of his door and waited for the door to open. Nothing happened. I waved down a cab and took it back home to call the embassy again.

"Is this Chloe?" Marty recognized my voice.

"Yes."

"Sorry, didn't Cian tell you?"

"Tell me what?"

"He requested a transfer back to London. Temporary, until he gets a new assignment somewhere else, of course."
"Wow. Really? He didn't tell me."

"Yes, do you want his number in London? I have his forwarding address."
"Yes, please."

"I should not be giving it out normally, but I know you two were close. Actually, come to think of it, I will be talking to him later; he agreed to call to discuss a business matter. I'll tell him you called."
Seizing the opportunity that my parents were out, I made a call to England from the Taj Sheba. We could not make international calls from home. An answering machine picked up, "This is Cian, you know what to do," his voice sounded warm.
"Cian? This is Chloe. I heard you left Sana'a. Marty told me and gave me your number," I paused, "I would like to speak to you. Will you please give me a call? Soon? Bye," I tried to sound cheery.
He called late at night, "Sorry, I just got your message."
"Good to hear from you," I said wanting to dissolve into tears.
"I've been concerned about you," he said, "Had no idea how to get in touch with you at all."
"I know. It has been very crazy for sure. We were like vagabonds all over the place," I said sitting down on the cold tile floor of Paps office.

"So you heard?"

"Yes, I did, you're back in England?"

"Yes, it kind of developed very quickly and I had no way of saying good bye."

"Mm," I struggled for words as I traced the grout lines, "Well, I might as well come out and just say it."

"Say what?"

"I am pregnant," I confessed. The long silence on the other end made me nervous. I said carefully, "Cian? Listen, I would have told you in a different manner, but you are there and I am here and that's just how it is."

"Sure."

"Look, I will figure it out, you really shouldn't worry," I said feeling slightly guilty.
"Worry? No....um...it's mine?"

"No, I am just telling you to share the information. Of course it is yours, why else would I be telling you?" I said somewhat annoyed.
"I need a moment to process this."

Suffering an anxiety that our relationship was now compromised I felt as though I needed to negotiate an appropriate response, "Okay. Take your time. I am not going anywhere. Call me when you like."
"Forgive me if this sounds untactful right now, but are you keeping it?" he asked.
"I think I am over three months along by now and yes I plan to have the baby."
"Can I call you back later?"

"Sure, anytime, I'll be home most of the weekend," I said ending the call and then retraced every letter of every word in my mind while I sat with Ronny and Tanner watching a movie.

Patty Smith

Chapter 25

The visas were ready the next day as promised. Andreas and Sofia travelled to Dubai where Andreas met the Secret Service agents at the Marriot Hotel lobby. He identified the men by the Frankfurter Allgemeine newspaper clutched under their arm. The agents brought Andreas a sixty-centimeter long tele-lens for his camera and an updated copy of the encryption-software. Andreas placed the lens back into the bag and immediately knew he would have a large problem taking it back to Yemen. Yemenis were very nosy, did not even respect diplomatic mail and inspected everything: broke locks if necessary, read all the mail, searched containers without care of the treaty from Vienna that regulated the privacy of diplomatic mail. They signed the treaty, but did not abide by it. Andreas entered the hotel room with the black duffle bag in hand.

"Are you ready to go out for dinner?" Sofia asked famished.

"Mm….uh…yes."

"What's on your mind?"

He would have to think of a way to get the new software and lens into the country. Fibs, who worked at the German embassy, Andreas would need to contact him. Fibs, he was the person who used to film all the girls he took to bed. Regardless of his character, he was a smart person, and by now, virtually everyone at the German embassy knew Andreas worked for the Secret Service.

"Okay, you know, I am going to go ahead to the restaurant and grab a table. Please change and come down," Sofia said noticing Andreas was deep in thought and she had no chance of breaking through to him, "Andreas, did you hear me?"

"Yes, yes, sure, I will be there in a minute. Need to make a quick call. Why don't you go ahead and grab a table?"

Sofia shook her head and left the room slamming the door into the frame shifting the picture on the wall into a crooked position.

"Come to the airport with a bag full of dirty laundry," Andreas requested, feeling fortunate that he had travelled with the large black duffle bag he purchased at a store in Sana'a. He gave Fibs instructions where to purchase the same bag.

"We will not talk. When you see us, just leave your bag, and pick up mine," Andreas said and then discussed a few more details about the exchange. Andreas repositioned his new spy toys inside the black bag, wrapped the lens inside a shirt, and placed the disc into a book.

Fibs had a special badge giving him quick entry and exit from the airport. He arrived, just as planned, with his black bag. When he spotted Andreas and Sofia by the baggage claim, he left it unattended for a brief moment. As Andreas walked around waiting for his luggage, he discreetly made the switch. Then Fibs lifted the other bag and left at once. Andreas had asked him to take it straight to the German embassy and hold it there until he came to pick it up.

"What do you have?" Fibs had asked him.

"You don't want to know," Andreas had said, "The less you know the better for you."

Fibs shook one of the Yemeni's hands leaving a couple of Rial bills in his palm. He was the customs guy for the German embassy and at the airport daily. Yemeni's expected receiving tips and in return they looked the other way. Fibs strutted haughtily with the duffle bag out the Airport door.

Patty Smith

Andreas and Sofia placed their luggage onto a cart, gaped around the area, when out of nowhere two people from the Yemen Secret Service appeared. Tapping Andreas on the shoulder one of the men asked to check their entire luggage.

"What did you guys do in Dubai?"

"I went shopping with my wife."

"What did you buy?"

"We did not really buy anything except for jewelry. We did have a good time, but it's time to be back."
Facing the men, Andreas pointed to Sofia's gold necklace he purchased in Sana'a a while ago. The men looked questionably at Sofia's neck. She gently stroked the necklace with her hand forcing a smile. Andreas patted her on the shoulder wishing he had prepared her for that moment, but Sofia knew to remain calm.
"Did you bring anything besides the jewelry?"

"No."

The man with the straight line of thick frizzy eyebrows and piercing eyes returned a piercing stare.
"Look at our stuff," Andreas said.
The two men searched tirelessly through all the laundry inside the black duffle bag, pulling out dirty men's underwear that did not belong to Andreas, while Sofia fixated on the man's shirt; it bore the stains of his last meal. For nearly forty-five minutes, the men switched between one bag and another not finding anything. All the while, Andreas wriggled to keep a straight face. He had mentioned that he was helping the Secret Service, but Sofia had no idea to what extent. He had even shared his approach: "The best way to hide is in plain sight," Andreas had told her.

Uncomfortably, Sofia shifted her weight back and forth. She had misgivings about Andreas' approach. It could not be safe to go around telling people what he was doing.

He had even confronted the head of the Yemen Secret Service and said very commonly, "Hey, I work for the German Secret Service, let's exchange information and help each other out."

Standing there in an effort to enter the country, Sofia vividly recalled her lengthy discussion. She and Andreas had sat around the small table inside the hotel room when he proudly shared: "I have a colleague in Oman; remember he came to visit us once? The guy who brought us the bolts for the Ford Blazer?" Yemenis had kept unscrewing the bolts for the truck in an attempt to steal the tires.

"He told me that his wife didn't know of his work, I said *'honestly you think your wife has no idea about what you're doing'? She is not that stupid.'* I also know of a Secret Service Agent working in Baghdad and he worked very differently. He told everyone about what he did. He was convinced that one should simply ask people to share any information they have. I tried his approach, and it worked. Many ended up telling me they had already suspected I work for the Secret Service. They said that someone who knew so many people and spoke all these languages could only be an agent, and if I had lied, they would not have spoken with me at all. Then they proceeded to share what they knew. The same scenario played out every time. I sat with the German Representative for Mercedes and the one for Siemens. Both said *'Ok, I heard this and that story, you might want to know who is behind this or that deal,'*" Sofia had disagreed with Andreas although he continued to insist, "On the other hand I treat them nicely and help them out. I told the Mercedes person *'Oh you want to speak to General so and so, who is in charge of purchase for the Yemen Army? Ok, here, tomorrow at this restaurant, he will be there.'* It all works out. You shouldn't worry," he had said stroking her hand.

Patty Smith

Part of his reassurance came from someone else posing as an agent. Wagner, who worked for the German embassy drove around on his Harley in his leather coat and boasted that he worked for the German Secret Service. He did not. He was as an embassy secretary.

"The Yemenis have got to be confused by now with several people making a claim to this job," Andreas had calmed her.

Unfortunately, Wagner was not his deterrent for long, soon later he was dismissed from diplomatic service for pulling a gun on the Moroccan ambassador at a reception. Andreas always knew he was crazy. The Yemeni men gave up the search through the bags, zipped them up and pushed them forward, "Alright, you are good to go."

Eyes dry and irritated from lack of sleep and poor airport lighting, Sofia grumbled on their way out. She felt tricked having gone on a shopping trip to Dubai without actually buying anything. Early the next morning, Andreas picked up his original black bag at the German embassy.

Chapter 26

The Sky was harshly low against the mountains. Fine dry sand blew through the open roof door and settled into the grout grooves between the tiles. Perched on top of the small wall, I looked down to the patio below. The marijuana plant found a new home and gave birth to smaller sprouts in its place. Wearing a long loose dress that blew against the wind, I rubbed my belly to feel for a bump unsure if I could get accustomed to the discomfort, the weight gain, and bloated feeling. Soon I would have to muster up the courage to tell my parents. Cian was pushing for time to process that I did not have. Independently of his feelings, nothing would change the fact that I was pregnant and would need to see a doctor soon, lastly an upside to living in the Yemen as a female. My loose clothing easily hid any signs that my body was changing.

"Chloe?" Mom shouted up the stairs.

I jumped up and straightened my dress, "On the roof."
"You up there?"
"Yes, I am up here."
Mom glided out of the door and joined me by the wall, "Are you alright?" she took a long look at me.
"Yes, I am okay," I said with my best smile.

"Ronny and I are thinking of going to the Taj Sheba for some coffee and then maybe to the souk to exchange gold," she fumbled at the necklace around her neck, "I feel like something fresh."

It was how we passed time.

Shopped for jewelry, watched the gold market, and sold it when the price was high. Sometimes we made money and gave us reason for an outing.

"Oh, I forgot to tell you," she leaned against the wall,

"Cian called yesterday. Completely forgot to tell you."

"No way, how could you forget?"
Mom shrugged her shoulders and pushed herself off the wall, "Sorry, too much going on."

After an initial rush of irritation, I nearly took the opportunity to tell her, however then dismissed the idea. I knew she would understand and be supportive, that was not my worry. I was prepared to raise a child on my own and figure things out. I could stay with my parents or move back to Germany. Deep down, however, I had obeisance for Mom's traditional values and I wanted to make her proud. I wondered if Cian concluded to propose. She began to walk away then turned and said over her shoulder, "Mo's flight comes in a few hours. Are you coming to the airport with us?"

"Sure, I will," I caught up to her. We simultaneously crossed the threshold to the staircase, "Mom, what did Cian say?"

"Nothing, he just asked for you."

"Did he say he was calling back? Did he ask that I call him?"

"No, I just said I'd let you know he called."
I realized she did not know Cian was back in England, "He is back in London."

"He is? Is he coming back?"

"No Mom, he is not."

She placed her arm around my shoulder, "Ah that makes sense now. I have been wondering what was wrong with you. You have been behaving strangely and I couldn't put my finger on it."

I almost broke down in tears. I pushed her arm off and began walking down the staircase, "No biggie. He'll call back if he wants," my face was on fire.

An hour later, we drove down to the airport feeling that I had squandered far too much of my time inside airports. I could see Mo and her now fiancé, Joe behind the glass window looking cheerful. An agent probed Joe with questions, releasing them a few minutes later. Little Rubén was asleep slumped over Joe's shoulder. Mo fell into Mom's arms and then hugged every one of us. They would only be back for a few more months then return to the United States to start a new life as a family.

Joe's assignment was ending and he had secured a position with the police force in Texas. While driving back to our house, Mo talked uncontrollably, like a waterfall words kept flowing as she wound unconnected thoughts. First, she spoke of Abilene, her wonderful new hometown in Texas. Then, she asked about the war and before we could answer, she shared what she had heard in the States. Next, she said how happy she was about her upcoming wedding. It would be in a month in Sana'a. I thought I knew her better than anyone else did, she would not be able to live in a small town, and it was much different from living in Munich. Then again, after living in Sana'a for the past years and blinded by love, any small town in the States might seem wonderful.

Arriving at home, Mo and Mom discussed details of the wedding: Bridesmaid dresses, color combinations, food, venue, and so forth, while I trailed behind listening with interest. Paps and Joe were left with the unloading of luggage.

Patty Smith

I seized a brief break Mo took to put Rubén to bed and asked if I could make a super quick call to England. I drove our truck to the Taj to make a call. Eagerly, I dialed his number and simultaneously calculated that it would be seven am in the morning.

"Yes?" a sleepy voice answered the phone.

"Cian? This is Chloe."
He cleared his throat, "Oh, hey, how are you doing?"
"Sorry I did not call back any earlier. My Mom forgot to tell me that you called," I said.
"No worries." An uncomfortable silence followed and then he added," I called you to tell you to come here."
"Go to England?"

"Yes, you would have free medical care here and I could help you. You could get a job here in England."
"Cian, I am not sure if that will work. Where will I live? I don't have any money for the flight."
"Do not worry about that. I have the flight covered and you can stay with me until you find a job of course."
"Let me think about it, okay. I told Mom I would not make it a long call. I will have to call you back or can you call me tomorrow?"
"Yes, sure," he said still in a sleepy voice.

"Talk to you soon."

That night, I laid in bed with ruminating thoughts unable to sleep for some time. Forcing myself to lay on my back was a challenge. When I examined myself in the mirror before bed, I could see my belly had grown to a small bump. The black cloak and baggy dresses I now wore in Yemen helped to conceal my state; however, I was not far away from showing under regular clothing.

While pregnant, I would not be able to find work in London. Surely, he assumed that I would find a job right away and I did not expect him to maintain me until I gave birth. Once the baby was born, I would also need to find care in order to work. I tossed to my side and wedged a pillow under my belly and another behind my back to prevent me from rolling. Mo and I have had our moments of conflict; nonetheless, it unimpeded me from feeling happy for her. She would embark on a new life and provide opportunities for Rubén.

W ith mixed emotions,

feeling both disappointed at my carelessness and simultaneously thrilled that I achieved one of my ambitions and was having a baby, I decided that I could do it. If it had worked out for Mo and she had been so brave, than it would somehow work out for me. My jaw released from the tight clench it had been in for days. I knew what to do next and felt instantly liberated from further worry and fell into a light sleep interrupted by vivid dreams.

The next morning, I told Cian that I needed some time to discuss my options with Mom and I would call him back. With clarity, I reasoned that letting some time pass could not hurt. Mo was getting married soon and I wanted to be there for her wedding. After all, the baby was not going anywhere. Upon my return from the Taj Sheba, I pulled Mom away from washing dishes at the sink, "I really need to speak to you." "Wait," she said with her wet hands in the air. She twisted out of my grip, lifted a towel from the hook, and rubbed her hands dry.

"It's important we speak now," I motioned her to follow me into the nearest bathroom.

"Sit down please," I said and pointed to the covered toilet seat. She looked at me puzzled and took a seat.

"What is all this drama about?"

Patty Smith

Maybe it was my moodiness or the fact that I had been driving to the Taj to make call after call that gave me away. When I said, "I am pregnant," she looked unsurprised, reached for my hand, placed it in-between her hands, and rubbed it softly, "I suspected something."

I pulled and she tightened her grip, "Chloe, I am your Mom. Nothing gets by your Mom. When you are a parent, you will understand this. Cian? Is it?"

Often she was able to guess my thoughts while I still struggled to sort them out, an unexplainable gift, "Yes," I said with low eyelids, "He asked me to move to England."

"That explains why you are walking around so melancholically."
I nodded embarrassingly.

"Don't worry about anything, Chloe, it will be alright."
"Should I move to England?" Before she answered, she blurted, "Did he propose?"
I stood rigid unwilling to discuss.

"Okay, you know, he will come around in time."

"I know, but I don't want to put my life on hold until then."

"You don't. You just focus on being healthy. Take care of yourself. We are here to support you, always. We'll start with a doctor's visit."

"Mom, thank you," I hugged her so tightly I heard her back bones crack and felt like the sky opened up above me. "I do not want to tell Mo or Ronny. I am not sure if I want Paps to know yet either."

"Chloe, that is too much to ask. Your father and I do not have secrets. Besides, he loves you just as I do. He will understand."

I agreed and asked that she tell him in my absence as we walked out of the bathroom together. She squeezed my hand once more, "Don't ever keep me in the dark again."

"I'm sorry Mom, I won't," my face flushed warm.

It seemed like ages when I last spoke to Cian although only three days had passed. Patiently, he waited to hear if I would move to England and I was ready to share my decision. In truth, I felt without much choice in my situation. Until the baby was born, I would stay in Sana'a with my family, and then I might stand a chance to finding a job. I would reevaluate my situation after giving birth.

"I want to focus on having a healthy baby right now and don't want to worry about finding a job trying to hide a bump while interviewing. To be honest, I do not want to work just a few months while pregnant either," I said.

I could hear Cian breathe heavily and before he could formulate an answer, I said; "I do not want to live off you either."

"Bloody hell, that's a lot of don'ts. Does a bloke get a chance?"

"Sorry," I said in my kindest tone, "This is how I feel right now. I may change my mind later."

He gasped loudly, "Are you cross with me?"

"No, not at all, Cian. Just give me some time. Okay?"
"Alright then," he said through another huff.
"Talk soon?"

"I'll call again soon," he said and hung up the receiver loudly.

Patty Smith

Chapter 27

Andreas never declined to help anyone. Eagerly he offered his services; saw it as an investment, knowing that he might ask for a favor in return. Some time ago, he accepted a request from Claudio, the first secretary of the Italian embassy. Claudio asked that Andreas help an Italian engineer who managed a power plant sponsored by the Italian government. The engineer allegedly owed Yemenis a substantial amount of money. Yemenis were as money greedy as anyone else and had a knack for placing sudden arbitrary charges on foreigners. In this case, they had invented some sort of back pay charge, came up with fake documents to enforce it, and the engineer unexpectedly faced a twenty to thirty thousand dollar back pay charge. He refused to pay the imposed debt and consequently found himself in danger of abduction.

"They claimed to have a food shortage and we sent a large shipment of wheat," Claudio said with an irritated tone,

"Yemenis accepted the gesture by asking for a large sum of customs duty pay. Well I will be damned; we were not going to pay the duty on top of sending them food. The wheat ended up on the bottom of the ocean as fish food instead."

Embassies paid around the order of a hundred thousand dollars to place a customs officer. In addition, embassies paid large sums for bribery. Steadfast with their fees, Yemenis requested the payment of charges over humanitarian aid. When Andreas shipped medical equipment into the country, he found himself in a similar position.

He got around paying fees by threatening to destroy the equipment in the presence of the international press. Meanwhile, the Italian embassy was giving the engineer refuge. He could not leave the country via the airport and there was no other feasible route to leave the country. Yemenis searched for him. Andreas got creative, smuggled him out of the embassy in the trunk of his car, and put him on a fishing boat to Djibouti from where he flew home to Italy. Claudio's home was across from the Lebanese restaurant where Johannes sometimes ate lunch, and now, Claudio owed Andreas a favor.

After some failed attempts to retrieve Johannes' fingerprints, he had to think of another strategy to prove that Johannes was hiding in Yemen. During his meeting with the German Secret Service in Dubai, he had reported his struggles, "I hate to say the man is smart, obviously only an idiot becomes a terrorist, but he is good at erasing his trail. I will give him that. It is nearly impossible to retrieve evidence. Several of my men have followed him into restaurants. We can't even get a cigarette butt."

"We have read your reports and thought about this. We are going to have a team of people join you in Sana'a and help you with this. We will send two agents for a couple of days. They will be in and out. Otherwise, it is too obvious. You will have to do all of the preparations for us," the agents had said.

Meanwhile, Andreas prepared for the agents' arrival. The long camera lens he smuggled back would come in handy. They would require a stake out location near Johannes and that is where Claudio could repay the favor. Andreas had come close a few times, thought he hit the jackpot when he received a retrieved beer can and a cigarette butt, and believed he had a sample of Johannes' fingerprints and DNA.

The analysis report returned negative.

The prints came back unusable and the DNA analysis was inconclusive. Then he followed Johannes himself to the Lebanese restaurant and failed to retrieve anything. Now he hoped to get a photograph. The agents arrived and Andreas had already prepared with a stakeout location and a VW-camper. They parked the camper inside Claudio's driveway. With black bed-sheets, borrowed from Chloe's bed, draped inside the camper as a backdrop, they performed an old magic trick. Dressed in black clothing to hide their skin, they concealed themselves against the dark background and blended in. Then they sat inside the van and waited for Johannes to appear. They took several photos of him entering and leaving the restaurant that confirmed his existence. Their stakeout ended when an old woman's goats walked past the driveway and chewed at the sheets.

Chapter 28

"The jackal rips out the hare's bowels, but the world rolls on."

— J.M. Coetzee, Waiting for the Barbarians

Joe looked deeply into Mo's eyes. Sofia dismissed the stresses of chaotic preparations relieved that all came together in the end. A most bestowing banquet of international foods, tables beautifully decorated in blue and white, chairs adorned with sheer white cloth and tied into large bows at the back, stretched out on the deep green lawn of the American embassy grounds.

The wind was perfectly still in anticipation for the sun to set high above the clouds and the smell of lilacs and lavender calmed guests that sat holding tiny paper umbrellas dipped inside Pina coladas handed out in welcome by Taj Sheba staff. Birds chirped beyond the wall and majestic brown mountains stood in whiteness of the ceremony. Andreas had exhausted all of his connections in hiring a catholic priest to perform the ceremony who was from India and flown in from Egypt.

Patty Smith

Weeks before Sofia initiated the work on bridesmaids dresses, a tailor prepared two prototypes that Mo declined. She wanted the dresses to match the perfect royal blue of the Marine Corps uniforms as well as have a European cut, simple, without bows, tiers, or lace.

Six marines altogether walked down the grassy slope, slowly, one-step, then paused, another step, then paused again. Threaded and holding their white gloved hands, walked six bridesmaids in matching colored simple long elegant satin dresses. The first two couples paced down the sloped lawn still smelling of fresh cut grass.

A Marine guard each also guided Mo's two sisters. Everyone else followed in perfect procession. Chloe had struggled with the dress design. Her belly was bulging and Mo would not allow her to place a bow or tier into the design to disguise her awkwardness and save her from questions, although people who took notice dismissed it for a little weight gain.

"As much as I hate to say this, people will forget the details of everyone else. This is Mo's day. Everybody will remember that two lovebirds vowed to dedicate themselves to one another for life," Sofia had said helping Chloe into her dress. "Besides, you're beautiful and your good looks take the attention away from that little tiny bump only you can see."

Andreas played *'Fuer Elise'* on the violin. Guests stood up and keenly waited for the bride's arrival. Andreas stopped playing the violin and the hotel band took over the performance of the wedding march. The past week Andreas obediently ran errands to help with preparations, picked up flowers, made calls, and arrived an hour ago, had hauled the catholic priest away from his hurried curry at the Taj. Wiping the sweat that shined his bald head with the white handkerchief in his left pocket and ran excitedly up the slope to the Marine home where Mo waited. He proudly wore a black tuxedo and polished black lacquer shoes. 'Only two more daughters to go, one as good as promised,' he thought.

He delivered Mo at the bottom of the hill. Mo and Joe stood shoulder to shoulder under the charmingly decorated arch. Its white flowers and silvery streamers took Sofia an hour to attach. Mo struggled to pay attention to the priest who read an indistinguishable verse with a strong Indian accent from the bible. She recalled her bachelorette party the night before when Marines dressed in combat clothing had stormed the home.

Everyone had been in on the plan except for Mo without considering the consequences of such a surprise until Mo's face turned ghostly from the shock of having men enter the home without forewarning again. One man placed a blindfold over her eyes, swiftly hoisted her into the air over his shoulder, and marched out the door followed by the other men, and Mo's family. The truck pulled up at the Marine house to a small horde of expat friends that had already taken a head start on the barrels of beer Andreas had smuggled into the country before the war. They greeted her with a loud singsong and clapping. In her pink pajamas, she sat tied to a chair at the center of the room. Gunny's dancing skills and his body captivated the attention of the women who stuck dollar bills into his pants. He moved sensually toward Mo, pulled the blindfold off with his teeth, and after some undulating over her lap, he untied her hands.

His performance ended with the flexing of his arm muscles and his perfect six-pack. Another marine had handed Mo a can of shaving cream, which she happily emptied onto Gunny's chest while people screamed, "Lick it off!"

The priest proclaimed, "You may kiss the bride," forcing her to focus on Joe who lifted her veil, and looked deeply into her eyes. They kissed far too long to a joyous crowd and someone screamed, "Get a room already!"

The married couple danced to a few songs while guests pinned large sums of money onto Mo's wedding dress. It was a Yemeni wedding tradition she appreciated. All the men jumped away when Mo flung the beautiful flower bouquet high into the air, making it easy for Chloe to catch it.

Tanner and Mike drove to the Taj Sheba Hotel and turned the furniture upside down inside the wedding suite. They carried out the mattress completely hiding it inside a linen closet. Meanwhile, Mo finished out the party that lasted into early morning hours in a pink satin dress and the two stumbled into their room without care for the missing bed and fell into each other on the carpet giving Mo rug burns and bruises that took a week to heal, the week she had left to pack things and say her goodbyes. It was a terribly sad and simultaneously happy moment.

That same week when Mo left to live in the United States, Andreas worked on a plan to capture Johannes. He now had the photos substantiating Johannes was hiding in Yemen. One evening, Halal, the President's mistress, showed up at his door. She was in the company of her cousin. Andreas had not met her in person and had not seen her cousin since meeting him the first time, all their communication was via a telephone.

H alal was a slender woman,

from what Andreas could tell through the dark Hijab she wore. Veiled, she revealed only her big dark charcoaled rimmed eyes. She could be anyone, Andreas thought caught by surprise and a bit confused. He offered them tea. She irreverently turned it down. He offered her a drink, and she asked if he had gin. She really liked the booze and knew about Andreas's special access to alcohol, "My favorite drink is a Gin-tonic," she whispered although the three of them were alone in the low-lit mafraj. Andreas poured her a glass of wine, the only thing he had, and offered to procure her Safire Gin soon, "It is the best I can get my hands on," he said.

Halal and her cousin stayed for a short twenty minutes. When they left, Andreas was unsure about the real purpose for their visit and told himself that it was probably to make certain he knew she liked to drink Gin.

Soon, he began to go to the Taj Sheba hotel on a regular basis and dropped a bottle of Gin off at the door to her room. That evening, at his house, was the only time he saw her in person. The President's details who guarded her room always received the liquor. Halal became his direct conduit and passed on his suggestions to the President. He also continued to speak to Halal's cousin, "It's the Middle East, and you have to bargain like a souk-trader," Halal's cousin had said one day.

"I know that. So tell me. How can I get the President's attention?" Andreas asked.

"You know what he really, really wants? He wants un-interrupted power supply for the Presidential Palace," Halal's cousin had said.

Electricity went out all the time in the Yemen. Sometimes an outage could last hours, but more often, it would be just a few minutes here and there. No matter how brief the outage, when working on the computer, work shot up the electronic nirvana. That happened a couple of times to the President's aids and to the President himself, which angered him. The President had many generators. However, generators could not deliver automatic power supply within a split second, instead the President needed to have a big wheel with sensitive reactor elements that could kick into gear within a split second.

"The President knows you have something that can provide un-interrupted electricity to your CT-scan machine," Halal's cousin had said, referring to the Siemens DR in the military hospital. It was the only CT scan machine in all of Yemen.

"How does he know this?" Andreas asked.

"In the past, if the machine failed, people called the president's office and complained. It meant they needed to fly to Egypt to get a cat scan. The absence of calls since you have taken over the management of the hospitals had the President thinking that you must have found a solution." Andreas's first job when moving to Yemen was making sure to have an uninterrupted power supply, a large UPS, for the CT-scan machine. Andreas purchased one. It was basically a big spinning wheel that connected to a generator and constantly hummed along at high speed. As soon as the electricity failed, it kicked in, "I do have an uninterrupted power-supply unit," Andreas admitted.

"The President would need something like that, perhaps on a larger scale."

Andreas wondered how he could set one up for the presidential palace suspecting that the project could run a couple of million dollars, money he did not have.

Tired of racking his brain, he crawled into the crisp cool sheets and cuddled up to Sofia. She wrestled some of the blankets back and pushed herself closer to the edge of the bed. A shaving of silver touched his hand as he waved it before his eyes. He had friends who worked for Westinghouse.

Next to him, lay Sofia, she was calmly breathing. It took weeks for her to sleep through the night again. The stress from the robbery and then the war stole her sleep many nights.

Andreas smiled, "I've got it," he whispered.

"Mm...what is it?" Sofia murmured.

"Nothing Maus, sorry go back to sleep."

Westinghouse engineers were designing turbines for the Marib Dam power plant. He rolled over and pulled the blanket with him, away from Sofia, and fell asleep instantly.

The next morning he called his friend: "You know I have a little project for you."

"I have not spoken to you in a while. How are things going?"

"They are going well, thank you. I am calling to see if you are interested in a favor for the President."

"A favor for the President?" His voice had elevated.

"Yes," Andreas said.

"What is it that we can do for the President?"

"Well, I thought you might be able to help with an uninterrupted power supply for the Presidential Palace."

"Mm…well….yeah, that should be a piece of cake," the engineer said.

"Really?" Andreas was not sure if he was on the right track by asking them for help and was now elated discovering his luck.

"We just did a project study; we can take one of the blue-prints and slap another heading over it saying Presidential Palace."

"Wow that might do the trick. So you'll give me the blueprint?"

"Sure, it's yours, but you know we might need a couple of bottles of liquor soon."

"You name it, it's yours."

He took the blueprint to Halal's cousin, who happened to be in town and passed it on via Halal to the President.
A day later, Halal's cousin called Andreas: "The President was pleased, he said '*Yea that is what I want. What can I do for him?*' He asked what he can do for you, Andreas."

"Perfect, tell him I want Johannes."

"Johannes?" the cousin asked.

Patty Smith

"Yes, just tell him I want Johannes."

Andreas' plan worked like a charm and he spent the next few days discussing strategy directly with the President who agreed to notify Andreas when Johannes purchased a ticket for travel. When Andreas received notice, he passed the message on to the German Secret Service.

Yemenis issued special badges giving the carrier permission to move throughout the airport in an expedited and unchecked manner. Johannes was relieved of his badge when entering the airport and then subsequently checked, "No, sorry we have a new rule. You cannot enter the airport with your weapon. We will return it to you when you come back."

Airport security disarmed him. When Johannes entered the airport, the German Federal Police waited for him. Amidst the men waited a woman in uniform.

Johannes hated women,

perhaps because of his relationship with Maggie. Maggie had dumped him and married Carlos 'the Jackal'.

> 'You did not allow me to take care of him myself. I am making the request that you send at least one female Police Officer who will be in charge of placing the cuffs on him.'

Andreas had typed into his laptop.

From afar, he watched Johannes face turn furious when a female officer slapped the cuffs around his wrists. Later he learned that Johannes sang giving away connections and information the Secret Service had been looking for.

Chapter 29

Chloe ran three to four miles every day. Her belly swung loosely underneath her sweatshirt. Staples dug deep into the skin of her underbelly as she pushed through pain and sprinted a steady cadence through snow and icy dirt. She drove the muscles in her legs to break with every step.

"Jeez, I am out of shape," she said to herself through a rough breath.

She focused on making it to the lamppost first, then the mailbox, from there to the corner of the fence, and then all the way back. Her gasps froze firm against the woolen scarf around her mouth and chin. She had enjoyed the time she spent with Cian up until the delivery of the baby. The meek fourteenth-century cottage near Strood Green Farm in Dorking, Surrey was his parent's home out of which they ran a limousine business. Cian had convinced her to move in with his parents temporarily to ensure she had company during the last two months of pregnancy.

She had looked radiant. The pregnancy became her. When he saw her disembark the flight, he instantly remembered that he loved her. He had considered proposing and could not shake the thought that it felt rushed, pressured, even uncertain, so he decided to wait. He could not explain his fear and wanted certainty beyond any doubt. Chilly cold air filled her nose when she inhaled and she remembered her breath tasted sour against her dry tongue and recalled how much she shivered cold under the white crisp sheets. She thought of how much she had wished to relax her body and her body did not listen.

Patty Smith

"We are ready," the doctor had said and wheeled her into an icebox of a room, prepared for delivery.

A nurse had washed and shaved Chloe for the operation. Each evening for weeks, she drank a cup of tea with a ham and coleslaw sandwich, and then ran a warm bath. She had shaved and washed herself just in case that night would be the night to go to the hospital. Every morning, Cian took the train to work and back. It was a long ride and the train often delayed his arrival home. The last few days he had looked exhausted of the set-up and Chloe was sure he longed for his apartment that saved him the two-hour commute.

"I'll be looking for work as soon as I can," she had found herself promising and missed the baby before she had mumbled the words.

A cold damp air had crept through the plaster of the old cottage in places where one could see right through to the outside. Chloe had looked at the walls as she kneeled on the bottom of the tub. The water ran tepid against her thighs. The white plaster had peeled to reveal horsehair within. Inquisitively she pulled at one of the hairs and the dry mud crumbled around it. Tiny speckles fell into the water. She had not felt well, had been queasy for hours.

Cian's parents had been out of the home, making runs that day, and stopped in periodically to check on her. Cian's Mom had left saying she would not be gone too long. Chloe had felt sick and thought a bath would help her feel better. She knew she was close and thought perhaps she knew how it felt to be in labor.

Overwhelmed by a feeling of sadness,

she had cried uncontrollably, naked in the tub. She also knew not to sit pregnant in hot water, so she did not put the plug in, and watched the water flow down the drain. It had felt safe that her loud cry was disguised by the sound of running water, even though she was alone.

With her cupped hands, she sprayed her shoulders with warm water from the faucet and scooped more onto the top of her back where it touched warm then turned ice cold as it flowed down her spine. She had complained about the heat in Yemen. The last few months were challenging, she had felt broad and swollen.

"I'll never complain about the heat ever again," she huffed over a heavy pant and pushed herself through freezing wind, "Just a few more steps."

Her feet slipped on icy patches of dirt beneath her runners. She paused to catch her breath and looked around. White roofs topped with smoky blowing chimneys in the distance, behind her a wide-open pasture. Some of the fields filled with colorful flowers that produced a Rembrandt like painting Cian had told her. She would not see the fields turn. This winter, in England, was like none she had felt before, a wet, freezing, debilitating cold that seized joints, the kind of cold that one could never gain warmth from and caused uncontrollable shivers even when sitting right by a fireplace. It was worse than winters in Germany or even Canada for that matter. At least in Canada the sun was always out and warmed the windows.

Looking out into the grey fields she thought back to the afternoon before her baby was born. She had stepped out of the tub carefully onto the ice-cold slate rock. His parents had remodeled the bathroom. Back in the day, it was some sort of pantry, a cold room, to keep foods fresh.

The home did not have an attached bathroom. In the fourteenth century, the outhouse stood all alone, separated by the house from a faraway distance, and the pantry stuck out of the building, away from the original structure, like an add-on. Chloe did not understand why someone would think of transforming the coldest room in the house into a bathroom. She had hated taking baths there.

They had left her feeling colder than before she stepped into the tub. Getting out, wet, was pure torture. Cian joked that it was as cold as Ice-station Zebra with the windows open. With chattering teeth, she had wrapped herself into a rough textured towel and slipped into her flip-flops.

Patty Smith

She had rubbed her big belly gently and whispered, "It is okay. I know. We will go warm up. You seem to be sleeping and probably warm and snug in there. Aren't you?"

Then she had sobbed again, unsure why she felt the need to cry so much. Her eyes swollen red, her nose runny, she walked into the main room of the home. Ceilings were so low that Cian needed to duck his head to get past the beams. Barefoot, Chloe fit right under them. The fireplace crackled hot. She took baths when the family was gone so that she could warm up by the fire afterwards. Kneeling close to the fire that had dried her face red, she wanted to continue knitting the baby blanket. Knitting the blanket was all she had done the past weeks. In Yemen, she had produced an entire wardrobe of woolen sweaters, jumpers, hats, little baby shoes. Unsure of the baby's gender she had knit mostly in yellow. Her last visit with the doctor had revealed it was a girl, so she had begun mixing in pink into the baby blanket. The front door squeaked open and she pressed herself up onto her feet.

Cian's Mom stepped into the home, "Are you alright?" she asked closing the door into the old metal latch.

"Yes," Chloe clutched the towel against her chest, "Sorry, I will go upstairs and change."

She had walked up the narrow winding staircase to the bedroom carefully.

The bedroom had once housed several cats.

Cian's Mom loved them and all the cats slept inside the bedroom until Chloe woke up one morning covered in a strange itchy rash. Embarrassed, she had discovered it was fleabites. Fleas had infiltrated her bed and covered her body with tiny red bumps that itched so badly she asked for advice to find relief. Cian's Mom felt the need to place the cats with a friend.

Chloe stepped into the upstairs room, low eaves did not allow for much furniture. She had dressed herself in comfortable clothing that she retrieved from the small dresser. On top sat a framed picture of her Mom. She missed her tremendously and cried again.

"Are you well?" Cian's Mom had called.

"Yes, I'll be right down," Chloe wiped her tears with the wet towel she had pulled off her head and descended to meet her at the bottom of the stairs.

"Actually, I have not been feeling too well. I have not felt the baby move much at all and I am feeling melancholic. I can't explain it."

"Have you been crying?" she asked and placed Chloe's face between her cold hands. Chloe worked hard against the urge to pull away.

"A little perhaps."

"Sorry, we have both been very busy today. I will call the doctor."

"Yes, please. I would like to make sure everything is fine," she said. After speaking to the doctor, she turned to face Chloe, "Chloe pack a small overnight bag. The doctor suggested we have you checked out."

Chloe packed a nightgown, fresh undergarments, and a clean pair of clothes. Before leaving for the hospital, she called Cian at work. He had already left his work.

"We will leave him a note," his Mom had said, took Chloe's bag and walked outside.

Chloe followed her to the long black limousine. Cian's parents owned two limos and a regular Mercedes. His dad had the Mercedes that afternoon.

His Mom had insisted she lay across the back seat of the limo and she had felt embarrassed arriving at the hospital in a limo.

Patty Smith

His Mom had held the back car door open and a nurse had rushed to help her step out. She had requested Chloe sit in a wheelchair and pushed her into a room where she placed probes onto her stomach to monitor the baby's heartbeat and before Chloe had realized what happened, the nurse prepped her for the delivery saying: "It is time," is the only explanation she had received.

The operation room was so very cold her body shivered uncontrollably when she was transferred onto a table, laid on her side, felt a giant needle pierce her spine, and the entire bottom half of her body went numb in minutes. Next she remembered, she had woken up in another room, one just as cold as the operation room. Cian had stroked her hand looking exhausted. She had cracked open her eyes and saw the doctor standing next to Cian, "I am afraid we have bad news," he had said with a creased forehead, "Your placenta ruptured, and you leaked blood for some time. The baby lost far too much blood, hence the C-section."

"Is the baby alright," Chloe had asked with her throat so dry her tongue glued to her tonsils.

"I am afraid not," the doctor had said, "she is on life support, she lost too much blood and will most likely not live without the machine.

We wanted to give you the opportunity to see her, and then we will have to take our chances and see if she can make it on her own. We have the father's permission to shut it off, but I will give you time to discuss," the doctor had walked away.

Shocked to her core, Chloe could not utter a word and simply looked at Cian with disdain.

"Chloe it's the right thing to do," he had said, "There is more. If the baby should breathe on her own, chances are she will come away with substantial brain damage. She was simply far too long without oxygen."

"Can I please see her?" Chloe had asked, unable to think about anything else but seeing her face and folding her into her arms.

Doctors had pushed her bed into a room where she found the baby attached to machines. They positioned it closely to see her. Dazed and confused Chloe reached, held her tiny perfect foot, wiggled her tender white toes, and then warmed her plunged cold hand, her skin like translucent fragile rice paper. She had pushed herself up. The baby had Cian's thick dark hair. Her face buried under tubes.

"Her eyes are blue," Cian said expressionless.

"I want to hold her, can I hold her?"

"I'm afraid that's not possible right now, but you will soon, when we stop the machines."

"Can we take Chloe back to the other room?" Cian whispered.

Chloe had looked up at the bright white ceiling examining the fuzzy edges of the tiles. The stench of bleach permeated the room. Half-conscious and disoriented she worked to center her gaze. A man stood at the end of her bed. A priest smiled and asked if she would like to baptize the baby. Cian had brought all of the knitted baby clothes and the nurses had dressed her in a light yellow woolen baby jumper, matching knitted shoes, and hat and placed the unfinished knitted baby blanket at her feet.

"It won't matter," Cian said, as he had tucked the unraveled blanket's corners beneath her cold little feet.

They named her Darcy.

Chloe's mother had always said, "Don't mourn or regret the things you have done." Doubled over, Chloe clutched the fencepost with the regret of a memory that would never leave her.

Patty Smith

www.ingramcontent.com/pod-product-compliance
Lightning Source LLC
Chambersburg PA
CBHW061951170626
46813CB00006B/2610